The White List

Nina D'Aleo

First published by Momentum in 2014
This edition published in 2014 by Momentum
Pan Macmillan Australia Pty Ltd
1 Market Street, Sydney 2000

A CIP record for this book is available at the National Library of Australia

The White List

EPUB format: 9781760081218
Mobi format: 9781760081225
Print on Demand format: 9781760081331

Cover design by Matt O'Keefe
Edited by Kate O'Donnell
Proofread by Thomasin Litchfield

Macmillan Digital Australia: www.macmillandigital.com.au

To report a typographical error, please visit momentumbooks.com.au/contact/

Visit www.momentumbooks.com.au to read more about all our books and to buy books online. You will also find features, author interviews and news of any author events.

Nina D'Aleo wrote her first book at age seven (a fantasy adventure about a girl named Tina and her flying horse). Due to most of the book being written with a feather dipped in water, no one else has ever read "Tina and White Beauty." Many more dream worlds and illegible books followed. Nina blames early exposure to Middle-earth and Narnia for her general inability to stick to reality. She also blames her parents. And her brother.

Nina has completed degrees in creative writing and psychology. She currently lives in Brisbane, Australia, with her husband, George, their two sons, Josef and Daniel, and two cats Mr Foofy and Gypsy. She spends most of her days playing with toys, saying things like "share," "play gentle," and "let's eat our veggies" and hearing things like "no," "no way" and "NEVER!". She is also working on more books—including the next book in The Demon War Chronicles series.

Also by Nina D'Aleo

The Last City: The Demon War Chronicles 1
The Forgotten City: The Demon War Chronicles 2

For my brother

Part 1

1

My brother had always insisted that humans were nothing more than shaved apes and now, sitting sixth row at my first commercial wrestling match, I couldn't help but see his logic. Not that there was anything wrong with wrestling, or with apes for that matter; there was just something simian about a big man wearing shiny underpants and a superhero cloak body-slamming another muscled-up guy in a unitard. There was a lot of grunting and chest beating. There was a lot of tight Lycra riding up into sweaty cracks and crevices better left unseen.

In actual fact humans were a ninety-six to ninety-nine point four percent genetic match for chimpanzees. Zero point six percent and shrinking, I thought, as the hefty guy on my right leaped to his feet and screamed, "Take him, *take him*!" showering everyone in the rows below us with spittle and half-chewed popcorn. I sighed and gave the I'm-not-with-him headshake as disgruntled victims wiped their necks and shot poison looks in my direction.

I glanced at my partner, sitting to my left. Fists clenched in his lap, body tensed and pressed forward, Dark's eyes darted left to right, following every move of the match. What had he called wrestling? "Ballet for the real man"? At the moment he looked like a real man who needed a serious boost of fiber in his diet.

"Bos." I nudged him.

He twitched, grunted, but remained in his happy place of contact sports, thousand-horsepower supercharged V8 engines and hot girls who never ask, "But do you love me?"

"You do realize this is all staged, don't you?" I said and got an angry mass shushing from everyone around me. I covered my laugh with a cough and checked the time. Two whole minutes had elapsed since the last check, two hours since our arrival, and still no sign of our guy. I faced the fact that, given there were only fifteen minutes left of the event, it was highly likely he was a no-show. That meant one of two things—his condition had spontaneously resolved itself or he had 'gone green' sooner than expected and other agents had picked him up and not yet called it in. It also meant I'd cancelled girls' night for the fifth time in a row because of work, essentially for nothing. A rare chance to wear heels, talk boys and potentially find *the one* traded in for steel caps, man BO and being stood up by a walt.

I blew through the next quarter-hour lost in my own thoughts, which these days mainly rolled around someone with dark eyes and dark allure, and a far more attractive, interesting, and successful version of me, meeting in all kinds of ways and going wherever the mood took us.

I blinked back to reality with Dark's elbow digging into my ribs. The show was over and the crowds were massing toward the exits. I rubbed my forehead and yawned. Dark nudged me again and I pushed his arm away with a bit too much force.

"What?" he asked.

"Nothing," I muttered, standing up and grabbing my coat off the back of the chair.

"Nothing," my partner repeated, following me along the line of seats. "Nothing as in actually nothing, or as in the lame, girly nothing that means something I'm supposed to magically know?"

"I had plans tonight." I glanced back at him.

"To do what?" He smirked as if it was laughable that I'd have plans.

Boston Bonacci-DeScuro (Codename: Dark). My partner. My best friend. Most of the time I felt like kicking him in the head. "I was going out with the girls."

"So what? Go out tomorrow night," he said.

We joined the jostling crowd filing up the stairs. I did a halfhearted scan of the people around us. There was the usual smattering of odd, awkward and intoxicated individuals. No one matched the surveillance photos we'd memorized before coming out after tonight's walt.

"That's not the point," I told my partner.

"So what is?" he asked.

A trio of skimpily dressed petite blondes crossed our path and Dark shoved me to one side to let them cut in front of us. They giggled and gave him the cutie-pie-baby-wave popular with girls fond of wearing belts as skirts. Dark ogled. He grinned. I noticed he was clenching his fists to pump up his muscles. Pepé Le Pew, tattooed on his left bicep, took on a strained expression.

"Pathetic," I told him.

He watched the girls until they vanished, then turned back to me. "So—what is the point?" he repeated.

I pushed ahead of him and climbed the stairs.

"What?" He followed me.

"You wouldn't understand," I told him, knowing he hated when I said that—almost as much as he hated being told he had short man's syndrome.

He grabbed my arm and pulled me to a stop. "Cough it."

"It's really nothing." I faked indifference. "It's just— everything is always *tomorrow night* and tomorrow night never happens ... and no one's getting any younger here."

Dark quirked up one side of his mouth—his ah-ha expression. "I knew it," he said. "It's about a guy. Who is he?"

"He's no one," I said. "And *that's* the point."

"Okay ..." Dark processed for a moment. "So you want a boyfriend." He looked around. "Well what about him, right there?"

"Who?" I followed his line of sight.

"The guy in the flannelette and the AC/DC shirt. Crew cut. He's checking you out."

"That's a girl—obviously," I snapped, annoyed I was still falling for his *jokes* after all these years.

"Really?" He squinted with mock confusion.

I turned my back on him in disgust. As I did, the random blur of the crowd snapped into sharp focus on the face of our walt. He and a bunch of other guys were exiting the glassed-off VIP section of the entertainment center. Based on their behavior—their sloshed, giddy, dog-on-the-loose frolicking around one central guy wearing a Hawaiian shirt open almost to the waist and a pair of Christmas reindeer antlers usually reserved for babies, dogs and retail assistants, I guessed it was a bucks' night. To the untrained observer our walt would have just looked like that guy in the group who always takes things too far—he's drunker, rowdier, more obnoxious. My eyes, however, picked up all the signs, now that I'd seen the face I'd been looking for. The walt was lurching left to right, stumbling, shouldering into people, blinking his eyes, shaking his head, biting his lips. His hands slid along the walls, along every surface. I saw a tremor run through him. I yawned and looked away, but all my senses had jolted into work mode.

"Bos. Walt in sight."

His dark green eyes sharpened. He picked out our guy and confirmed, "In sight."

The walt and his friends headed toward the closest exit. We mirrored their movements, palming the crowd aside. A few people gave us dirty looks and one guy stubbornly refused to move. Dark flashed his badge and said, "Cops. Move your ass."

The guy moved, double time, which may have had more to do with the gun he'd glimpsed inside Dark's jacket than with the prospect of us being the law. We reached the top of the stairs just as the bachelor party vanished through the exit. We stepped up the pace to keep them in sight, trailing the group through the lobby of the complex and out to the driveway, where a limousine sat idling. The chauffeur opened the door as the men approached. They tumbled in. A blue light flashed from the depth of the vehicle to the sound of a techno bass and a chorus of giggling girls.

"Strippermobile," Dark told me.

"Combining high-performance engines and naked wo-men—how could you ever go wrong?" I muttered dryly.

We passed the back of the limo as it pulled away from the curb. Once the vehicle was in motion, we sprinted to Dark's car, parked nearby. A drunken night on the town with the boys gave us the perfect cover to take our walt—but if we lost him at this stage of break-thru, it was not just a failed assignment, it was life or death.

2

We tailed the limousine through a stretch of backwater highway before reaching the city limits. I watched out the window as we buzzed by streets I knew so well I could walk them blind. High-rise lights sparkled across the windscreen—hotels, luxury apartments, and office buildings where corporate slaves still sat hunched over their desks at past eleven on a Friday night. But then again, who was I to judge? I hadn't seen leisure time in so long we were virtual strangers. The car's heater warmed my legs while an unforgiving cold buffeted my face from Dark's open window. No matter how freezing, boiling or in between, my partner was incapable of driving with his window up. He said he needed fresh air. I questioned his mental health.

The usual massing of clubbers and pubbers crowded the popular nightspots. People mingled, lingered, flirted and flaunted. The meat market in motion. A group of black-shirt bouncers tried to break up a curbside fight. Alcohol fueled a fire lit by the frustration of life stuck in a rut. Change the setting and the scene remained. Wherever people went, there were loving, fighting, desperation, exhilaration—life in polar extremes. This city was one of many, but also one in a million. Our City. Codename: *Toran-Rabbin-Es.*

I felt Dark's vehicle slowing and concentrated my attention ahead on the limousine. It had turned into the parking lot of one of the city's largest strip joints, or as certain patrons liked to call it—*casa della performance erotica.* Next thing Dark would be trying to convince me that stripping was art too. The limo double-parked across a row of cars. We eased into a spot behind them and watched as the bachelor's buddies exited the car and stood around it, talking and smoking, tapping on the windows. More girls came out from the club and sidled into the limousine. Our walt was at the front of the car, leaning against the hood. His sides were heaving. We needed to grab him and quick, but we couldn't do it yet. Not with so many witnesses. We had to wait until the bachelor was done.

"Compromised visual," Dark muttered. "Switching to halo."

He killed the headlights and switched on the halos. Imperceptible to normal sight, they gave us, via a screen embedded in the center console of Dark's car, an X-ray view of everything, including the X-rated goings-on inside the vehicle.

"Great," I complained. "If it takes one guy with one woman an average of two point four minutes, how long does it take one guy with six women?"

"Two point four seconds," Dark suggested. "Lucky bastard." He tilted his head, staring at the halo screen. "Hey, do you think X-ray porn could take off as a new fetish?"

"Maybe for frustrated radiographers," I said. "It's doing jack all for me."

Dark snorted. He dragged gum out of his pocket and offered me a stick.

I shook my head.

"Take some," he insisted.

"Why—do I stink?" I asked.

"You never chew gum," he said.

"I prefer mints."

"Who prefers mints?"

"Obviously some people do," I snapped. "They're not putting them on the market just for me."

"Name one other person who prefers mints," he demanded.

I searched my mind for a name and came back with nothing. "Too many to name," I said. "Besides, this isn't about mints, this is about your inability to see anything from anyone else's point of view."

My father had taught me that the best defense is a good offense. Unfortunately he ran his marriage under the same principle.

Dark clicked his tongue and gave me an Italian 'get lost' gesture.

We watched the monitor in silence for several minutes.

"You know you've been friends with someone for too long when you start arguing about breath fresheners," I muttered.

"You know what this is right here?" Dark tapped the steering wheel. "This is marriage. Two people forced together arguing about every pointless anything that comes up. And you still want to get married."

I knew I wanted to *get* married, the *being* married part—well, I was choosing to be ignorantly optimistic about that.

"Maybe you should just face facts," he continued. "Some women never get married and you could be one of them. I mean, you don't even know how to cook."

"Really, Boston? That's the bar I'm aiming for—knowing how to cook?" I said. "I have a PhD. I speak eleven languages. I have a ninety-nine-percent shot accuracy rate and I'm fabulous with kids, but because I can't cook, I'm unlovable?"

I didn't mean to bash him over the head with my CV or come across conceited—self-praise was not my usual style, but his words had hit a raw nerve and I felt like I needed to defend myself.

"You're lovable, you're just not wife material," he replied. "Who the hell wants a wife who physically and mentally kicks his ass and then serves him instant noodles every night?"

"Why would she need to *serve* him anything?" I pointed out. "Is he somehow incapacitated? What century do you think we're living in?"

"Century irrelevant," Dark said. "This is a man's world, baby—like it or lump it."

I turned in my seat to focus the full force of my glare on my partner. "I find your statement offensive on so many different levels, I don't know where to start."

"So don't," Dark cut in. "Just accept it as fact."

"I will accept *nothing* as fact," I hissed.

"Silver—seriously." Dark met my stare. "Look at us. Do you really want to spend the rest of your life living with someone you have to lie to every single day until you die?"

My insides knotted. Dark knew all my buttons and weak spots. Lying to my family all this time had been almost unbearable. If their safety hadn't been in jeopardy, I would have broken a long time ago. My greatest fear on this earth was something happening to the people I loved.

"I could marry an agent," I said.

It was Dark's turn to stare incredulously. "Are you forgetting Dale?"

I sighed.

"Three years together and he breaks up with you *with a text message*."

I rubbed at a building pressure behind my eyes.

"What did he say again—that you were an emotional cripple—?"

"I remember," I cut in.

"—that you made him feel like he was going crazy and—"

"Bos!" I said. "*I remember.*"

"Then why the hell are you talking about marrying an agent?"

"Because not all agents are like him."

"Who? Who isn't like him?" Dark demanded.

I sighed. Why did he always have to have a name? "There's you," I said.

My partner laughed. "Me? I don't hold doors open. I don't bring flowers. I don't call girls back—ever. And it's not because they're not nice girls—some of them are very nice—trust me. It's because I know who I am. A relationship is just not an option for me. Any agent who is *compos mentis* knows that." He tapped the side of his head.

"There are actually plenty of agents who are happily married," I reminded him, and it had nothing to do with them opening doors or bringing flowers, or whatever other stereotypes Dark was imagining constituted a healthy relationship.

"If they're married to a civilian then they're living a lie," Dark said. "No matter how nicely you dress up the relationship—it's a lie. Correct? And if they're married to an agent, it won't last. You know our divorce rate."

I felt my dreams hit the wall and splat. I must have looked especially pathetic because Dark's expression softened so that he looked uncharacteristically boyish and bashful.

"Don't worry." He thumped my arm. "I'm here. I'm not going anywhere. We're stuck together forever."

"Awesome," I said. "But I have needs too. Unmet needs ..."

Since Dale there really hadn't been anyone, serious, or even casual, and it was coming up to two years now. I didn't like to use the words 'dire' or 'desperate' but it was getting that way.

"Fine—how about we stop by Walmart after this and I'll buy you some flowers—would that satisfy you?" he asked.

"Again with the flowers," I muttered. "And no—it wouldn't."

"Spoilt—that's what women are these days—they want everything and they want it now. It didn't used to be like this. Men were men and women knew their place."

"I could literally punch you in the face right now, Dark," I said. "I'm this close."

"And right there is why you're not wife material. Case proven. End of story."

"You are a gigantic a-hole, do you realize that?" I told him.

Dark grinned. We turned back to the screen and several moments later the bachelor staggered out of the limousine to the exuberant cheers of his friends.

"Cheating rat," I muttered.

"What happens on bucks' night stays on bucks' night," my partner said.

I rolled my eyes.

The group bunched together and headed up to the club. Our walt straggled at the back of the pack. His feet dragged with every step. He was right on the edge of going green and not in the eco-friendly way: more like the incredible hulk. One of the other guys put an arm around walt's shoulder to support him.

When they were at a safe distance Dark said, "*Andiamo.* Let's go."

We left the car and headed for the club. I was freezing but sweaty, weary but wired, hoping for the best grab scenario and preparing for the worst.

3

In this club, La Nox, the term *exotic dancer* didn't quite cut it. Seriously I had to admire the athleticism of those girls. They were managing to maintain sexy while performing major feats of strength and acrobatics. They were flipping, jumping and kicking, dancing and sliding up and down poles that extended the full two stories of the club—all this while virtually nude. I had a mental flash of myself up on stage, out of breath and sweaty, mascara running and flab flying as I failed at cartwheels and fell into the crowd. Not a pretty sight. Maybe the imagery was overly self-critical. I did maintain a certain level of fitness—it was necessary for the job—but even so, the usual extent of my nude escapades involved dashing from the bedroom to the shower and back and I couldn't imagine that changing any time soon.

Not surprisingly Dark knew exactly where he was going, so I trailed him through the club, which was crowded with patrons both male and female. I spotted the bachelor party, now one of many, settling into a corner booth. Dark and I took a position by the bar where we could keep them in sight and wait for our chance. A topless waitress came to take our drink order. She recognized Dark and spoke to him by name. They exchanged niceties and, to my partner's credit, he looked her in the face the entire time—which was surprisingly more difficult than it sounds. In most human cultures, staring directly into someone's eyes while talking, other than in intimate situations, comes across as threatening or strange. Our eyes naturally wander, especially to anything unusual—like a gigantic pair of double-Gs covered only in body glitter. She tried to strike up a chat with me as well, but I gave closed answers and kept my arms by my sides—my Italian parentage tended to make me talk with my hands, and the last thing I needed tonight was to accidentally grope some unsuspecting exotic waitress mid-conversation about the sunny weather we were having. She left and Dark glanced at me and snorted.

"What?" I asked.

"Could you be any more uptight?" he asked.

"We're not on vacation here," I told him defensively. "We are actually working."

He shook his head and muttered, "Another arrest by the fun police."

I gritted my teeth. I *hated* when he called me the fun police. It made me feel like he was some young springbuck cavorting through the fields of fun while I was the grumpy frumpy killjoy chasing him down with an oversized net, trying to foil all his good times. In reality, whatever Dark did with his time off was his business. Whether he felt as if we were married or not the fact remained we weren't. I didn't keep tabs on him and I didn't try to curtail his fun. I could be fun and spontaneous too … At least I kept telling myself that and hoping it was true.

It was something I questioned, though: how did people see me? How did I want to be seen? How did I even see myself? Who was I? I'd heard that whoever we really are emerges when we're all alone, unobserved. Well, when I was alone … I was usually asleep. It was the only chance I got. I wasn't sure what that said about me, but now wasn't really the time for self-reflection. Now we were working.

A group of lap dancers had surrounded our bachelor party. One girl stood gyrating in front of the walt. He was rocking, but not in time with the music or with the hypnotic circles of her hips. He was moved by an even more savage, primordial drive, one that was about to rip through his reasoning and send him green. The dancer would be the first one hit. I imagined pieces of sequined thong, silicone and lower intestine splattered across the walls and this time the imagery was not exaggerated.

"Bos, we've got to move now," I said.

"No shit," he muttered back.

"I'll try to get him to the bathroom," I said.

"I don't think there's time," Dark replied.

The walt staggered to his feet, knocking the dancer out of the way. Dark reached into his jacket and drew his primary weapon. If the walt lost it before we could get him, there would be no other choice but to put him down—not a concept that sat well with me. As a partnership, we'd never had a fatality before and that wasn't pure luck. I put myself on the line every time to stop a shoot. The put-downs were murder—no matter how you dressed it up. Not that I had ever mentioned this conviction even to my partner, let alone any of our colleagues.

I moved past Dark, weaving a quick path through the crowd. I reached the walt and, with a glance to make sure none of his friends were looking, took hold of his wrist and directed him away from the dancers. He resisted, pulling back sharply. His otherwise handsome features twisted with anger and confusion. I tried to give him a reassuring smile and spoke close to his ear, "It's okay, buddy. I know you're not feeling great. Come with me, I'll get you some help."

I touched his hand lightly, slipping a sedation patch onto his skin. I noticed the spot from the laser sight of Dark's weapon vibrating on the side of his head. I tried again to lead him away. This time, the sedative working fast in his system, he followed with minimal struggle. I took him down a crowded hall toward the women's bathroom.

In most clubs on a busy night, the line to the ladies' room would be a mile long, but here, with women guests the minority, it was inhabited by only two other girls. They were dressed in super short dresses and heavily inebriated. They were hugging each other and singing loudly into the mirror, using their tiny shiny purses as microphones. Their ankle-breaking high heels slipped around on the tiles. They cheered as we entered and both tried to high-five me on their way out, missing completely. One slapped my shoulder and the other lost her feet and fell over—legs in the air, flashing her underwear to the world. She lay where she'd fallen, paralyzed by hysterical fits of laughter. Her friend joined her on the floor and the two of them rolled around wetting themselves with the hilarity of it. The scene didn't look quite so riotous from where I was standing, but I'd had my fair share of drunk and disorderly nights in my younger days so I really couldn't judge.

I managed to shuffle the blitzed duo gently out of the bathroom and close the door on them. I moved the walt into a cubicle and sat him down on the toilet. I turned and locked the door, but as I turned back, it happened. He gasped. His pupils went from pinpoint to fully dilated in one second. All his muscles tightened. The veins in his neck bulged. I only had time to duck as he lunged at me, taking a swing that ripped the cubicle door off its hinges and sent it flying into the bathroom. It hit the mirror with so much force the glass exploded. I twisted and lunged backward, trying to get out of his way, but the walt caught me with an upper cut to the stomach. My ballistic vest absorbed the impact, but it still knocked the air out of me. I landed sprawled on the tiles and the walt rushed me. Completely disoriented by his condition, he misjudged the distance between us and smashed into the wall instead with a brutal whack that rattled my teeth and broke a row of tiles.

He reeled around, blood streaming down his face. He tried to charge again and toppled sideways, taking out a sink. It shattered to the floor and water gushed from the fractured pipes. I took the chance and leaped at him. I caught him around the middle and crash tackled him to the ground. I tried to pin him, but I may as well have been wrestling a rhinoceros. He flipped up with so much force we hit the ceiling and crashed back down to the tiles. His body mostly broke my fall, but then he was on me, his fingers clenched into claws, reaching for my neck. I went for my TRANQ gun.

The bathroom door flew open. Dark charged in with his weapon drawn and took aim at the walt. The young guy broke for the window, smashing through the glass and a good part of the wall. Dark and I both cursed and rushed for the damage. We looked out and saw the walt crashing down the fire escape. He found his balance and jumped from the structure down to the alleyway—a good twenty-five feet below. He landed on his feet running. We scrambled out onto the metal steps and flew down after him. We reached the alley and sprinted toward his fleeing shadow.

"No good," Dark yelled out to me. "He's heading for the road."

We couldn't allow the walt to cause a crash. Dark pulled up and dropped to one knee. He took aim at our walt's back. I kept running, drawing my TRANQ and firing before he could get a round off. The dart struck dead on, into the back of the guy's neck. He ran at least another two yards with enough sedative in him to drop an elephant, and then the effects hit him and he stopped. He didn't fall, which would have been normal: he just froze. We ran the distance and as soon as we got to him, Dark threw the stocks around the walt's arms and locked him down. We were literally five steps from the end of the alley, where sidewalk met a busy inner-city road. A constant stream of headlights passed before us. Our walt was shaking.

Tears shimmered on his cheeks. He looked young and scared, confused. He was struggling to whisper, his lips reluctant to move, "I'm sorry. I want to go home. Where's Mom? Where's Dad?" Then he bucked back and shouted. "Fuck *off*!"

Dark fought to hold him. I ripped a syringe off my duty belt and pumped another dose of paralytic into the guy's neck. His eyes rolled back and his head hit his chest.

Dark and I exchanged a glance. This one was a real fighter. He stumbled to one side and we struggled to right him. His wallet tumbled out onto the ground. I crouched to pick it up, while Dark started walking the walt back down the alley. A honking horn drew my attention and I glanced up. Across the street, I saw the silhouette of a man in black standing, watching. I couldn't see if his eyes were on me or not, but somehow I felt they were. A bus crossed in front of my line of sight and when it passed the person was gone. I dismissed him as a random passerby.

"Sil," Dark called for me from halfway down the alley. I shoved the walt's wallet into my pocket and rushed to catch up. Dark was already on his cell phone calling in the catch and ordering a clean-up crew for the bathroom and a tech to check for CCTV footage. For sure Chapter 11 surveillance would have recorded the catch—including my use of the TRANQ, which was, as I well knew, against Chapter policy. Since every person is different we couldn't be sure of the exact amount of drug needed to bring down any one individual, so we couldn't be sure that one hit would be enough and that wasn't good enough as far as the Chapter were concerned: regulations were to go straight to lethal force. Even so I'd always preferred to answer to my superiors than to my conscience.

"I'll lay the cover for the friends," I told Dark as reached the parking lot.

"No, you take him. I know who to ask," he said. He handed over the shackled man and flipped me his keys. I headed for the car while he jogged back up to the entrance of the club. We needed to get someone to tell the friends the cover story—that our walt had decided to call it a day and had caught a cab home to sleep it off. I assumed Dark would ask one of the girls he knew in there to pass on the message. I looked around for witnesses to refute the story, but there were only a few knots of people up near the entrance of the club and no one was looking. The clean-up crew would double-check that.

I reached Dark's car and directed the walt into the caged-off back seat.

"Watch your head, buddy," I said, helping him to lower in. I locked the door and went around to the passenger side. The adrenalin was draining fast from my body, leaving my limbs weak and heavy. It hadn't exactly been a flawless catch, but the job was done. Zero fatalities.

4

We escorted our restrained and sedated walt along the streets of central Toran-R toward Chapter 11 Headquarters. At this hour, the business district was virtually deserted, save for patroling security guards and a random partyer who had taken a wrong turn and was now trotting down the semi-lit street, glancing behind him and peering ahead with an anxious look on his face.

Once we were out of the car and crossing the sidewalk to Headquarters, a chill wind from the river howled through the center of the city and ripped at my jacket. It slid icy hands along my back. I clenched my teeth to stop them chattering. We approached the darkened glass doors at the front of Headquarters, walking to meet our reflections. As expected, my hair looked tragic (curls plus windy weather equals frizz); otherwise we were deliberately non-descript. Both Dark and I wore duty belts, jeans, black T-shirts, black jackets—mine was Kevlar lined, his all leather. I also wore body armor, but Dark wore none. Apparently my partner thought just looking cool would save him. The walt staggered between us. The poor guy was a little the worse for wear. He reeked of vomit and blood. His head still hung to his chest and we had to drag every step out of him.

"Almost there, buddy," I murmured as we entered the lobby. It was a bland, emotionless space. It had a modern look and layout but zero personality. Like us: inconspicuously inconspicuous. The tap of our boots echoed in the silence. We headed for the elevators, passing a man dressed in janitor overalls mopping the floor. He was Norman—a C11 agent—our *just-in-case* man. I smiled at him as we came even. He returned an awkward shifty-eyed grimace. Some people just don't have a face for smiling. Norm was more of a surly nod kind of guy. We directed the walt to the last elevator on the left. Dark swiped his hand across the sensor panel. The doors parted and we stepped in. A line of heat from the security check ran down our bodies from head to toe and a voice from the speakers above us said, "Silver, Dark. Please state today's password."

"Moncrieff," we repeated in unison.

The elevator began its descent. Soft jazz hummed in the background.

Floors one to thirty-six of the building housed conventional federal offices. Chapter 11 operated in the building beneath the building. No buttons could take you there—just the highest security clearance possible, which no one outside the Chapter possessed. Even presidents, prime ministers and V-VIPS were all fed our cover story: that the agency was a deeply buried unit working on counter-terrorism and international security. Not a lie, but not the whole truth. C11 had branches across the world, with main centers in all the major cities, Moscow (Codename: *Mosaics-Arc*), New York (Codename: *Eastmark-Rye-On*), London (*An-lend-long*) and so on, but central Headquarters was right here in Toran-R. Hidden in plain sight.

"What a night," Dark commented. "Great entertainment, fast grab—Why can't every night be the same?"

I sniffed indifference.

"What?" he asked, then narrowed his eyes. "You think you're too good for wrestling, don't you?"

"No." I glanced at him. "I don't completely understand the attraction but—"

"The attraction is," Dark cut in, "our human—inbuilt—need to witness competition."

"Violent competition?" I said.

"Whatever. Look at history—the Roman gladiators—fighters pitting their strengths against each other for the entertainment of the masses."

"Difference was that was real, this is pretend. No one is actually getting hurt."

"It's not about someone getting hurt," Dark said. "It's about the process—and there is actually a lot of skill involved in fighting and not hurting your opponent—have you ever thought about that?"

"No," I admitted.

"Well maybe you should." Dark took on a fake high and mighty tone.

"So sorry for questioning wrestling." I laughed. "It'll never happen again."

"See that it doesn't. It's art."

"Well ..." I considered the concept "... it is one of the only public arenas where it's okay to put your ass in someone's face. You even get applauded for it. So I guess it could be art of some sort."

"And so is this." Dark smirked.

I rolled my eyes and held my breath. My partner thought breaking wind in closed spaces was the height of hilarity. Actually, he thought farting anywhere was side-splitting humor and he always had to share both the joke and the subtle variances of flavor and sound density. Unfortunately I found his noxious flatulence distinctly unamusing. Fortunately walt was too chemically lobotomized to care either way. The elevator came to a smooth stop.

The doors opened to reveal the entrance hall of Headquarters, lined with shiny black marble threaded with gold for as far as the eye could see. Unlike the lobby above, this room did speak: it said *Expensive—Very Expensive*. The Chapter 11 seal—the Uchelpaix, mythical bird of peace—was stamped across the center of the floor. We crossed it as we headed for reception at the far end of the hall.

"I'll take him to lock down if you script the report," Dark told me as we neared the front counter.

"Five minutes of walking versus an hour of writing—sounds fair to me," I said dryly.

He pushed ahead with his cocky strut and flashed a cheeky grin back at me. Desk work didn't involve enough shooting, punching or full-frontal nudity to interest my partner. Marissa, at reception, was attempting to look serious and focused as we reached the counter. She had a thing for Dark, but the poor girl didn't stand a chance. She'd committed the cardinal sin in his eyes. James from Accounting had told Beck from Surveillance who'd told Terri in the tea room that Marissa had said that Dark was *cute*. For him it was a four-letter word so offensive that even I didn't go there. Sadly, there were no second chances as far as Boston Bonacci-DeScuro was concerned.

Knowing this made her nervous fluttering painful to watch—and even more painful still was the fact that she reminded me of the way I used to act around guys I liked when I was a teenager. The hair twisting, the awkward laughter, the stilted conversation crammed with things you later relive and repeat to yourself under your breath in the hopes that it didn't sound as bad as you think it might have—and yes, it definitely did. Finally she gave Dark a temporary clearance for Medical and buzzed us through to the offices. I exited the cringe-fest, embarrassed for her, embarrassed for me, and pretty much over men in general.

Dark nodded to me as he led walt toward the internal elevators heading for Medical Division, where our guy would be locked down and re-capped, after which time he'd be returned home with a significant gap in his memory. I paused to watch them go. I'd conducted the same LIA (locate, isolate and apprehend) countless times before, yet I still felt moments of unease. I knew we were doing the right thing, saving the walts from themselves and protecting others, but they were just so vulnerable and unaware. They were watched and controlled and they never knew a thing about it. Exactly how the operatives in Medical Division reversed their break-thrus and re-capped them I didn't have clearance to know and, admittedly, I probably wouldn't have been able to understand the process anyway. There was an emergency boredom override switch in my brain that activated at the onset of any scientific, mathematical, mechanical or technological conversation, mentally transporting me from reality into fantasy. Incidentally, I'd spent a lot of my teen school years and adult work life in fantastical places, at least inside my head.

The 'why' of the process was more my level of operation. walts were people identified as having a syndrome discovered in the early nineteen-forties by Dr Douglas K Whitman, whose name inspired their codename 'walt'. *Shaman Syndrome* was a genetic disorder characterized by a mutation across numerous chromosomes. It was passed through certain families. However, its sequence was not the same in each person and had not been mapped with any exactness, prompting the discoverer of the syndrome to famously ponder: *if not explicable by science, could this aberration possibly be considered in the realm of magic?* (Thus the name *Shaman*) The symptoms of the syndrome in an un-capped or breaking-thru carrier were an uncontrollable, preternatural heightening of the senses, which made the person, the walt, superman strong and mentally unstable: basically homicidal and suicidal all in one hit.

Shortly after the discovery, a global meeting of heads of state unanimously voted that it was in the best interests of the human race as a whole not to have these people existing. They were extremely dangerous to themselves and anyone around them. The first suggestion was wiping them all out, but in the aftermath of the heinous genocide of the Second World War and the following international laws and conventions on group extermination, less horrendous methods of controlling the walts were sought. Someone came up with the idea of inventing a disease with symptoms mirroring those of a person close to breaking-thru. They thought it would encourage carriers to come forward and seek treatment, and that treatment would be specialized sedatives to keep the symptoms in check, as well as a sterilizing drugs to stop the syndrome passing on to another generation of walts.

The planning was solid, but the operation failed. They hadn't taken into account that the condition manifested itself differently in every carrier. For some the medication worked, and for others it didn't at all, plus somehow the walts were still falling pregnant and giving birth, despite the sterilization. The science at the time just couldn't explain how, but as an outcome, a new group of researchers, recruited from the very top of their fields, developed a method to suppress the symptoms, to 'cap' the current generation of walts as well as those being born. Chapter 11 was established to monitor these individuals and, in its modern form, was the longest-running, largest-scale surveillance operation in the history of the world.

Most walts lived their lives never knowing what they were. A small percentage 'broke-thru' and started exhibiting symptoms. Then agents like me and Dark acted to bring them in to be re-capped. We were operatives, we were the clean-up crew, we were spin doctors. Most of us had an inborn propensity to stretch the truth, which made trusting anyone difficult, but imagination was like any other beast—it was either chain it up and hear it roar, or run with it. Of course, with any operation of this magnitude, questions regarding preservation of secrecy were always thrown around. How did we function without anyone finding out?

That wasn't a brain-teaser. Either we kept the secret alive, or we kept it in our graves, and anyone we told outside of the Chapter also had an immediate target on their backs. It wasn't written in any operational manual, and certainly not mentioned during recruitment and training, but the fact was the Chapter had long outgrown its former constraints and had evolved into a self-regulating, self-enforcing machine. We operated beyond any government, above any law and outside of any help should we run afoul of the company. It was something agents learnt quickly, mostly through rumors and sometimes with first-hand experience. Agents and their families had vanished. The official response was always that they had been relocated for debriefing and retraining, but we knew this wasn't the case.

When it came to saving the world, the Chapter had an extremely cold-blooded approach that, at times, ran in opposition to the beliefs of their individual agents, and there was definitely a climate of fear governing everything we did. And I could understand why: if the general population of the world found out what we were doing—watching one in three people worldwide, twenty-four hours a day, and performing non-consensual medical procedures on them—there would be a mass uproar, maybe even revolutions—wars—and then what? What if all the walts started breaking-thru and killing civilians and themselves? It was our moral obligation to stop that—I understood that—it was just the 'at whatever cost' that stuck in my throat.

Mostly the Chapter hired agents who could easily fall into line with the operational ideology, but there had been many times when I wondered how I'd slipped through, why they'd accepted me knowing how I'd felt and thought. I'd been honest during the recruitment process, if not extremely naïve. When I'd discovered how things really were, I'd wanted to leave, but by then I was trapped by the fear of something happening to my family—so now I just did my job, inflicting as little damage as I could, while trying to pretend everything was okay. But every day the things we did were getting harder and harder to justify, and more questions about the Chapter were forming in my mind.

Dark vanished down the hall and I turned right. I passed through frosted glass sliding doors into the offices of my division—Operational Services.

5

Compared to most agents operating in other intelligence services and organizations around the world, I was elite as far as security clearance went, but inside Chapter 11 Headquarters, the reality was significantly less grand. I was a small fish in a big ocean of sharks. I was a regular field agent and regular field agents didn't get their own offices; we had cubicles within kissing distance of each other. I had Dark's desk in front of mine, a colleague, Dragomir Jovanović (Codename: Jovic), on the left and his partner, Mai Lin (Codename: Feng), on the right. They called it a pod of desks. It was kindergarten all over again.

I received and returned a few hellos from fellow agents as I weaved my way toward our pod.

"I thought you were on morning shift this week," an agent codenamed Boots called out.

"Called in," I replied to a chorus of sympathetic groans.

My regular shift would start in five hours—seven am. I'd had exactly two hours off in the last forty-eight hours.

Jovic and Feng, looking like the dictionary definition of mismatched, were already standing at our pod. Jovic was of Serbian descent with deep Mediterranean skin, a blond crew-cut and a squat weightlifter's physic. His claim to fame was a walk-through part in an eighties Schwarzenegger film. I hadn't personally been able to catch sight of him in the millisecond of footage, but I'd told him I had, as friends do.

Feng on the other hand had Chinese parents. She was vampire pale with flowing black satin hair and a statuesque frame that made even a tracksuit look elegant. Her family had disowned her after a string of embarrassing, rebellious acts. She described the event as *my emancipation*. That was before the Chapter had recruited her. Feng was the archetypal agent—a single loner with estranged or deceased family and a flexible conscience. But that wasn't her complete persona. She was also a Gemini, a boating enthusiast and three quarters of her way through a PhD studying the positive or otherwise effects of physical contact on the human psyche.

"Hey you," Feng said to me as I reached my desk. She rubbed my arm affectionately and I smiled. Her attempts at "reaching out" always made me smile. Despite countless hours of laboratory observation, role-playing and modeling of culturally normative behaviors, Feng's physical contact always came across as mechanical and was often situation-inappropriate. She was trying to prove that a person who had grown up in a physically cold environment and who wasn't naturally demonstrative with affection could become viewed as such by forcing him- or herself to make regular contact with other people. I wasn't holding out much hope for the evidence supporting her hypothesis, but I did appreciate the effort she made. Our society could be so cold—people too afraid to touch in case they got sued for sexual harassment or contracted some horribly mutated animal flu. Every little bit of human contact helped.

I turned my smile to Jovic and winced at a pain in my jaw. I couldn't remember getting hit in the face; maybe it was from smacking into the ceiling.

"Tough night?" Jovic asked.

I shrugged. "Not so bad."

"Clean catch?"

"Cleanish. Just a totaled bathroom at La Nox."

"The strip club?" His eyebrows shot up.

I nodded.

"Damn!" he cursed. "Why does Dark always get the good jobs?"

I decided against telling him about the wrestling—that would have just been cruel.

Feng fixed her partner with a down-the-nose stare and said, "Men, monkeys and dogs."

She used the saying a lot and even though I wasn't exactly sure what it meant, I could hazard a guess. I loosened the straps of my body armor and sat down at my desk. My whole torso felt tense and bruised.

"Where's the man?" Jovic asked, leaning around his computer.

"Medical," I said.

"Leaving the hard stuff up to you again, is he?" Feng spotted her blonde nemesis passing our pod and shot the girl a threatening look.

"What's new?" I grumbled.

"Smart man," Jovic put in. "I should take some tips."

Feng gave an annoyed grunt and said, "Dream on, Dragomir." She turned to me. "We have to go. One of the walts on our strip is starting to look green."

"Is it just me, or does it seem like there've been a lot more break-thrus lately?" I asked them.

"Maybe," Jovic said. "Maybe it's just age catching up with us. We're not so young any more, yes?" He grinned and patted me on the shoulder. "See you later."

"Do good work." I gave the standard alternative to "Good luck," which was incidentally bad luck to say aloud.

"You know it," Jovic responded. He took his sidearm off the desk and slid it into his hip holster. "Say hello to the man for me—tell him I hate his guts."

He turned and headed for the external elevators. Feng paused beside me. She leaned down and whispered close to my ear, her dark hair spilling across my desk, "Heads up. Twenty's foul today and it's that time of the month again."

I inwardly groaned. Monthly unscheduled performance reviews with our boss, Agent Twentyman. The man had perfect elocution, a penchant for tweed jackets, and the worst god complex I'd ever seen. I'd expected the reviews to be soon, but the thought was still putrid. They never went well for me, and for some reason, I felt particularly vulnerable today. I wasn't sure I could handle it. I could hope for Feng to be wrong, but her intel was never off. She always knew the latest office news or gossip before anyone else. She was carrying on a clandestine relationship with one of the bigger bosses from another division. She'd told me once that it wasn't love, more like, in her words, he had a thing for Asian chicks and she wanted a promotion, and she was more than willing to use both her racial heritage and her feminine wiles as weapons to advance her standing in a kingdom ruled by men. I didn't know whether to think of it as a modern form of feminism or that we'd actually slipped back to square one in racial *and* sexual terms. So I deferred to my dad's life motto—when in doubt, mind your own business.

"Thanks," I mumbled to Feng. She gave me a sympathetic pat on the shoulder and said,

"We definitely need to reschedule tonight."

Feng was one of the friends who I was supposed to have met up with that night. She'd been called in as well. We were all agents, so we understood, but being able to coordinate time off together was almost impossible. She must have read my expression because she said, "Don't worry, we'll find another time. Leave it up to me—I'll organize everything."

I murmured a thanks and she smiled and headed off.

I slumped back heavily into my chair and rubbed prickling eyes. My cell phone vibrated in my pocket and I jolted and grabbed it out. The Caller ID said *Dark*.

"Hey," I answered.

"You've got his wallet." My partner's voice came through the phone lowered and urgent.

I cursed and quickly patted down my coat. I felt the square bulge and dragged out the walt's wallet. One of his cards was sticking up. I forced my eyes away. We weren't supposed to know anything about our targets. No names, no addresses, no personal details, no nothing. Their identities were classified and I was currently in breach of policy—for the second time this shift—on the same day as performance reviews.

"I'm stalling them. Bring it down—now!" Dark said.

He hung up and I jumped out of my chair. I hauled ass out of the office and headed to the front desk. Another agent was talking to Marissa when I got there and I stood behind her, stepping impatiently from one foot to the other, peering over her shoulder until she got the message and moved on. I rushed the desk and said, "Can I please get a temp pass for Medical—Dark needs something urgently."

"Oh." Marissa straightened at the mention of my partner. She quickly formatted a pass card and handed it to me. I snatched it up and hustled to the elevator. Of course it was down on the lowest level and was the slowest ride in history, hitting every single floor as it made its way up to mine. I watched the numbers creep up: nine, Corporate and Conference; eight, Medical; seven, Strategic Intelligence and Liaison; six, Security; five, Legal; four, Surveillance and Technical Operations; three, Support to Operations; two, Human Resources; and, finally, one, Operational Services.

The doors parted and I rushed in, bumping into the people coming out. We did the awkward sideways shuffle with mutual fake-laugh apologies, then I was in and heading down. I shook my head, silently telling myself off. Seriously, where was my brain? I should have put the wallet straight back into the walt's pants as soon as it dropped out, or at least remembered I had it and put it back before we reached Headquarters.

The elevator stopped on level eight and the doors parted. Dark was standing right there, jittering with impatience. He still had the walt beside him.

"What took you?" he demanded in a hushed tone as I stepped out. "Have you got it?"

I glanced at the Medical Division agent at the admissions desk. She seemed otherwise occupied, but I knew the surveillance cameras everywhere in Headquarters didn't suffer from such human limitations. I stepped close to Dark to obscure our actions and slipped the wallet into the walt's pocket.

"What did you tell her?" I whispered, nodding to the admissions agent.

"I just said I'd forgotten the drop-off ticket—used the charm," Dark murmured back, showing me the exact ticket he'd pretended I was bringing him. He clicked his tongue at me and shook his head and I nodded, Yeah I know. The walt shuddered and Dark moved him over to the desk. I watched them for a moment as my partner cleared out the guy's pockets and the Medical admissions agent ticked off the items. Most walts, most people, carried wallets or purses and if one came in without one it always raised questions.

My eyes wandered past the admissions desk down the narrow white corridors of Medical Division. This level was hospital-esque—it smelt sterile and felt cold—and all the agents wore white coats. I thought there was something very creepy about all the closed doors lining the corridors, something unsettling about the absence of sound. It was unnatural.

Laughter broke the unsettling silence and my attention went back to Dark. He was flirting with the admissions agent—or actually they were flirting with each other. I left them to it and took the elevator back up. It stopped at several levels, with agents getting in and out. A couple of them were talking about something to do with archival footage and it made me think. I needed to talk to someone. The elevator stopped at level four, Surveillance and Technical Operations, and I followed a group of people out.

Op Services and Surveillance and Tech agents had dual clearance because we moved between the two floors so much. I stood beside the elevators looking around. There were only four floors between Medical and Surveillance, but they were worlds apart. Here it was non-stop banter and calling out, clattering of keyboards, phones buzzing, chairs squeaking, coffee percolating. In fact it was almost too much—stimulation overload. My head was starting to ache and the skin of my face felt like a mask tightening over my skull.

A pair of large, cool hands slipped over my eyes from behind and a familiar voice said, "Guess who?"

"Just the man I was looking for," I replied.

"And I was just on my way to see you. There's our telepathy again."

The hands slid away and I turned to my friend Evan Ostby (Codename: Byter). Dark and I had met him at basic training and we'd been close ever since. He had a frightening intellect, and with very little effort he could have made everyone else feel like complete imbeciles, but he never did. He was one of the good guys. A rare breed. He would have been quirky-handsome too—if not for *The Beard*. Long, thick and bushranger bushy, it made him look like Santa, The Teenage

Years. Even if a girl decided she did want to kiss him, despite the facial forest, it was highly probable that the hair itself would prove an impassable barrier. I looked away from the beard to the rest of my friend. His outfit today was boho meets gamer, a bit of both, but achieving neither. I guessed that was how new trends got started. I, myself, had no style whatsoever—unless 'cat fur and washing-machine lint on black' suddenly came in. Not that it stopped me buying beautiful clothes, but most of them just hung, like works of art, in my wardrobe. Still, if Byter didn't lose the beard soon, I was going to break into his apartment and depilate him in his sleep.

"You're thinking about my beard again, aren't you?" he said.

"I can't help it," I said. "It's just so—"

"Sexy, manly, playful—like Sean Connery and Harrison Ford's love child." He raised his eyebrows.

"Not exactly," I said. "More like Hagrid crossed with Gimli the dwarf."

"Awesome! Even better!" Byter seemed genuinely delighted.

I shook my head and said, "No. Not awesome."

He laughed. "Don't worry—it will grow on you."

"I hope not." I touched my face. "I'll have the biggest waxing bill in history. Listen …" I searched for the right words. "I may have discharged an extra amount of sedative into a walt tonight at La Nox. It *may* have happened instead of lethal force." I raised an eyebrow and Byter caught on immediately.

"Ah," he said. "Well no worries. I'll look into it." He gave me a smile that said if there was footage of me using the TRANQ in the laneway, no one would be seeing it.

"Thanks," I said.

"Is something else wrong? You seem stressed," he told me, massaging my shoulder.

"Just one of those days," I said. "or nights … day-nights."

"Yup, I'm hearing you." He nodded in understanding. "Just a while ago I locked myself in the toilet—I had to SMS for help, so now I'm officially known around the office as the Toilet-Bowl Bandit."

I smiled. Byter could make fun of himself and I admired that.

"Speaking of the bathroom," I said. "I gotta go."

"When you gotta go—you gotta go," he said. "But before you go—where's Dark?"

"Medical," I said. "Dropping off a walt."

'Well, when you see him, can you tell him I scored those tickets? The game is a go." He did a happy dance.

"What game?" I asked.

"Football—don't worry, you wouldn't understand it," he teased.

"I'm sure I would if I bothered to try."

"Well I only got two tickets."

"Just in case I try to intrude on your bromance with Dark," I said.

"Hey, what can I say? He's very," he lowered his voice, "*cute.*"

I sucked the air in through my teeth. "You're skating on thin ice," I warned him.

"I live life dangerously," he grinned. "Hey—what did you think of the whole 'guess who' intro there?" Byter liked to re-visit and over-analyze mostly everything he did. "Too high-school?"

I laughed and said, "It seemed fine to me. I probably wouldn't use it for a first date or anything though—might come across a bit …"

"Stalker-ish?" Byter asked. "Over-eager-beaver?"

"Something like that." I laughed again and started to turn away.

"Oh and hey—sorry—just one more thing," he called me back. "How's *it* going?" He made a gesture to his arm.

I automatically squeezed my forearm and said, "Great."

"So it's working?" He raised his eyebrows.

"You haven't been tracking us?" I asked.

"No," he said and I could immediately tell he was lying. "Well not much," he clarified. "Not to keep tabs or anything, just now and then to check how it was all looking from a tech perspective."

"It's okay," I told him with a laugh. "We signed up for this."

Dark and I had agreed to be test subjects for one of Byter's new tracking systems. It was the tiniest of microchips embedded into our forearms. It communicated with an app on our phones and showed our precise locations. It wasn't highly confidential, but Byter had asked us to keep it quiet due to some issue in his division of design copying.

I took out my phone and opened the app—it showed a map of the city and rushed down and down until it pinpointed Dark's location as below us, still on Level Eight.

"Any pains?" he asked. "Any pins and needles or numbness?"

I shook my head. "Nothing."

"Cool," he said. "I'm working on the next stage now—establishing visual—RFID implants are not new technology by a long shot, but it's new in the way it interacts with the body … You know how previously we couldn't physically tag walts because of the way their bodies responded to the implants? Well I don't want to jinx myself," he lowered his voice, "but I think I may have cracked it."

Whenever Byter talked about his work, his face lit up and his words raced. He loved his job, but I felt suddenly ill-at-ease. Swallowing it down I said, "That's good—but I better go and get this report done; apparently we have a performance review today."

He grimaced, and said, "Fun times." He knew my history with the boss. We said our goodbyes and I headed for the ladies'. When I went in, I checked that the outer door was definitely unlocked. I didn't want to repeat Byter's mistake and become known as the Toilet-Bowl Bandit's less intelligent accomplice. Things like that tended to stick. Another friend for Op Services had been saddled with the codename Brownman after an unfortunate incident during basic training involving too much curry and a lack of public-toileting facilities. Still I could think of worse names that could have come out of that particular event.

Afterwards, I made my way back to the elevator and got in line behind a pair of colleagues, who I recognized as fellow Op Services agents. They were partners with the codenames Omen and the Rose. With my mind on other things, I didn't immediately notice the tension between them, but then it hit me like a physical shove. Their bodies were so tight and upright, their silence so suffocating, I wondered if either of them was actually even breathing. I seriously considered taking the next ride up, but I really needed to start the report and it was only a few floors. So when the doors opened, I shuffled in. The pair stayed to the front of the elevator and I moved to a back corner. I knew these guys were intense—they had a reputation as ruthless operators in the field—but they were usually icy emotionless, like Feng but without the well-intentioned heart. Today they seemed volcanic. The Rose was smoulderingly beautiful as always, with waves of shiny chocolate brown hair cascading down her back and a curvaceous body poured into a tight red dress. It wasn't exactly subtle agent garb, but it was possible that she was on a specific assignment that required that kind of clothing, and I highly doubted she'd get any complaints from the bosses either way. The Rose was the type of girl I tried not to stand beside, in case I looked like the ultra-unflattering *before* shot from an extreme makeover show.

Her partner, Omen, was similarly searing, with infinite dark eyes and heavy arched brows, a face with a million expressions a minute, all equally unreadable, and all laced with an undercurrent of contempt for everyone and everything. As well as being ruthless, I'd heard they were also elite—consummate professionals—but at this particular moment it was difficult to imagine either of them being able to blend in anywhere—let alone everywhere. They both looked pale, sweaty and, in short, extremely pissed off. Omen's hand was jittering at his side. I looked at it and it stopped. He had a black sun, split in half with a jagged line, tattooed on his wrist. The Rose huffed heavily and crossed her arms across her chest, and I got the distinct feeling then that the tension between them was sexual tension.

As I thought the thought both agents turned to look at me with an eerie synchrony. Their eyes had an uncomfortable intensity to them. Thankfully the elevator stopped and I maneuvered my way past them and out into the entrance lobby. They exited as well and headed toward the external elevator. I guessed they wanted to get out of Headquarters, find somewhere in the city where C11 cameras weren't watching and have a massive screaming argument. Or some massive screaming sex. Or both. There was another reason agents shouldn't date agents—especially not their partners. If Dark and I had no escape from each other, there was no doubt it'd be war—nuclear. I headed back to my desk, composing the report in my mind as I walked.

6

I pushed my hand into the device on my desk that we called the Shake. No one could access C11 files without first 'shaking hands' with the most advanced computer security system in the world. The Shake read my fingerprints and skin density and a hundred other things in one second then logged me into the system. A box popped up on my computer screen asking for my name, codename and password. I typed in *Silvia Denaglia—Silver—Yzzirf* (the name of one of my cats spelled backwards). My desktop loaded and Dark and my open cases flashed up. I had a few low-priority tasks to deal with, but they would have to wait until after the report. I opened a template and sat for a long moment to gather my thoughts.

A shiver ran through me. It was hard to think with the air-con gusting at sub-arctic temperatures, not to mention the low lighting. After a Workplace Health and Safety report suggested that the blaring office lights were contributing to agent psychological ill health (though somehow neglecting to address the ridiculous air-con), they'd changed all the fluoros to mood lights, which made it feel as if we were out to dinner instead of at work. So now we were all cold, depressed *and* hungry.

My eyes ran over the objects on my desk—a photo of my cats, a photo of my family and Dark at my brother's wedding in New Zealand, a multiplying random stack of papers in my inbox, my coffee cup, which I wished was full and not bone dry, and a somewhat sickly pot-plant geranium that I'd felt sorry for and purchased even though I definitely did not have a green thumb. I noticed the edge of a bag of chocolates peeping out of my top drawer. They called to me with tiny delicious voices. In what state of mind had I ever thought I was strong enough to have a stash of "emergency" chocolates? Just one, I thought—knowing full well there was no such thing in my world. I broke my junk-food-on-weekends-only promise to myself on a daily basis. Why did chocolate have to taste so good? No-no foods and long hot showers topped my list of vices. I liked to read those health articles they put out every now and then with experts claiming chocolate was good for you—though I tended to skip the paragraphs where they talked about limiting intake to like one square a fortnight or whatever. Who only eats one square? Actually, I did have a particularly regimental friend who only allowed herself to *smell* chocolate and not actually eat any. Whenever she felt depressed she went around inhaling peanut butter cups. I admired her resolve, but I also sort of felt sorry for her. Was that much deprivation necessary? Each to her own, I guess.

I leaned back in my chair and glanced around the office. My eyes were drawn to my latest office crush, Wyatt (Codename: Adonis). But he really wasn't Adonis, just the most attractive of what was currently available. I sighed. I was like a man-seeking missile sending every male in my path running for cover. Maybe a little self-critical again, but still sometimes it definitely felt like that. When I was younger, I'd felt a quiet excitement about the prospect of meeting the man of my dreams. There was something magical about the idea of eyes meeting across a room, a first kiss, shared interests and experiences and now ... I just wanted to know exactly where all the normal, non-personality-disordered, caring guys hung out and I wanted exact directions how to get there.

I realized I was procrastinating, but instead of getting straight into the report I found myself checking my work email. There were a couple of forwards, and way too many anal, annoying memos from my direct supervisor, Eric Wickwhitter (Codename: Turbulence)—delete, delete, delete—I made it my mission in life never to read any of his emails. I wasn't against authority. I would stick by a leader I respected to the ends of the Earth and back, but I had no time for connivers who expected respect without doing a thing to earn it. They weren't great men. They were just men who thought they were great. Eric fitted solidly into the category. He lurked, he lied, he came in on the joke just a few beats too late. He wormed his way out of work. He passed the buck. Because of him I had perpetual backache—not because of the completely unergonomic chair he'd assigned me, but from the knife he put in every time I turned away. I flicked over to my personal email.

"Silver." Eric's weasel face popped up beside me. I tapped Ctrl F4 rapidly to close the screen. "Have you read my emails?"

"I was just about to get to them," I lied.

"Great. How's the workload?"

"Well actually it's a bit—"

"Great." He handed me a heavy stack of papers. "Can you process and file? I've got a long weekend coming up and my secretary can't get to them. Just shoot off an email to me once you're done. I'll give you a call later to touch base—and if you wouldn't mind answering my phones for me. Just jot the messages onto the yellow pad beside my computer and at the end of the shift type them up and save to desktop. Thanks a whole bunch."

"Right," I said, keeping my voice civil, while I gave him the finger with both hands under my desk.

"Agent Wickwhitter." A voice, deep and mellow, spoke just out of my sight.

I straightened up as Landon 'Jack' Marshall (Codename: the General) stepped around the pod divider. He gave me a conspiratorial smile and lifted the papers Eric had just given me off my desk. He spoke genially, handing the papers back to my supervisor. "I'm afraid Agent Denaglia will be tied up with something for me for the next few weeks, but thank you for considering her worthy enough to take over your role."

Eric's Adam's apple bobbled as he swallowed the lump in his throat. He took the papers and said, "Absolutely, sir, and may I say what an honor it is to have someone you personally trained working under my direction."

"You may," the General said. He turned to me. "Do you have a moment to take a walk with an old man?"

I jumped up and followed him through the desk maze. Awed eyes tracked the General everywhere he went. There was some jealousy there too. I knew a few of my colleagues felt threatened that the General had been my Case Officer during training, and I understood why, but to me he was much more than an ex-mentor. He'd changed the whole path of my life. I'd first gotten into law enforcement, despite the needs and expectations of the job being totally contrary to my nature, because of an incident in my neighborhood that profoundly affected me as a child. A few twists and turns had led me into the Federal Police, where I was partnered with an officer by the name of Boston Bonacci-DeScuro. It had turned out we'd gone to the same high school, though had of course never socialized. According to him, I'd been a nerdy, book-hugging overachiever and, according to me, he was a crass, moronic, sports fanatic—cheating on all his exams, smoking dope behind Block A and doing burnouts in his pickup truck. Despite this unfortunate history, we'd managed to bridge the gap and discovered we actually worked well together. We even had things in common.

Although we achieved at work, however, we never progressed in rank. For whatever reason—Dark's temper, me being female—we were held back year after year and I started to feel like a bird running along the ground trying to take off—maybe not a majestic bird like an eagle, more like a seagull or a magpie—but still I wanted us to fly and I was desperate for someone to believe we could. The General had believed.

He'd recruited me and Dark into C11 and personally acted as my Case Officer and mentor. He'd counseled me through the grueling training in the tradecraft. He'd given me assignments above my level that no one else would have given a woman in an organization still controlled by a boys' club of aging male bosses, all scratching each other's backs raw. To me, the General was a great man. He wasn't afraid to challenge convention. I had all the respect in the world for him, and I wasn't alone. Everyone knew who he was. His reputation loomed large and so did he. He was a hulking force—tall, wide—sixty-something, but ageless. He spoke softly, listened intently and remembered everything. He could verbally eviscerate someone and never lose the jovial twinkle in his eyes, which, understandably, some people found unsettling. But I understood—he liked to play with words and didn't take anything too seriously. He ranked way higher in the agency than my biggest boss, Twentyman. In fact he sat on the Conference—the ruling board of Chapter 11, but he never acted like it. Instead he made plebs like me feel important. Obviously I couldn't say enough about him.

We headed down a long hallway into a lounge area overlooking an interior garden—another WH&S attempt to booster our sanity. The General made a sweeping gesture for me to sit, then went across to the vending machine and got two hot chocolates.

"Thank you, sir," I said as he handed me one and sat down in the lounge chair opposite mine. "Is there a special project you need me for?" I couldn't think of anything I wanted more at this moment than to escape from Twentyman and Eric.

"I'm sorry, my dear, not at this stage." He chuckled at my visible disappointment. "There will be something. You know I have your professional development always in my mind. And I keep telling you," he added, "to call me Jack."

"I can't," I said honestly. I felt it would be physically impossible to call him anything but 'sir'. Which made me sound like a bit of a brown-noser, but around him I couldn't help it.

He took a sip and murmured, "Wonderful and terrible. Just like life." He gave an enigmatic smile. "So—tell me everything—How's the family?"

"Everyone's good," I replied. "Just working. Benny and Gemma's baby is due in July."

"Aunty Silvia, hey?" He beamed. "My fifth grandchild is due in August."

"Wow, congratulations," I said.

"I think so," he agreed. "Anything I've accomplished in this life shrinks to the minutest insignificance beside the magnificence and privilege of being a granddad."

He glowed with pride and I smiled. I could imagine he'd be a fun grandpa—always teasing and playing.

"They're all coming to our house for a few weeks over Christmas. I'm counting down—six and a half weeks to go," he said and I shook my head.

"I can't believe how fast this year's gone. It's crazy."

"Wait until you get to my age," the General said. "Time flies—it really does ... And how's work?" he asked, turning the mood of the conversation back to business.

"Okay," I lied.

He lowered his head a little and repeated, "And how's work?"

I searched for the words, not wanting to come across as whiny and ungrateful. "It's okay, really. I just ... You know how I always said I got into this line of work in the first place to actually help people? I'm just still not sure that I am. I feel like I could be doing more."

What I really wanted to say was that I felt like I could be doing more to change how C11 was currently handling walts. I'd been questioning our procedures for a long time and feeling more, now than ever, that there had to be a better way—like getting to the walts earlier, educating them instead of forced capping, integrating the syndrome into mainstream society so that the Chapter no longer operated in secrecy, killing off innocent people whenever they deemed it necessary. But I couldn't say any of this aloud—even to the General. It was the agents who started speaking about change who vanished. "Good—because there is more to be done." The General leaned forward and set his cup down on the table beside us. "The face of this earth, of humanity itself, is ever-changing, presenting new opportunities and new challenges. You are in a perfect position to reach out and grasp life with both hands. My worry for you is the same as it has always been." He touched the left side of his chest. "You feel too much. You're circling brilliance like a falcon on the wing, but you don't have the killer instinct that's required to move into positions of power in this game."

I nodded. He was right, of course. I wasn't a killer—not in the actual sense. I wouldn't even squash spiders or roaches. I caught them in jars and took them outside to freedom. I wasn't a killer in the corporate sense either. I had my faults, but I wouldn't lie and backstab my friends just to be promoted.

"I know what you mean," I said. "But I can't be who I'm not."

"I understand," the General said softly. "Not so long ago, I felt the way you feel, that I could do more and be more, but I was stuck as well. I think you should spend the next little while really asking yourself the hard questions, reorganizing your priorities, getting back to who you are and preparing yourself to walk through the doors of opportunity when they open. There is actually—"

He paused, glanced over my head and smiled.

"Agent Marshall," Dark spoke just behind me. The General stood up and he and my partner shook hands. Dark pocketed his phone. He'd been using Byter's app to track me.

"How're things, my friend?" the General asked Dark.

"Couldn't be better. Easy assignments, overtime wages, and a hot date tonight after knock-off."

The General laughed. "Ah, I remember those days all too well … But, believe me, one day you'll meet a girl who will tame your wild ways."

Dark shook his head. "No, thank you. Not for me."

The General continued smiling and said, "I'm betting you're married within the year."

It was Dark's turn to laugh. "I think the dementia's starting to hit you there, sir."

"Maybe," the General said, his bright blue eyes twinkling with mischief. "But I think not. I'm quite good at predicting these things, you know. I have a one hundred percent accuracy rate."

"I'm sorry to be the one to bring you down, but it will never happen," Dark insisted.

"Okay." The General gave a teasing smile. He checked his watch. "Well, I'm sorry but I have to head off. Talk to you soon," he said to me, then to Dark, "Enjoy your last year as a free man."

"It'll never happen," Dark repeated.

"Of course not." The General grinned at him.

We watched him walk back up the corridor. He looked back to wave before he vanished. He never stayed anywhere very long. He was a workaholic, spreading his time between Headquarters and the various other C11 facilities around Toran-R, plus international travel for meetings and conferences.

When he was out of sight, Dark turned to me and said, "Report done?"

"Not even started," I replied. "But I'm over this. I need to get out of here."

"Your place for breakfast?" he suggested.

"My place," I agreed, and we headed for the entrance lobby.

"Who are you going out with tonight?" I asked as we walked. "Natasha?"

He scrunched up his face.

"I thought you liked her."

"I did; she was perfect until she started talking."

I sighed. "With that attitude you'll be lucky if you don't go home alone after your *hot date*."

"Oh well." He shrugged. "If it doesn't work out with this one, I've always got Mrs Palmer and her five lovely daughters." He held his hand out in front of him and grinned.

"So wrong," I said. That image was going to stain.

"Silver. Dark." An announcement. "Agent Twentyman's office in ten minutes."

The voice inside my head screamed an expletive. "I forgot to tell you—performance reviews," I whispered to Dark.

He cursed—not in his head. "There goes the perfect night."

7

Dark and I perched on the hard, narrow chairs outside Twenty's office. I kept shifting uncomfortably, disturbed by the terrible flashback to standing outside my principal's office in primary school. He was also a man who had taken himself way too seriously. I was guessing it wasn't too difficult to feel big when you're yelling at trembling kindergarteners. A headache had set in behind my eyes. I'd always dealt with regular migraines, but it felt like something had been setting them off more lately. I felt for my pills and had just started to consider making a dash to the water cooler when Twentyman's door swung open and his PA, Agent Kenealy, appeared. She was a forbidding, matronly type with a bulldog face and enormous bosoms that emerged a good second from a room before she did. She gave us a curt nod. We stood and followed her down a hall into the boss's office.

"Sir, Silver and Dark," she said into the room.

Twentyman (Codename: Wrath) sat at his desk reading a document. He held up a finger to tell us to wait. He continued reading for what felt like half an hour before he put the papers down and looked up. He wore tinted glasses that made it impossible to see where he was looking. In larger meetings, people had to keep pointing to themselves and glancing over their shoulder to check who he was talking to. On the up side the lenses dulled down the ferocity of his eyes. Nothing, however, could tame the bite of his aftershave. It was something pungent and old school—hell for a migraine sufferer like me. I could feel the pounding behind my eyes building.

"Let's get to the point," Twentyman barked. He had a scar near his mouth similar to one I had—except his looked like a knife wound and mine had been from a parrot I'd been trying to save and which had bit through my lip.

"Dark, your performance is acceptable," Twenty said. "Silver, yours is unacceptable. Your field work is sloppy, you take unnecessary risks and ignore protocol, you're still questioning your superiors despite previous warnings, and according to your line supervisor, you spend more time reading personal emails than meeting your KPIs."

Damn you Eric, you complete turd—I thought, but just nodded.

What could I say? I did check my emails a lot and I did question my superiors and ignore protocol—and I did take risks, but to me those risks were very necessary to prevent fatalities. No matter what he said, I knew I always worked to a very high standard—but unfortunately my standard and Twenty's standard were two completely different things. What he wanted from me, I felt, was everything superficial that could be ticked off a list and filed away neatly—and nothing that actually mattered—like life and death. He didn't want me to ask questions or try to search for better options; he just wanted me to do the job exactly as he thought it should be done. And that was where the relationship had broken down.

At first, I'd struggled between trying to impress him and listening to my instincts, but as my respect for Twenty had plummeted, so had my desire for his recognition. Coming from a past of overachieving and people-pleasing to the point where even I wanted to punch myself in the face, part of me still cared—a lot—about the negative evaluations, but there was another part of me now that completely rebelled against the idea of him dominating me. It was a silent rebellion, because it had to be, but it was still there, and I think he saw that. As much as I disliked him, he was sharp and he made it pretty clear that if it wasn't for my connection with the General I would have been demoted to coffee-stirrer long ago. And as for Eric, he was just the type who needed someone to bitch about and blame. Twentyman's attitude toward me gave him permission to exercise all his favorite humiliations on me. In a way I'd definitely brought everything on myself by not being more subtle with my feelings, but, in another way, they were both just pricks.

"You seriously need to step up your game, girly. You need to make yourself a useful part of this division," Twenty continued.

"Agent Twentyman," Dark spoke and I cringed in anticipation. "Respectfully—your assessment is bullshit."

"You watch yourself." Twentyman whipped off his glasses and burned Dark up with his acid stare. "You're way out of line."

"Am I?" Dark shot back. "You're passing all this judgment on her, yet I'm the one working with her twenty-four/seven. I see her breaking her back every day. She doesn't sleep. She doesn't eat. She puts everything into the job."

"Well maybe she should consider transferring to a more administrative role, because her everything is nowhere near enough."

Dark clenched his jaw and pressed his thumb against one side of his nose—a 'catch gesture' the good people at anger management had taught him to make himself stop and think before physically attacking someone. I tensed, ready to grab him if he made any move whatsoever.

"Silver, I'm putting you on probation. Step up or transfer out. Understand?" Twenty bellowed.

'Yes, sir," I replied.

"You're dismissed." His phone rang and he picked it up, swiveling his chair away from us and starting to talk as though we were already gone.

Kenealy appeared and ushered us out.

We moved fast to the entrance hall, and rode the elevator up in silence. We made it to the lobby. Then Dark erupted like Vesuvius. He yelled a curse and kicked over the nearest bin. He punched the wall. I grabbed him and hustled him outside. Norm was coming over to assist and we didn't need the kind of help he had on offer.

"Easy, Bos." I tried to calm my partner on the sidewalk. "Do you really want to re-do anger management—again?" I asked.

"He has no right to pass judgment!" Dark shouted. "He doesn't know shit-all about what we do. He just sits in that office and answers the phone. A monkey could do his job! We have a hundred percent success rate—one hundred! He's not mentioning that, is he?"

"He's the boss," I said. "He can say whatever he wants to say and since when are they required to know anything before spouting off?"I was trying to lighten the mood but it didn't work. "Don't let it get to you. It doesn't worry me," I lied.

"Bullshit it doesn't worry you," Dark said. "I know you."

It was true—he knew me way too well. It did hurt, but unlike Dark, I did most of my melting down on the inside. I shrugged, faking nonchalance. "What can you do?"

We looked at each other. We both knew the truth to that question.

"Forget it," I urged him. "Come on, let's walk it off."

I took his arm and forced him into motion. Several thousand blocks should be enough to cool him.

8

In this generation of delayed launching—longer years of study, a later start to earning, thirty being the new twenty—it wasn't quite so embarrassing to admit I still lived at home. I had tried independence. It just didn't take. I'd managed the practicalities. I made rent, I balanced my budget, I cooked and cleaned for myself, despite Dark's opinion on the matter. It was the emotional disconnectedness that had worn me down. Coming home to an empty space, eating alone, watching television alone, going to sleep alone in silence. Some people would have relished the privacy. I'd missed being part of a family, and since I was one of those fortunate enough to actually have a family I could mostly tolerate and who could mostly tolerate me, I'd packed up my stuff and moved back home. I knew it was the right decision because it'd felt effortless. Friends and colleagues had given me flack for what they saw as a backslide into dependency, but to be honest I was too happy to listen.

That said, I was well aware of the seeming incongruity of an intelligence operative living at home with Mom and Dad, but obviously our work wasn't all international jet setting, martinis at high-society functions and random steamy encounters, so there wasn't that much to cover up. For me it was mostly paperwork, endless hours stuck in Dark's car monitoring walts, and an abundance of time to contemplate the meaning of life. Never a good thing.

It took just on half an hour to get to my parents' house from central Toran-R. The area was suburban/rural, full of Italians, Macedonians and other southern Europeans. That meant lots of manicured hedges, water features, and miles of concrete. A rising sun cast shades of fairy-floss pink and orange across the sky as Dark swung into my driveway. We rumbled up the gravel stretch.

My parents were already awake and out in the front yard. It seemed the older they got, the earlier they woke up. Soon they wouldn't be sleeping at all. My mother was throwing feed to her chickens and various flocks of wild birds. Dad was attempting to construct cages around his palms, which Mom's birds were using as beak sharpeners. From their tense body language, I guessed it had been one of *those* mornings. Dark parked the car and we stepped out. I'd known Dark for so long he was practically family, which meant no holds barred for his benefit—unfortunately.

Mom and Dad stopped what they were doing to wave. I waved back to them—my parents—day and night of my existence. They were proof that opposites did attract. Opposites sustaining a thirty-year marriage—that was another story. I was saving it for therapy. Mom, survivor of an abusive childhood, was an all-creatures-great-and-small kind of person. She could be found by the side of the highway checking roadkill for signs of life, adding to an ever-expanding menagerie of lost and broken animals. She was an introspective thinker, struggling with self-doubt and questions of worthlessness, constantly worrying about offending people. She cried when others cried, she felt others' pain profoundly, and took on the world's sorrows as her own. She couldn't bear to watch the news.

Dad loved the news. He loved mafia movies and foreign-language films. He said he watched them for the *real* storylines. We teased him that it was for the gratuitous sex and violence, which he continued to deny. Dad was loud. He spoke loud, laughed loud, moved loud. He shouted at the television when he watched soccer, which made Mom curl into a small, silent ball in the corner. She hated shouting. She loved quiet mornings—Sudoku, crosswords and fine-bone china. She loved her cats. Dad tolerated her cats—with frequent complaints that their importance eclipsed his in his own house—*I don't have a chair to sit on!*

I knew my parents loved each other—despite everything, I saw that—but as for *liking* each other ...

"Your mother's birds have destroyed all my plants," my father called out to us. "I've been nurturing them for ages."

I gave the usual neutral nod.

"They're not *my* birds. They're wild birds!" Mom said, exasperated, as though this was a repeat run of an argument they'd just had. It very likely was.

"But you're feeding them!" Dad said.

"I'm feeding the chickens!"

"The chickens—the chickens," he muttered. "Do you know that your mother spent four hours this morning patting those cats—*four hours?*"

"It was five minutes!" Mom said.

I gave the same nod. Dad was prone to exaggeration; Mom to understatement. I thought the time spent on cat-patting had probably been somewhere between fifteen and forty minutes. Not that the timing actually mattered in any conceivable way.

Dad laughed. "Five minutes! You're off with the fairies." He did a dance around his palm trees, flapping his hands like little fairy wings. Not my dad's best look. Mom glared hard at him as he started talking Italian in an unflattering high-pitched voice.

"See you inside," I called and Dark and I left them to it. An audience tended to spur on Dad's performances.

We went up to the house—my home—and stepped inside. It looked like it always did: as if we were either just moving in or moving out. Mom was a hoarder, Dad a chucker. One of my earliest clear memories was of sitting on the driveway watching Mom making trips into the house with a bunch of odds and ends she'd picked up at the local charity shop. At the same time, Dad was sneaking out the back door and around the side of the house with armfuls of other random stuff and stowing them in the boot of his car for a stealthy trip to the dump.

I paused in the hallway to let the tension drop from my shoulders. I'd taken my migraine pills in the car and the pain was starting to ease.

A fur tumbleweed drifted across the tiles in front of us, coming to rest beside a toy rat. Dark picked up the squeaky toy and threw it to a cat who was stretched across the hall-way. He was a big, pink-nosed, ginger-and-white Turkish water cat we called Mr Foofypants.

"Fetch," Dark said.

Mr Foofy eyed the toy with sluggish indifference, then started grooming his back as if to say, I feel embarrassed for you.

"What do they do all day?" Dark said as if for the first time. He, like Dad, was more of a dog person. I didn't reply. He had already heard everything I had to say on the matter many times over.

We headed out into the lounge room, where my brother, Benicio, sat on the couch in front of his laptop. A muted basketball game played on the television beside him. Benny worked as a prosecutor for the government and, like me, couldn't get a handle on the notion of work/life balance. Maybe we were just victims of our time. He and his wife, Gemma, also lived with my parents, but were actually saving for a house, so they at least had an excuse. Gemma was just over two months pregnant and suffering serious morning sickness. Even the passing notion of food made her throw up. We only glimpsed her these days as she ran through to the toilet.

"Hey, how's it going?" Dark went over and slouched down beside Benny.

My brother removed his glasses, looked over at Dark and said, "Hell is other people."

My partner snorted. "Tell me about it."

"You working on a case?" I asked my brother.

"Yep."

"How's Gemma?" I asked.

"Pregnant," he replied.

"Still sick?"

"Yep."

"That's no good."

"Nope."

That was a typical conversation for us. I asked, he answered, a teasing glint in his eye. *Little sister trying to act like a grown-up.* Getting information out of him was like wringing a dry towel for water. He would have made a good C11 agent—better than me. We'd always communicated best through movie quotes.

The bells on the front door jangled and Mom came in, windswept and flustered. "I'm so sorry about us," she said to Dark.

"Mom," I warned her.

"Oops, sorry."

"Mom." I raised my voice.

She put a hand over her mouth and I heard a muffled 'Sorry'.

She was a serial sorrier. She said sorry at the beginning of almost every sentence. She said once it was because her father was angry about everything. In truth, her father wasn't angry, he was a psychopath. The fact she'd come through a childhood with him at all, let alone as healthy and loving as she was, was a miracle. Still, after I caught her saying sorry to a cushion she'd accidentally knocked off the couch, I decided enough was enough. I was myself a recovering apoloholic, so I understood it was a long road.

"Not a problem," Dark replied.

"Would you like a drink?" she asked him. "There's juice, water, tea, coffee, decaf, herbal teas, soda, milk, flavored milk, soy …?"

"How about a beer?" Dark teased her. "And a shot of tequila."

Mom gave an obliging chuckle. She was a teetotaler and there was no alcohol in the house, except for Dad's vino, which he kept with his own 'emergency' stash of chocolate and thought no one knew about. Dark himself never drank, which most people found to be a surprising fact about him. He'd said once that his grandfather had told him not to start something he couldn't finish.

"Coffee would be great," he said.

"And how about breakfast—toast, cereal, fruit, yoghurt …?"

"Mom." I stopped her before she listed the entire contents of the fridge. "We don't really have time to eat." I checked my watch. "We're on double shift."

"But you haven't slept." Worry overtook her face.

I shrugged. "I'll catch up tomorrow."

My family thought we still worked in federal law and were not allowed, under legislation, to talk about our cases. That was as close to the truth as they would get.

"She may not have time to eat," Dark said. "But I definitely do. Give me the usual."

Mom beamed at him. I knew she secretly hoped Dark and I would end up a couple.

Dad wandered into the room and said, "Five and a half million this Tuesday." He rubbed his hands together. My father's two greatest dreams were to go to space and to win lotto. He always spoke about winning as if it was inevitable and not a virtual statistical impossibility. Benicio, Dad and Dark started debating which sports car they'd buy with the money, so I escaped the conversation and took the chance to go upstairs to my room to change. As I passed the bathroom I heard my sister-in-law hurling into the toilet and cringed in sympathy. Getting pregnant may be a gift, but being pregnant sounded like hell. Still I secretly wished it were me—more than I ever let on.

I went into my room and locked the door behind me. I stood for a moment breathing in the familiar and safe—touching sight with all my 'things'—my desk, my bed, my bookcase. Everything was animal patterned. Dark said it made the room look like a poor man's brothel, but I wasn't about to take fashion advice from a man who thought underwear wasn't dirty until you'd worn it inside-out as well. The bookcase was jammed packed with books, mostly classics Mom had passed on to me from her literature degree days. I'd only read a fraction of them, but I had good intentions and they made me at least appear well read. Mom had also given me her vast collection of Men and Women Relationship Self-Help books, of which I'd read exactly zero. Judging by her relationship, they didn't work.

My phone vibrated in my pocket. I dragged it out and saw a message from one of the other girls from my group of friends—Gloria (Codename: the Terminator). She was into body-building and close-combat fighting styles. She was a tough, make-no-excuses sort of person, but if a man with an accent, particularly French or Irish, spoke to her, she melted on the spot. The message said, *Hey luv. How was the night? We missed you!*

I smiled and wrote back, then threw the phone onto the bed and crossed to my favorite part of the room, an obscenely large walk-in wardrobe. (Another big reason I'd moved back home.) I slid open the glass doors and looked around at all the clothes and shoes, color coded and gorgeous. Many were unworn, seeing as I spent most of my waking hours in blacks for work, but still the sight made me happy. Because of what I was, I couldn't talk about everything that was bothering me, so I attended retail therapy instead—mostly over the net, which was horribly addictive, but it made me smile. I walked to the back of the robe. I keyed the passcode into my cell phone, wirelessly disabling the wall-safe's security. The fake wall panel slid up and lights flashed on around the various weapons and agency gear I had in my stash. I pulled the TRANQ gun off my belt and pushed in into its mold. It was probably better if I rested it until I was off probation. I re-placed the TRANQ with a standard, live-ammo weapon and re-stocked my duty belt. I undid my body armor and lifted it over my head with a groan of pain, then inspected the damage. Despite the protection of a medium-weight ballistic vest I had light bruising across my ribs. I shook my head. That walt had been a real fighter. I started wondering if he was home by now, but stopped myself, instead focusing on grabbing a shower and changing my clothes and armor.

When I went back downstairs, the guys were still talking cars, and the conversation had gotten loud and animated—as though their opinions on the matter actually made a difference to anything. Mom was cooking in the kitchen, humming along to her blaring stereo, zoning out to Mozart. I decided to do the same. I dragged one of the cats off her favorite sunflower cushion and inconvenienced her with a cuddle. I sat down and switched off for a few precious seconds as the smell of toast and pancakes wafted through the air.

9

"She could have just left. She could have said, 'This isn't working—I'm sick of you—it's over—I'm leaving—goodbye.' She could have. The fact that she chose to completely trash my entire life first and not even face me. I just can't get over that," Dark called out to me.

And he wasn't wrong. Seven years on and he was still talking about the break-up like it was yesterday fresh. He didn't know what was harder to believe—that he had spent five years of his life with someone and never really understood her, or that she had changed so much seemingly overnight. He would never admit to it, but I suspected that this heartbreak had more to do with why Dark never wanted another serious relationship than did the constraints of our job or whatever macho bravado of Chosen Singledom he put on.

"She even took the bulbs out of the sockets so that when I arrived home I couldn't turn on the lights. Who the hell does that? Can you tell me who?"

I stared out the apartment window and drifted. Replies were unnecessary. Sometimes Dark just got into a rant and needed to see it out. His ex had ended it with a very low blow: she'd left without telling him, taking every single thing they owned with her, even his clothes—even the light bulbs, but he hadn't exactly been the dream boyfriend either. He'd taken her for granted, spent excess time working on his cars and going out with his friends, he'd forgotten all their special occasions and flirted with other girls. Basically he'd continued to live a single life while reaping all the benefits of having a relationship. What had he really expected would happen? These were the things I thought, but never said aloud. I loved Dark too much to tell him the truth.

I leaned my head against the windowpane and waited for him to finish changing. Dark's apartment building stood right beside the river, several blocks from work. Six bridges, in various places, joined the CBD with other parts of the city, including the arty south bank. Ferries crisscrossed the river transporting passengers up and down to various terminals along its length. An early sun warmed the backs of people strolling, jogging and bike-riding along the boardwalk. In a few more hours the place would be packed with tourists enjoying the sights and sounds. A thought occurred to me. If I could see two hundred people now from this kitchen window, sixty of them were guaranteed walts, and that meant those sixty were not only in my sight, but under the constant eye of C11—on the streets, at work, at school, in their homes—everywhere, everyday, men, women, children. Disquiet slithered down my spine. It was necessary, but still a privacy invasion of epic proportion.

A smell like some kind of organic rot disrupted my thoughts. I peeked into a pizza box sitting on the bench, then gagged and slammed the lid back down. Pizza à la fur. The stench complemented Dark's current décor theme: mess layered on mess with a shade of mess. He had clothes everywhere, so many it was a wonder he wasn't running around naked. A dirty-dish Leaning Tower of Pisa stood in the sink, the soda-can Coliseum on the coffee table.

Ice-cream sticks, corn-chip packs, newspapers and (ewww) condom wrappers littered the floor. I needed to go to the bathroom, but I didn't dare brave the sight of his toilet. I wasn't a neat freak by any stretch of the imagination, but this place was giving me palpitations.

My eyes settled on the only clean spot—the cabinet Dark's grandfather—'Nonno' in Italian—had made for him. It was now a shrine to the old guy. Framed photos of him and Dark's grandmother sat on top with an ever-burning candle lamp beside them, along with a small collection of personal items he'd kept—rosary beads, the gold cross and chain, an old bible, a cloth map of Sicily.

I knew my partner could come across as shallow, but there were other deeper, well-hidden sides to him. I seemed to spend a lot of my time trying to convince other people of this, but they didn't know about Dark's childhood, about what he had suffered at the hands of people who should have been protecting him from all the dangers in the world. That had left scars beyond anything physical, beyond anything explainable or fixable.

He never spoke of it, but his grandfather had told me some things that had haunted me ever since and made me a lot more understanding of Dark's mood swings and blunt ways. As soon as the grandfather had realized what was happening, he'd stepped in and taken Dark—and had never let his mother or her boyfriend near him again. I'd known Nonno as a little old man, but in the nineteen-thirties he'd been a champion boxer in his native Palermo, and there was something else about his eyes that, old man or not, you just didn't want to mess with him. He'd become Dark's protector, his parent, his mentor and guide, his best friend. Who knew what sort of person my partner would have become without him, or if he'd even have survived childhood? I didn't know where the mother or boyfriend were now, but part of me really wanted to track them down and make them suffer. Maybe one day I would.

I went closer to the cabinet and leaned down to look at the shelves where Dark kept a collection of rocks he'd chiseled to look like animals, a couple of terrible vases I'd made in my attempt at pottery class and, at the very back, hidden behind a framed photo of me and Dark, a small photograph of his daughter. She was seven now and they'd never met. He kept tabs from a distance, mostly checking she was okay, but that was the line for him. He'd never said it, but I knew he thought he'd be a bad father. It was funny how we'd been partners for so long and still thought we could hide things from each other.

"What?" Dark had come out of his room and seen me thinking.

I gestured to the sty around us. "How can you live like this?"

He looked around. "What?"

"What do you mean *what*?" I said. "Your whole place looks like a fourteen-year-old boy lives here."

"My cleaner's on vacation," he said defensively. "What am I supposed to do?"

The man was an expert in armed combat and espionage but the concept of a vacuum cleaner and a bin baffled him? Whatever he paid his cleaner, it wasn't enough.

"Hey, perfect opportunity for you to practice," he said, handing me a broom and patting me heavily on the back.

"Not in a million years," I replied, handing it back.

I checked my watch and my partner raised an eyebrow. He thought I had an unhealthy obsession with checking the time. I disagreed—I thought my time checking was well within the normal range. I couldn't help that we lived to such strict schedules.

"Are you ready?" I asked him.

He fastened his shoulder holster and duty belt, shrugged into his leather jacket and said, "Let's go."

10

The night before the gods of pro wrestling and gratuitous nudity had smiled on Dark; today, however, belonged to me. Our first assignment for the shift landed us just west of central Toran-R—at the expansively green and irresistibly romantic botanical gardens. It was one of my favorite places to be: a peaceful oasis in the heart of the concrete jungle. It was especially beautiful now with the new sun's rays streaming through the leafy treetops and glistening silver across the pond, where ducks and swans swam, glided, in the still quiet. The air was chilled but fresh, perfect for relaxing in the sun. I sat beside Dark on the park bench where we could observe the garden's entrance, the walking tracks all around the pond and halfway up the hill to the lookout.

It was ten-sixteen am and the first wave of early Saturday brides, arriving for their photographic sessions, had just rolled in. A relatively calm few. Come one o'clock, just past the more popular wedding times, and there would be a bridal stampede for the most romantic spots, with impatient jostling and the frantic camera clicks of self-proclaimed creative geniuses. I watched the arriving limos, and the disembarking groups, fascinated by the bridal dresses, the bridesmaids' colors and hair-dos, and the inter-group dynamics playing out like mini soap operas. The men in general looked the same—insert Guy In Suit here. Some grooms had taken a different angle—one was wearing a bright yellow tux. His bride wore black, so collectively they looked like a very large bee.

Some of the brides appeared ultra relaxed, chatting, strolling, glass of champers in one hand, their heels in the other, train dragging along the ground. Others were uptight and jittery, forcing smiles, checking flowers and veils, constantly reapplying lip-gloss and powder. And yet another group—the sergeant-major brides—came through at a march, barking orders, death-staring bridesmaids who weren't keeping up with their train-holding duties, and God help anyone who stopped for a bathroom break or tried to take off her heels. I guessed everyone handled the stress in a different way and big family events tended to bring out the best and the worst.

I had a flash of memory of my uncle's wedding. Dad was the best man and over the course of the day had become staggering, slurring drunk, and with my dad, being that drunk inevitably meant dancing—enthusiastic, uncoordinated, sweaty dancing. He was hopping and bopping all over the dance floor, sending all the female guests running for cover. He proceeded to initiate a two-person conga line with the bride, only to knock her over and trample her tiara. He continued doing the twist, oblivious, grinning lopsided, suit in disarray, hair disheveled. One of the bride's older relatives had asked me and mom if we knew *that man*, to which we'd replied in unison, "Never seen him before."

After the fallout from that event, and subsequent death threats from my mother, Dad was much more reserved at my brother's wedding. But where one ridiculously drunk person abstains another steps up to the plate—or the bar, as it were. The resident drunk at Benicio and Gemma's wedding had started off being loud and tragically unfunny, went on to engage in rum-breathed flirting with anyone who'd stand still long enough and ended up doing the chicken dance wearing my mother's bra on his head. (Apparently it'd been so un-comfortable that she had taken it off and left it on a chair in the women's bathroom—and somehow—this guy had got his hands on it.) You had to laugh … sometimes hysterically.

I nudged my partner and said, "This is nice."

Dark turned and gave me a look of supreme indifference and unmitigated boredom.

"Romantic," I added, to tease him.

His expression took a vaguely ill turn.

"Look at the brides." I gestured to the entrance. "What do think of that dress? Would that suit me?"

Dark stared at me until I said, "What?"

"I hate weddings." He over-pronounced each word. "And everything to do with weddings."

"Oh come on," I said to him, undeterred. "You had fun at Benicio's wedding."

He winced and shook his head. "Didn't we just decide last night that neither of us is getting married?"

"I don't recall deciding that," I said. "I remember you telling me I wasn't marriage material."

Dark threw up his hands and sighed: *Here we go again—the marriage conversation.* "Don't you think of any-thing else these days?" he asked, pained.

I shrugged. "Not really—no."

"Okay, listen," Dark said. "If nothing else puts you off, think of this. I read a study recently about marriage styles or something like that—whatever—basically what it was saying was—no matter what we do most people end up repeating the relationship patterns of their parents."

"Well we're screwed," I said.

"Exactly." He tapped my arm. "So no weddings—no rings, no flowers, no 'Does my butt look big in this shade of white?' Okay?"

"Well maybe not for me," I said. "But apparently you'll be saying 'I do' before the year is out."

Dark groaned and toppled over to his side. "Don't encourage him. He has no idea what he's talking about. No one's getting married,"

"Okay," I agreed. A few seconds later I asked, "But if I was—do you think I'd look good in that dress?"

Dark slid out his sunglasses and pushed them over his eyes. He crossed his arms and clenched his jaws. As far as he was concerned the conversation was over. I laughed quietly to myself. Some days he was so easy to tease.

My smile faded as a bad idea came to me. We'd viewed an image of the walt so we knew who we were looking for, but we didn't know what she was dong at the park. What if she was a bride? How the hell were we going to vanish a bride on her wedding day? She wasn't exactly replaceable. I'd turned to Dark to ask the question when I spotted our walt, thankfully not in white. She was wearing a pink velour tracksuit and had a short blonde bob that didn't quite suit her skin color. She was jogging alone. Perfect. Dark hadn't shifted his position, but I felt the focus of his attention. We watched the walt jog around the pond. She looked out of breath and uncomfortable, but aside from that I couldn't see any symptoms of a break-thru. There was a possibility it had spontaneously resolved. I hoped so. I felt sore and tired and I really wanted to stay sitting in the sun for a while longer. The walt stumbled and confusion crossed her face as she noticed her feet felt different, faster, unstable. I sighed—here we go again. She jogged past and Dark and I got up. We started onto separate paths to cut her off near the lookout. I heard a *tsk* sound and glanced behind me. Two Op Services agents, Hawk and Chewy, were heading our way. Hawk, whose nose was indisputably beakish, raised his eyebrows at me, beckoning.

"Bos," I called my partner. He turned and headed back. As we moved together toward our colleagues, a call from Headquarters came through on Dark's radio. He responded and the switchboard operator said, "Dark and Silver, you are reassigned. There have been two walt fatalities—9 Bank Terrace. No surveillance intact."

"Confirmed," Dark said.

The connection cut and I said, "No surveillance intact?" There were always multiple cameras hidden in walt houses, for them all to fail was very strange and extremely rare.

Dark shrugged. Rare but not unheard of.

We passed our replacements halfway around the pond. We acknowledged each other with a nod and kept moving. They headed after our target and we moved toward the garden's exit. I glanced back toward the walt jogging her way up to the lockout. I spotted someone else standing on the hill—a man wearing black. I halted and Dark stopped beside me.

'What?" he asked.

"I thought I saw that guy at last night's job," I said.

A girl who had been heading down from the lockout tapped the guy on the shoulder. He turned and they kissed and hugged.

"Something?" Dark asked, his sharp green eyes studying the couple. He waited for my reply. My intuition had always been stronger than his. Seeing the guy again definitely felt wrong, but I had to admit I wasn't a hundred percent sure it *was* the same person. It could just be paranoia—an occupational hazard.

The couple walked off with their arms around each other and I shook my head,

"Nah … just … nothing."

We moved fast to Dark's car and headed for the inner-city address.

11

By the time we arrived, the refurbished colonial-style house was already swarming with uniforms. Dark and I ducked beneath the yellow tape and headed up a path. No one gave us a second glance. We looked like we had the authority to be there. That was part of our training. It was about the walk, the posture, the facial expression. Humans went a lot more on body language than most people realized. We climbed the steps to the front door, which stood blocked open. First thing I saw was a thick drag line of blood leading from the door back into the house along a polished wood hall. Blood was also drying on the inside door handle. My first thought was someone had tried to escape and been caught. My second thought was that I was glad I hadn't eaten much for breakfast. We had the training in crime-scene investigation, but it was definitely not my forte.

We edged inside and followed the blood trail to the victims—according to Headquarters they were both walts—one man, one woman, lying facedown. Both had gunshot wounds to their heads. From the similarity of their positioning, it looked like an execution-style murder. But it wasn't really our job to determine the whos, hows and whys—just to make sure that the killings weren't related to *what* they were and to ensure the secrecy of the agency hadn't been breached in any way. I looked over the murdered walts: they were maybe middle-aged, both well dressed, no obvious abnormalities. I crouched carefully beside the male victim. His arms were splayed, hands sprawled out. I couldn't see any bruising on his skin or any other signs of a struggle. He did have a distinctive tattoo on his wrist—a black sun split in half with a jagged line. It immediately clicked that I'd just seen this tattoo on Omen, the agent from the elevator. Weird. They taught us not to believe in coincidence, but this couldn't be anything else: a walt and an agent with similar tats. Maybe it was the symbol of some eighties rock band or something. I checked the woman and saw she had the exact same tattoo on her wrist. My suspicion deepened.

"Do you recognize the tats?" I asked.

Dark studied them for a second then shook his head.

"Do you?"

"Omen from Op Services has the same symbol on his wrist as both the vics."

Dark's eyebrows lowered. "The same one?"

I nodded and he said, "We'll have to look into it."

We exchanged a look. Agents investigating agents—it didn't sit well with us but we couldn't just ignore something like this.

I took out a notepad and sketched the mark, finishing up as the lead investigator entered behind us and began dishing out orders.

"Better do the intro," I said.

Dark gave a nod and I got up and approached the officer, while he stayed by the bodies. It was an unspoken arrangement between us that on jobs I generally did the talking. Dark couldn't help but antagonize and mock people.

"Hi there." I flashed a federal badge at the police boss. "I hope you don't mind us having a look around."

"As long as you don't mind me asking why the federal interest," he said.

"Just had some gang-related activity in the area." I kept it vague. "Do you have a theory on the deaths?"

"Not really: too early," he said cautiously. "We'll know more after the autopsies."

"It doesn't look like forced entry," I prompted him.

"No," he agreed, but gave me nothing else.

"Would you mind if I took your name and called you for further information at a later date?"

"Sure," he said, "Damon Walsh—Sergeant."

"Great." I jotted it down. "We'll just have a glance around and then we'll get out of your hair," I added, which was probably not the best cliché to use, considering he was virtually bald except for a good attempt at a comb-over, but his attentions were already elsewhere. I hadn't made much of an impression, which was exactly how it was supposed to be. I returned to Dark.

"Guy's a real chatterbox," I said. "Couldn't shut him up."

My partner smirked.

We did a quick scan of the lounge room, which apart from the dead bodies was neat and tidy, with nothing in particular out of place or noticeably unusual. We headed through the doorway into the kitchen. The smell of baked banana saturated the air. I tapped the oven—still hot—and kneeled down in front of it. There was a cake inside. I called Dark over and he crouched beside me.

"Talk about life cut short," I said. "One second you're baking, the next you're … gone."

"Do you think anyone would notice if—" Dark started.

"We're not taking the cake."

He muttered something under his breath that sounded a lot like *fun police* and stood up. I stayed where I was, feeling more aware than usual of the C11 surveillance cameras I knew were planted all around the house.

I imagined the dead walts alive—cooking, watching something on the TV that sat on the kitchen countertop, or maybe just talking to each other about their days. Everything they did, someone was watching, every private mo-ment—going to the toilet, having a shower, having sex … An invisible witness judged their every step.

"What's wrong?" Dark peered over the bench at me. I shook my head and tried to hide my anxiety. When I didn't answer he crouched back close to me. "What, tell me?"

"Are we doing the right thing?" I whispered, as quietly as possible.

"What do you mean?" he whispered back.

"With the walts—watching them, bringing them in."

"Of course," he said without a flicker of doubt. "It's for their own good."

"Is it?" I asked.

He looked at me as if I'd lost it. "You've seen what hap-pens if they're not re-capped."

I nodded. He was right. I had seen it—a thousand times.

"Here, have some gum." He pushed a stick into my hand. "Stop thinking so much." He stood up, patted me on the head and moved out of the kitchen and through a doorway into the dining room.

I used the counter to drag myself up. Past partially open French doors, the backyard hedges swayed in a slight breeze and brightly colored parrots hopped across the lawn. The sun shone. Life continued, oblivious to the loss. Sounds in-truded into my thoughts: footsteps, conversations, the click-ing camera of the crime-scene photographer, Dark scraping a chair across the wood floorboards. Then I heard something else—something out of place. I held my breath, and in the si-lence someone else breathed—behind me, in the pantry. As I turned, the door burst open and a person shoved me hard in the chest, slamming me backward into the edge of the counter.

I crashed to the ground and staggered up to see the person leap off the back porch.

"Dark!" I yelled to my partner and took off in pursuit. I barged through the doors and bolted over the railing. My boots slammed down on a concrete path. Dark landed just behind me. We saw the person jumping over the backyard fence.

"Where was he?" Dark called as we sprinted across the lawn.

"Pantry," I said. We scaled the wood boards of the fence and landed in a back road behind the block of houses. The suspect was already halfway to the other end of the street. He was moving way too quickly. We thundered after him, pushing our bodies to maximum speed. My muscles knotted and lungs burned.

"Stop or we'll shoot!" Dark yelled at the fleeing stranger. He drew his gun.

As the guy reached the end of the street, a car screeched across his path. Two men, dressed in black, stepped out of the vehicle. Dark took aim. The suspect skidded to a stop and looked back at us. I caught the sense that he was crying. One of the men from the car lifted a hand.

An incredible force rushed toward us with a tidal wave of destruction. It snapped fenceposts like toothpicks and ripped up the concrete. It struck us, sending us both flying backward. I smashed down on the ground and rolled over and over, coming to rest against an uprooted tree trunk. I lay there stunned, with my face pressed to the ground, the smell of soil close to my nose. I blinked to focus and finally rolled over to sit up. I squinted through the settling dust. The suspect was gone. The men and the car were gone. The street was demolished and Dark … I scanned the wreckage and couldn't see him. I struggled to my feet and still saw no sign. Panic seeped through the shock and spread quickly through my body. Where was my partner? Halfway down the demolished road I spotted a bloodied hand protruding from beneath a slab of rock. I ran.

12

I wandered directionless through the hallways of the hospital, peering through doorways at strangers. The foreboding feeling, the labyrinth of winding corridors and, more than anything, that smell, disinfectant washed over sickness, reminded me of when Dark's grandfather had died. Visiting his bedside had been like visiting his gravesite—he just wasn't there any more. Dark had never really dealt with the grief. He just kept burying it and re-burying each time it clawed its way up—zombie pain. My partner had no idea how to deal with emotions. He usually just punched his way through.

Since the emergency crew had brought us in, I'd been stitched and patched and had given my statement to a pair of agents from Support to Operations Division. They'd asked me if I had seen whether our attacker had thrown or propelled an explosive device, or if he'd been holding a detonator. I'd said I hadn't seen, and, in fact, I hadn't heard an impact explosion either, prior to the rush of damage. Which to me seemed strange, but everything had happened so quickly. Maybe I'd just blanked it out. Maybe I was concussed. The doctors had said I needed to sit down and rest, but I couldn't. I couldn't stay still, so I limped on. I had a banged-up knee, some cuts and bruises—one on my forehead that looked worse than it was. The body armor must have saved me from any major damage. It shouldn't have, especially since I hadn't been wearing a helmet, but somehow it had.

My cell buzzed for the zillionth time. Jovic and Feng, Gloria, Byter and the others from our closer circle of friends had been calling, and so had a whole host of more distant people from the C11 world, but I hadn't answered at all. I didn't want to talk to anyone. I just wanted to know if my partner was alive. It felt like every clock in the place was ticking backward second by ever-slowing second. Finally, *finally*, I heard my name called over the hospital intercom. I ran to the elevator and slammed the button until the doors opened, then ran through the ward hallways until I arrived at Intensive Care, where they'd told me to come when they called.

The nurse at the front desk directed me down the hall and I arrived at Dark's room out of breath.

I went through the open doorway and saw my partner lying on a gurney bed. He was chalky white, battered and bruised and breathing through a machine. I started to cry and couldn't stop. I went to his side and took his hand. He felt so cold. I didn't even notice there were other people in the room until the surgeon started talking. He was still wearing his operating cap and gown. A C11 Conference official stood beside him taking notes. The surgeon explained the extent of Dark's injuries—broken ribs and arm, dislocated shoulder, collapsed lungs, internal bleeds, skull fracture—the list continued. He talked about prognosis—that he expected with extended physiotherapy and occupational therapy Dark would make a reasonable recovery with some long-term reduced capacity. He was lucky, he said, very lucky. I thanked him and he left. The Conference guy loitered for several more minutes, he said a few well-meaning words that sounded rehearsed and patronizing, then he was gone as well and Dark and I were alone.

"Bos?" I whispered to him. I leaned in close. "Boston?"

If I lost him … If I lost him … I couldn't even think of it. I dragged a chair close and sat. I leaned my head against the bed beside his arm and let time slide. I was vaguely aware of people coming and going, checking machines and charts. Somewhere in the depth of the waking nightmare, I felt Dark's hand close over mine. I jolted upright and found him watching me through slitted eyes.

"How long have I been out?" he whispered, his voice raspy.

I blinked and checked my watch—just after seven am.

"Almost twenty-two hours," I said. "It's Sunday morning."

He scrunched his eyes shut.

"Are you in pain?" I asked. "I'll get someone." I jumped up and the room spun around me.

Dark grasped at my arm again and tried to drag me back down. "I don't want drugs," he said. "I want to get clear."

"You need something," I told him.

"Sit … sit," he murmured.

I hovered uncertainly then sat back down. I perched on the edge of the seat and stared at my partner. New tears stung my raw eyes.

He lay for a while with his eyes closed, listening to me gulping and sniffing, then he sighed and said, "Sil—go home."

"No," I replied.

He looked at me and repeated, "Go home. I don't need you sitting here sobbing over me like I'm about to die. I can't take it."

"I'm not going anywhere," I said.

"I'm fine, see." He tried to move and collapsed back, groaning in pain.

I leaped for the red button on the device lying ignored by his hand and pressed it. A nurse appeared in the doorway.

"He needs something for the pain," I told her. She came in and checked his vitals and charts, then amped up the dosage of his morphine drip.

Dark's body relaxed and he mumbled, "Sil—go. I'm not resting till you've gone." He stubbornly kept blinking his eyes open. The electrocardiograph output started spiking as his heart rate picked up speed.

"You're stressing him out," the nurse told me sternly. "You have to leave. He needs rest and so do you. Come on." She tried to manhandle me to the door, but I resisted.

"Fine, I'll go," I said. "But just give us a minute."

She looked reluctant, but left the room, saying, "Two minutes."

I went back to stand close to Dark. "Your watch, cell and wallet are in this drawer," I told him, trying to keep myself official so I didn't start crying again. "They said I have to take your duty belt and guns—hospital policy ... I'll be back really soon."

Dark shook his head. "Don't ... I don't want to be that person ... lying ... lying in hospital ... people around them." His words ran together. "I don't want anyone else seeing me like this. I'll be out soon ... Go home, then go to work—find the psycho ..."

"I will," I said.

"Go home ..." he whispered again. "Now." His eyelids flickered.

"Okay," I whispered. I turned and headed for the door.

"Silvia!" Dark struggled to call me and I rushed back to his bedside. "My car ..." he said.

"It's fine," I told him, smiling because I'd thought it might have been something profound. "They took it to the compound. I'll make sure it's okay."

I settled him back down and arranged the pillows behind his head. The nurse popped her head around the corner and said, "Two minutes."

"Equals a hundred and twenty seconds—thanks I can count," I snapped, my tolerance severely stretched.

I kissed Dark's cheek and backed to the doorway. I stood there for some time before finally leaving.

I caught a cab back to the city and picked up Dark's car from the C11 impound where the clean-up crew had taken it the day before. I turned over the engine and it spluttered and growled unhappily. Dark never let me drive it and with just cause. Despite scraping through all the agency driving requirements, I was still an iffy motorist. It was an effort to get behind the wheel every time I drove, to the point where I had to admit it was probably some kind of phobia. I thought of Dark's expression if he knew I was actually driving his baby. That made me laugh, which made me cry, which made my driving even more hazardous, but it felt wrong to just leave the car there. I composed myself, adjusted the mirrors and headed out of the city.

13

I made it home, but stayed in the car. I sat shivering, waiting for the feeling that I was falling apart to fade. An hour turned around—maybe two. After arriving at hospital, I'd texted to ask my brother to tell our parents I'd had an extended shift. I didn't want them to panic. Mom had phoned a few times and left messages. I knew there would be a scene when they saw me. I would make a scene if I saw one of them in my condition, but still, I was dreading it. I wasn't sure if seeing them upset would make me break down and I didn't want them to see me crying. The more something hurt the less I wanted to show it, especially to my family. For some reason them knowing I was hurt made it hurt all the more. But I couldn't stay in the car forever. The combined odors of blood and hospital stink clinging to the fibers of my clothes and hair were starting to get to me. But I just couldn't make myself open the door.

Eventually Dad came out with the trash and saw me there. He waved. I waved. I forced my face into a mask and finally got out of the car. I watched his expression as I limped nearer and saw the change—the Hello Happy to See You becoming the What Happened?—a lowering of the eyebrows, the apprehension darkening his eyes. He glanced past me to Dark's car and his forehead creased into heavy lines. He lowered his head. I'd seen that look before—it was the anticipation of pain. Dad knew a bad sign when he saw it. Mom was an academic, but he was street smart—one result of growing up in a Sicilian orphanage in the height of the mafia reign. As soon as I was close enough he said, "Is he alive?"

I nodded.

The front door rattled and Mom came out with the compost bucket. She saw me and stopped sharp. Her hand shot up to her mouth.. I must have looked even worse than I thought.

"There was an incident." I got in first. "Dark's in hospital. He's okay."

Dad shook his head; Mom teared up. I braced myself. There was a lull and then they both launched in—asking questions, demanding answers, voicing their united hatred for the job that put me and Dark in this danger. They didn't actually leave any spaces for me to answer, which was fortunate as I didn't know what to say.

Eventually the commotion brought my brother out. He saw my damage and started grilling me in prosecutor fashion about the whats, whens and whys of the accident. Finally I managed to move the interrogation through the front door and into the lounge room, where I threw off my jacket and slumped down into a chair. Now that they knew, I didn't want to be alone. I didn't want to think. Since my wounds were basically superficial the doctors had given me only low-grade painkillers, but now I wished they'd given me something much stronger. I wanted to pass out into chemical oblivion. Mind and body, I ached.

The day passed. My parents hovered, they worried, shot glances, gave me food and took every opportunity to tell me to quit. My brother put off the work he had been planning to catch up on that day. He had a bunch of downloaded series and started playing one that he thought I'd like. Even my poor sister-in-law struggled down clinging to her vomit bucket so she could sit beside me on the couch. They all wanted to go and see Dark, but Intensive Care had strict guidelines on who could visit and when. So I sat staring at the television screen, seeing the attack over and over instead of the show Benny had chosen for me.

Every time it replayed, my mind added new details. I was sure now that our attacker hadn't launched a grenade or missile, and there hadn't been an explosion, but before the impact I had felt something … something like a word on the tip of your tongue, like the tune of a song you can't quite remember, something half-forgotten, half-unforgettable. That feeling had made me throw myself to one side just before we were hit. Dark hadn't moved and that was the real reason he was lying in hospital and I wasn't. A terrible disquiet squirmed in my gut. I needed to figure out what had really happened. It occurred to me that there would be footage of the incident. I got up and everyone copied me.

"I have to call the office," I said.

"You need to rest," Mom insisted.

"It's okay," I said. "I'll only be a minute."

Before they could stop me, I shuffled to the front door and went outside. I dialed Byter and he answered after the first ring,

"Silver!" he said, his usually jovial voice strained. "Are you okay? How's Dark?"

We spoke for a bit about my partner and then I asked, "Have you seen footage of the attack?"

"No," Byter said. "I mean—we brought it up straight away after you called it in and there's a picture, but it's totally fuzzed out."

"Fuzzed out?" I repeated. "How does that happen?"

"Well, it can be a few things," he said. "Usually some kind of electrical interference."

"They told us that the surveillance footage at the Bank Terrace murder scene was also compromised," I said.

"Ah …" He tapped on his keyboard then confirmed, "Yes—yes it was. It's a similar kind of broken track, which makes sense since it's the same location."

"Is there any way to clean it up?" I asked.

"Already on it. I'll do everything I can."

"Can you do me another favor?" I asked.

"Of course."

"Can you find out if this kind of interference has happened before and where and when?"

"Sure—I'll check the logs," he said.

I thanked him and we talked for several more minutes before hanging up.

As I turned back to the house, I spotted a car with heavily tinted windows pulling into the driveway. I watched with suspicion as it crawled up the gravel stretch. It wasn't the smartest thing, to just stand unarmed out in the middle of nowhere watching a potential hostile approach, but my brain was functioning on low power.

Luckily, when the door swung open, a familiar figure stepped out. The General straightened up. He was wearing a fedora hat and a suit with the pants pulled up past his belly button, granddad style. I limped over, trying to put on a neutral face. He saw through me in a second.

"Silvia." He took my hand in his warm grasp. "What happened? Tell me everything."

I recounted the incident. I also told him what I hadn't told any of the others—that in my recollection the attacker had not been holding any devices nor thrown anything. When I was finished we stood in silence while the General considered my words.

"Sometimes," he spoke tentatively, "after a trauma, the mind can create or delete details of an event as it tries to make sense of what happened."

I wanted to agree with him but I couldn't. "No, I'm clear," I told him. "Something very strange happened back there."

The General gave a nod. He glanced over his shoulder then back to me and said in a lowered voice. "There have been cases like this before, where Shaman syndrome has mutated."

"What do you mean mutated?" I asked, disliking the sound of the word

"With an average walt it's the strength we have to watch for, correct? They have the heightening of the senses, but that mainly feeds into their physical enhancement," the General said. "But in certain individuals the syndrome manifests itself in different ways ... *unusual* ways after they've broken-thru."

"I don't understand," I told him. "Are you saying a mutated walt did this? He blew up an entire street with no weapons?"

The General was watching me carefully. He checked over his shoulder again and said, "Possibly. There's an investigation currently under way—but Silvia—" he fixed his blue eyes on me "—it's highly classified—highly—it's very dangerous for us to be even talking about it. I'm telling you this in the strictest of confidence and only because I want to warn you against saying anything to anyone about what you suspect." He glanced around us again, sincerely freaking me out.

I wrapped my arms around myself and said, "Dark is lying in a hospital bed because a walt is out of control. I need to find out who he is and bring him in."

"You need to leave this to me," he said. "You start looking into the wrong places and you'll get yourself into the kind of trouble even I can't help you out of ... Dark is alive and the right people are aware of what has happened. So get some rest and be assured I'm personally on it."

"Sir, how am I supposed to do nothing?" I asked him. "I can't. They could have killed him, they could kill others—and I know for a fact that C11 doesn't care how many people die as long as their objectives are achieved. I can't be part of that anymore—murdering innocent people—I didn't sign up for that! I won't do it! I want to fight against people like them—not be one of them!"

I knew I'd said more than I should have, but once I'd started I couldn't stop myself. The General swallowed, studying me. He sighed and ran a hand through his hair and I could see he was thinking fast.

"Have you said this to anyone else?" he asked me.

"No."

"Then for the love of God—don't," he said. "This is not an employer that you quit from, Silvia. I thought I was very clear about that when we signed you up."

"You were," I could remember him saying that, but I'd thought he'd meant that it was difficult to resign, not impossible—not dangerous—I'd thought he'd meant red tape not red blood.

"What do I do?" I whispered.

"You rest."

"Do you think people will really believe that I wouldn't try to track down whoever did this? He almost killed *my partner*." As I said it I felt tears swelling again behind my eyes and I thought—*He almost killed my best friend …*

The General considered it and said carefully, "I think people will expect you to start investigating—and it will come across as strange if you don't. So I think you should start looking into things, but—" he held up his hand "—only on a superficial level—don't dig. You've entered extremely dangerous territory and I'm trying to keep you safe. Please trust me on this."

I shook my head. The General was my hero, but right now I felt as though he really wasn't seeing things from my perspective and, even if he was, he was trying to downplay it, no doubt he thought it was for my own good, but I still felt unheard and angry.

I pushed down the bad feelings and nodded.

The front door to the house opened and Dad emerged, some antagonism in his eyes.

"Silvia needs rest," he said. "No more work."

'Dad, it's okay," I told him.

"No, your father is right," the General said. He spoke to Dad, "This was just a very quick visit to let your lovely daughter know we're here for her." He gave me a smile and squeezed my arm. "Goodbye, Silvia. Please get some rest." He turned away and I thought I saw a tear in his eye. He climbed into his car and started the engine. After we watched him leave, Dad steered me back inside. I told everyone I needed some sleep and retreated to my room.

Once I was alone, my body seemed to just crumble. My legs wobbled out from underneath me and I sat heavily on my bed. I closed my eyes my mind replaying the General's words " ... in certain individuals the syndrome manifests itself in unusual ways ... highly classified ... You start looking into the wrong places and you'll get yourself into the kind of trouble even I can't help you out of ..." It really didn't surprise me at all that there was more to the walts than the bosses let on. It was shocking and confusing, but not difficult to believe given the covert nature of C11. The bosses told us only what they wanted us to hear. We were just their flesh robots. Tears blurred my sights and I put a hand up to my face. How had Bos and I ended up here?

As I had neither the energy nor the desire to stop them, my thoughts returned themselves to when I was twelve. I had a friend, Amy, a neighborhood girl. She had a brother—two years old. He was kidnapped by two older boys, tortured and left to die. It had broken their mother: she'd split with their father and Amy had gone with her dad. I remembered the little boy clearly and Amy crying for him ... and the day she'd been bundled up into her dad's car with a bunch of boxes and bags. She'd looked so pale and frightened and just stared out the window at me as the car had pulled away. First they'd gone to another city and then back to England where her dad originally came from.

After she left I wasn't able to stop thinking about them. To the point where my parents had taken me to a doctor, then a psychologist, then a psychiatrist. The tragedy had ripped Amy's family apart, and, not to take the focus away from their grief and pain, it had marked me too. I'd been diagnosed with Post-Traumatic Stress Disorder. I'd developed an obsession with saving people. I was convinced I could be a superhero. I jumped off our balcony wearing a cape and broke my legs. Long story short the thoughts settled down with time, they changed, but never completely stopped.

And when I did finally accept that Superhero wasn't really a valid career option, I decided I wanted to become a cop.

And so the path had led here, but even though I'd spent my entire working life in law enforcement, I felt as if hadn't saved anyone—not even my own partner. Anger rushed in and gave my body back its strength. I stood and went to my desk. I turned on my laptop and used my portable Shake to access C11 files.

A knock disrupted me. I went and unlocked the door and found Benicio standing in the hallway. His eyes were worried. My brother had a hard exterior. He could come across as cold, but his heart was the opposite. Mom had told me that when we were kids she never knew who was hurt because he cried with sympathy every time I did—until he hit eight, and me seven: then we just wanted to kill each other.

"I wanted to check—are you okay?" he said.

I nodded. "Want to come in?"

"No, no—get some sleep," he said. He turned to leave then changed his mind. "Maybe ... and I know Mom and Dad have been saying this all day ... but maybe you could try a different job. Do something else less—fatal."

At that second—I really wanted to tell him the truth about the Chapter, about what I really did. If anyone in this world would understand it, it'd be him. We'd always been close, but now I felt as though we were standing on two separate islands with an ocean of lies between us. I almost broke, but managed to stop myself.

"Yeah," I said. "Might be time for a career review … I'm not exactly in my prime years any more."

My brother shrugged. He ran a hand through his hair and said, "It's a race."

"A race?" I asked.

He pointed to his hair. "Between the bald and the gray. It's still anyone's game."

I gave a small laugh and it hurt on all levels.

"See you tomorrow," he said.

I nodded, relocked the door and went back to my computer. I went into the work databases and started searching for mentions of anything like what had happened to us. I scoured countless reports, but there was nothing—at least not at my level of clearance. In the back of my mind I heard the General telling me to stop here—don't dig any deeper and draw attention—so I resisted the urge to make my search terms any more specific and just hoped I'd stumble across something. Somewhere in the ugly hours of predawn morning, I fell asleep with my head beside the keyboard. My dreams were freakish and confused. I was flying, but not high enough to escape shadow hands reaching up for me. I was screaming to my family and to Dark.

The screams of my dreams shook me awake the next morning. A timid light peeked around the curtain. I immediately called the hospital. A nurse told me that Dark was resting and that I could come in to see him, though they weren't accepting any other visitors at this stage. I got up and hobbled to the bathroom, where I downed a few pills and got ready. As I dressed, my mind kept going over the attack, and over my conversation with the General. Things weren't adding up. If they knew this mutant walt had broken-thru, why hadn't they brought him in for re-capping? Was he hiding and avoiding capture? Was that even possible? And if it was, what did that mean? Could there be other mutants walts out there—self-aware walts with dangerous abilities? I'd never thought about it as a possibility, but now that I'd started I couldn't stop. What if it was true?

14

Everything ordinary felt corrupted without Dark. I approached Headquarters and saw only my reflection in the glass. I limped past Norm alone. In the elevator the voice only said my name and only I recited the password. Before coming into work I'd gone to the hospital. I'd found Dark sleeping with his arms resting over his chest. His tattoo of Pepé Le Pew had looked deflated and tired. I'd kissed my partner's cold, battered face and told him I loved him, then started crying again. He'd stirred and let out a slurred, "Go home!"

He'd tried to roll onto his side away from me. Dark was afraid of emotions on a good day, or maybe, better put, he was a man of action not contemplation, and there was nothing he could do to stop me crying, so it was making him feel terrible, on top of already feeling like death. I attempted to control myself, but not before his rolling dislodged one of his wires and set off an alarm on his cardiac monitor. Nurses suddenly flooded the room, pushing me back to get to him. Once they'd seen the cause of the alarm, a few gave me irritated looks, but one of the others said kindly,

"He's doing real well, but probably best he gets some more rest."

I nodded and stepped closer again to say goodbye. Dark had slipped back to sleep. I really wanted to talk to him about what the General had told me, but he clearly wasn't up to it. I relied heavily on Dark's thoughts in most of my decisions, but this time I'd be going in it alone. He had to recover and I had to go to work and start investigating. The General had told me to keep it superficial, and I needed to listen otherwise it put us all at risk, but where the line between superficial and digging too deep lay I wasn't sure. I just had to hope I didn't cross it without knowing. I kissed Dark again and told him I'd be back soon to panic him further with my unrestrained sobbing. He didn't stir.

When I arrived at the entrance lobby, Marissa at front desk was also red-eyed and snuffling into a disintegrating tissue. I could see she was looking for a comforting word, but I had nothing. I was using all my reserve energy just to keep up a professional front. She buzzed me through and I entered the office. Colleagues were on their feet and coming at me from all angles. When an agent gets hurt everyone takes it personally. Agents I'd never spoken to before were hugging me, everyone was asking questions and telling me I shouldn't have forced myself to come in so soon. I lost count of how many times I heard some variation on 'You should be resting.' Even Adonis, my office crush was there, rubbing my back. I felt nothing. All I wanted was to find Byter and talk to him about the footage from the attack. Thankfully Jovic and Feng were in. They waded through the concern and hustled me to our pod. Feng started to go in for the hug, but then decided against it last minute and gave me a few awkward pats instead. Usually it would have made me smile.

"He'll be fine," Jovic told me, gruff from the effort to express emotion while remaining macho. "He's a tough guy."

"Should you be here?" Feng asked, staring at the wounds on my face.

"I need to find who did this," I told them and they both nodded in understanding, then glanced at each other, maybe thinking how they would feel if it had been one of them, or maybe that they were thinking they had to watch me in case I went off the rails.

"We'll find them," Jovic said firmly.

"Tell us what to do and we'll do it," Feng added.

Feeling many watching eyes, I looked around the office. "It seems crowded in here."

"Everyone's been called in," Feng told me. "Something serious is going down—I mean, other than Dark. I'm not sure exactly what, but all the big boys are in a tizzy."

She leaned in to tell me something, but before she could say any more, an announcement came over the intercom, "All agents proceed to Auditorium twenty-one. Repeat—All agents proceed to Auditorium twenty-one."

Twenty-one was the largest auditorium at Headquarters, situated at the far end of level one.

"Let's go," Jovic prompted us and we joined the crowd of Op Services agents shuffling toward the auditorium. A constant stream of operatives from other divisions was merging with us from the stairwells and elevators. I couldn't remember any other time when all agents from every division had been called in together. I kept my head down, trying to avoid attention, Jovic and Feng walking on either side of me like bodyguards.

We entered the darkened lecture theatre and I saw all the division bosses and a good number of Conference members standing up on the front stage. The General was notably absent, but Eric was up there handing out glasses of water, groveling and crawling. I scanned the crowd and finally spotted Byter sitting midway down. His beard stood out a mile away.

"Catch up with you after," I said to Feng. She seemed hesitant to let me go, but nodded and hustled to keep up with

Jovic, who was already halfway along a row of seats. I pushed down the stairs and climbed through to the spare one beside my friend.

He glanced my way with bleary eyes, registered it was me and jolted back. "Silver! Geez! You look …" He searched for lost words. "Are you sure you shouldn't be in hospital?"

"I'm all right," I told him. "Looks worse than it is."

"Try a lot worse." He stared at my face. "Seriously, you should be resting."

"So everyone keeps telling me," I replied. "But I don't feel like resting. I feel like finding whoever did this."

"I know … me too." Byter shook his head wearily. "I'm so sorry, Sil—I've been working on it non-stop, but I haven't had any luck with refining the footage. Everything from before the murders to just after the explosion is ruined. I mean, it sounds impossible, but there doesn't actually seem to be any footage … it's just gone. I've never seen anything like it before and I've done everything I can think of …"

"Damn," I murmured. "I really appreciate you trying."

"I haven't given up," he told me, looking into my eyes. "I'll think of something."

I patted his hand and thanked him again, half-disappointed he hadn't found anything, and half-relieved that he hadn't be-cause it would put him at risk. I thought about warning him, but that was a danger in itself.

The noise of the crowded auditorium quietened as the bosses on stage sat down and one of the Conference guys took the podium. A photograph flashed up on the screen behind him—a head-and-shoulders shot of a man. He was attractive, but his lips were twisted in a contemptuous, almost predatory way, and his dark eyes had a disturbingly deep stare to them. I immediately recognized Omen.

"Agents," the Conference man spoke close to the micro-phone, "memorize this face. This is the face of the enemy."

A murmur ran through the gathering. Beside Omen's picture, other photographs of his extensive tattooing and scars appeared. That tat of a black sun split in half on his wrist flashed up and made my skin prickle. How was Omen connected to the vics and what did he have to do, if anything, with the walt who had attacked us behind their house? I straightened in my chair and listened.

The briefing went for well over an hour, but it could be boiled down to these facts—Omen—real name Gabriel DeLeon—had, the night before, gone rogue. He'd murdered four fellow agents, including his partner Evelyn Drake—the Rose. I'd gasped along with everyone else when they'd announced this information. I'd seen something was strange between them in the elevator, but I hadn't thought for a second that he was about to kill her. After seeing her so vivid and fiery only two days before it was difficult to believe she was now gone. After the murders, Omen had stolen a whole lot of data from the system and vanished, which, considering the totality of coverage of C11 surveillance cameras, was not an easily accomplished task. In fact I'd never heard of any agent—anyone at all—disappearing so completely. I would have said it was impossible. The Conference spokesman informed us that the surveillance and management of walts should continue as always, but that a special taskforce had been set up to track and apprehend Omen, and that all agents should prioritize aiding said taskforce in any way directed by their division leaders. We were all expected to put in double shifts, triple if necessary, until Omen was caught.

As soon as the lecture finished, I murmured a goodbye to Byter and hurried up the stairs. I kept my head down, hoping to avoid all conversations. Byter caught up with me again in the hallway outside the auditorium and said, "I almost forgot. I went through the logs and recorded all interference to surveillance similar to when you and Dark were attacked. I compiled it on this, but I haven't had a chance to analyze it."

I took the portable hard drive he was holding out to me and thanked him. I headed to my desk, but before I could reach it, all the Op Services agents were called into Twenty's office to be given new directives and tasks. We packed in, everyone trying to get a back-line spot, as far away from our boss as possible. As he looked up and saw me, an expression came over his face which I would have described as suspicious, and it made me wonder why—what was he thinking? He started off saying a few words about the attack, and about Dark. He said nothing much about the explosion, framing it as an attack by an, as yet, unidentified civilian who was linked to the killings of two walts.

He said there was no evidence that being walts had anything to do with their murder and that they suspected their involvement with extremists. As he spoke all I could think about was the split-sun tattoo and that the couple being murdered and Omen going AWOL at the same time was not a coincidence—it wasn't extremists. Twentyman was just selling us a cover story. I glanced up and saw Eric watching me from where he stood beside Twenty's desk and I saw it again—suspicion. I looked down quickly. What did they think I'd done? Had I already said too much and was I being set up for a fall?

At the close of the meeting, I started heading for the door with everyone else but heard Twentyman say, "Silver, remain."

I stopped and stood against the wall to let everyone pass me. Feng shot me an anxious look as she exited. Finally it was just Twentyman and Eric left and my throat felt so dry I couldn't swallow. My fingers kept straying to my duty belt, toward my gun ... I had no idea what was about to go down.

Twentyman removed his glasses and sat back in his chair, scrutinizing me with those cutting eyes. I did my best not to squirm.

"In your own words what happened at the Bank Terrace house?" he finally asked.

Eric cleared his throat and I glanced at him, thinking he wanted to speak, but he gestured back to me and Twenty gave him a hard look.

"We attended the crime scene and while we were searching the house, a man jumped out from a cupboard in the kitchen. He fled, we gave chase along the street behind the house. Dark was about to drop him when a car pulled up at the end of the alleyway—two men got out and then ... then there was the explosion."

Twentyman nodded—he'd been watching my mouth as I'd spoken, now he looked up to my eyes. "And in your opinion, what caused the explosion?"

"I didn't see," I told him. "It was a shock ..."

Eric cleared his throat again.

"Was there anything of interest about the crime scene that you would like to report?" Twenty asked leaning forward and I got the feeling it was one of those questions where the person already knows the answer, but wants you to say it. I seriously considered telling him about the tattoos, but stopped myself, hearing the General's warning replay in my thoughts.

"Nothing I can remember at this stage, sir," I said.

"Nothing at all?" he asked.

I shook my head. "Nothing."

Eric gave what sounded like a snort and Twentyman shot him a glare then said, "Desk duties for the rest of the week, Silver. Take today off. I'll re-assess you on Friday."

I nodded.

"Dismissed."

I turned for the door, feeling them watching, and left. They were both acting out of character, Twentyman by saying too much and Eric by saying too little—and it felt like

Twenty was almost going easy on me … That made me extremely nervous.

I headed to my desk where Jovic and Feng were waiting.

"You okay?" Feng asked immediately.

I grabbed my jacket off my chair and said, "Just a debrief. I've been told to take the day off … got a killer headache anyway."

"Go and get some rest," Jovic said. "I wasn't going to say it—but you look like a zombie from that show … what's it called?" he snapped his fingers.

"Shut up, Dragomir," Feng said. She took my arm. "Do you want me to drive you home?"

I shook my head. "Thanks, but I really am okay—don't worry."

She nodded and released me. I lifted my arm and said, "Not a bad touch—felt natural."

She grinned. "Practice makes perfect. Call us when we can visit Dark. Get some sleep."

I thanked them and headed for the exit, with no intention whatsoever of resting.

15

I couldn't go home, where my parents would be hovering like well-meaning helicopters, so I went to Dark's apartment and used my spare key to get in. I booted up his computer and hacked into police records with C11 passcodes. I scanned the report from the murder scene. The only mention it made of the complete obliteration of the street behind the house was that there appeared to have been some kind of electrical fault that had caused a minor blast at the back of the place. The C11 clean-up crew had done their job—as usual. The murder victims were identified as Adam and Tracy Bushel. The cause of death for both was a single gunshot wound to the head. I searched for photos of their tattoos, but didn't find any, which seemed strange considering they were distinguishing marks. I saw Omen's face in my mind and picked up my phone to dial the General.

He answered almost immediately and said, "Silvia, how are you?"

"Sir, there's something I need to tell you," I said. "The vics at the Bank Terrace crime scene had black sun tattoos on their wrists, and the agent who's just gone rogue, Omen? I saw he had the exact same tattoo in the same place …"

There was a brief silence on the other end before the General said, "Okay ... have you mentioned this to anyone else?"

"No—Agent Twentyman questioned me earlier, but I didn't say anything."

"At this stage it's probably for the best—we're not sure of Omen's involvement in the wider situation we were discussing earlier," he said, avoiding giving details. Agent cell phones had security software installed named Fortress, which supposedly prevented anyone from tapping into them, but who knew if this was true.

"Do you think he could be involved with the people who attacked us?"

"It's uncertain," the General said. "Leave it with me—and please remember what I said."

I assured him I hadn't forgotten and hung up. I went back to the computer. The police report said nothing about a young man being discovered at the scene, though certainly someone would have seen us chase him across the lawn. There had been cops everywhere and we hadn't made a secret of it. For some reason, no one was speaking—it may be Chapter-directed or maybe it was something else. Maybe they were keeping details back to use once they identified possible suspects?

I found a list of names of officers and police personnel who had attended the scene and printed it. I'd have to question them individually. But before I did that, I needed to scan the failed footage Byter had given me for any connections. I dragged the external drive out of my pocket and spent hours trawling through its contents. Mostly it seemed like momentary glitches, but there were several prolonged incidences of fuzzed vision.

I used Dark's external Shake to log into C11's system and ran a search using the dates and times of these incidences.

Something came up—around each incident, at similar places to the footage disturbance, there'd been a report of the symptoms of a walt who was breaking-thru spontaneously resolving. I narrowed my eyes, staring at the information—this meant something significant. I could sense it. The most recent was a woman in her thirties who started going green at home. I wrote down the address. I needed to pay her a visit and ask some questions about what had happened to her while the surveillance was down. There was a chance it might shed some light on the whole situation.

I shut down Dark's computer and stood on numb legs. Pain shot through my injured knee and I groaned and reached down to hold it. A scratching noise near the front door froze me mid-motion. The door handle rattled. I drew my gun and moved soundlessly across the floor. The lock clicked and the door began to push in. A person shuffled into the apartment. I stepped into their path and pressed the end of the barrel to their forehead. Dark's cleaner, Mrs Smithy, gasped and stared at me with terrified eyes. I dropped my aim.

"What are you doing?" she shrieked at me.

"I'm so sorry," I said. "I thought you were on holidays."

She spotted the state of my partner's apartment behind me and I think her gasp was louder than when she'd thought some random psycho had a gun to her head. I quickly explained what had happened to Dark and that placated her somewhat.

"Don't you worry." She patted my arm. "I'll get this place spotless and then I'll take him some soup—my mother's recipe—magic."

"They're not letting him have visitors," I told her. "But you can still try."

I'd rung a few more times since I'd been there and been told the same thing—he's doing well and sleeping. Speaking of calling, my folks were hounding me, filling up my inbox with messages. I knew they were worried so I'd sent Dad a text: *At work, am totally fine. Relax. Be home soon.*

I took the address and left as the Smithy Cleaning Frenzy began. The elevator opened while I was still halfway down the hall. I rushed as fast as I could on my leg and caught it. Two people already stood inside, a nondescript guy in a suit with a briefcase, and a girl. She had short dyed-red hair, leather pants, a ring through her lower lip and steel-capped boots. She smelled metallic like a welder and had an angular, hungry look to her face. She turned to me and I thought she was about to say something, but then seemed to change her mind. She must have seen me coming out of Dark's place and was going to ask after him. All the girls loved him.

I headed out to Dark's car, which I'd parked out front of the apartment block. The sun was dipping low in the sky and my stomach snarled, reminding me I hadn't eaten all day, but I wanted to get to this walt's address and question her before it got too late. I could eat after that. I entered her address into the GPS on my cell phone. Dark didn't have a car navigation system. He didn't believe in them.

In rush-hour traffic, it took me a good hour to reach the destination. I parked under a streetlight and stepped out to look around. I'd ended up at an abandoned warehouse close to the waterfront shipping sector of the city. There weren't any houses in sight. I checked the address on my phone and it appeared to match what I'd written down—but it didn't even seem like the right suburb. Strange.

Night had now taken over from the light and heavy shadows stretched across the concrete square leading to the darkened warehouse. I shivered in the evening breeze. The air carried a tinge of smoke and the murmur of a storm. I stared at the warehouse. Smashed windows, graffiti marked, creepy and isolated—everything about the place said *stay away.* And I wasn't about to argue. I started to get back into the car, but then thought maybe Dark had an old street directory in the trunk that I could check. So I went around and opened it up, rummaging through Dark's duffle bag of tools. Footsteps sounded close by. I looked around the side of the car. A person, a woman, was approaching. I recognized her as the girl from the elevator at Dark's apartment building.

"I'm sorry," she said.

I stepped out from behind the car, not sure what she meant, confused at seeing her again, and by her saying but not sounding sorry.

She closed the distance between us fast and punched me in the face. A terrible debilitating pain crashed me to the ground and my eyesight blanked out then flashed back in. I rolled away as her boot rushed toward my head. I scrambled to my feet and grabbed for my gun. It was gone. The girl gave a nasty smile and opened her jacket. She was wearing my duty belt. I stared, shocked: how had she gotten it off me without my knowing? She took my gun out of the holster and held it up as if to say, Looking for this?

I struck fast, slamming my hand into her throat. She reeled and I bolted. There was only so long fists could hold up against bullets. Shots rang out and I lunged behind the side of the warehouse. The girl came after me, pulling on night-vision headgear as she ran. I crashed blindly beside the building, dragging my hand along the wall and stumbling over unseen rubble. I turned the corner into a lamp-lit area and saw a wall blocking my path. It was too tall to climb. I looked left and right searching for a way out and spotted an open window up about twice my height. I could hear the girl's running steps closing in behind me.

I darted forward and grabbed a discarded cardboard box. I shoved it up against the side of the warehouse and climbed on. It collapsed, dumping me onto the ground. I swore and grabbed another box. I leaped up and reached for the window, grasping at the ledge. I stretched up, every part of my body straining. My fingertips closed over the windowsill. A hand darted down from the window and closed over my wrist. It wrenched me off my feet and dragged me upward.

16

I landed on my back with a knee pressed down on my chest and a gloved hand covering my mouth. The shadow form of a man crouched over me. He whispered, 'Shhhh.'

I attacked, hitting him in the groin while arching my body up, sharp and fast to throw him. He gave a stifled grunt and shifted. I scrambled out from beneath him, but he was on me again straight away. He grabbed my arms, trying to pin me, while I thrashed wildly, kicking him.

"Stop!" the stranger whispered. "I'm here to help you!"

"Get off me!" I hissed. "And then I'll stop."

After a second more of struggle, he relented and released me. I flipped over and crawled away from him fast until I hit something solid and then I put my back to it and faced him.

My heart thudded heavily in the silence as I eyed the stranger. Though darkness hid his face, I could sense his eyes watching. A scuffling sound came from outside, and, keeping focused on the man, I edged over to dart a glance out the window.

I saw the girl who attacked me arriving at the end of the alley just below. She turned one way and then the other, searching. With the headgear she wore, she should have been able to see our heat, even through the wall. She should have been able to see the window with no headgear at all, but she didn't seem to notice either. She just kept turning and turning and turning, then she yelled a curse and ran back the way she'd come.

I exhaled slowly and turned my full attention back to the man. "I'm going to leave," I told him keeping my voice as even as I could. "And you're not going to stop me." I started to move with caution.

"Don't you want to know who she is?" The man spoke with equal control.

"I can find out for myself," I said, continuing to maneuver into a position where I could jump out the window.

"I doubt that," the stranger replied. "She's an Undertaker—Annrais Pope."

My nerves scattered. We'd all heard the Project Undertaker rumors. The story went that in the early nineties the Research and Development Department of the Chapter had procured a number of individuals matching pre-set personality and genetic requirements and, basically, had used a variety of inhuman, experimental methods to mold them into killing machines. After a series of failed tests and subject meltdowns, the agency had pulled the plug on the project and terminated all the assassins, except for a handful who had escaped and never been found. However, there had been no evidence to suggest this was anything other than an exaggerated, fear-mongering story. There were a lot of those floating around Headquarters.

"How do you know who she is?" I asked him.

"I make it my business to know things," he replied ambiguously. "Pope hacked your navigation and led you here to collect the bounty on your head."

I laughed involuntarily. "I have a bounty on my head?"

The shadowy figure said nothing, and I felt the truth of his words.

"I have a bounty on my head," I repeated. Obviously I'd crossed that line the General had been trying to warn me about and now the Chapter was trying to "relocate" me. I wondered if Twentyman had been the one to sign the order.

I opened my mouth to speak, but then I remembered something I'd learned during basic training about assassination protocol. If an assassin failed to engage a primary target on the first, direct attempt, standard procedure was to proceed to a secondary path, to use emotional bait to draw the target out. Which, in my case meant ...

"My family," I breathed.

I grabbed for my cell phone, but then remembered I'd left it in the car. My body moved on instinct. I leaped out the open window and dropped down to the alley below, crushing the cardboard box flat. I raced back along the side of the warehouse and rounded the corner. The space below the streetlight was empty. The assassin had stolen Dark's car. I ran out into the concrete square, turning everywhere, searching for another car, a person, a public phone, anything. The place was completely deserted and I heard only very distant sounds of civilization. I didn't even know which way to run.

The stranger spoke behind me, "By the time you make it anywhere, it will be too late. She led you out this far for a reason."

I spun around and faced the man. He was dressed in black, tall and strongly built with dark steely eyes. I blinked and it came to me that I'd seen him before—this was the man who had been watching us outside the club and again at the gardens.

"She'll take your family and you'll never see them again," he said. "Your best hope for them would be a quick end and even then you'll have no guarantees. Pope is crazy, blood-hungry. Her favorite trick is burying people alive."

"Why are you telling me this?" I yelled at him, my chest so tight I could barely breathe.

"Because I can help you."

I ran to him. "How? Do you have a phone?"

"Yes. But it's useless. Your parents' line is already dead. She doesn't work alone. She has a crew and she always has a Plan B."

"How can you help me then?" I demanded.

"My people will keep your family safe—if you come with me to—"

"Fine," I cut him off. "Whatever. Anything. Just help them."

He gave me a measuring look, then took a phone out of his pocket and pressed the screen. He held it up to his mouth and said, "Stop Pope's crew. Watch the family."

I unclenched my trembling fists. I had no idea who this person was. He could be lying. He could be working with the assassin, or even be her competition, but I had no choice but to agree to his terms. It was a rock and hard place to be. A freezing wind shrieked in the dark night. Rain started falling, sounding like bullets on the corrugated metal of the warehouse. I shivered, blinking to keep the drops out of my eyes.

The man slid the phone back into his jacket pocket. He turned toward a shipping container left on one side of the concrete yard. He pointed at it. The lamplights lining the street faltered. One bulb blew out in an explosion of glass. Before my eyes, the whole massive container lifted into the air, revealing a black four-wheel-drive vehicle underneath. The man lowered his hand, bringing the container silently down beside the vehicle.

It felt like my heart stopped beating for a second. Had I just seen what I thought I just saw? Did he shift something with his mind? The thought immediately took me back to the attack at Bank Terrace. Someone had destroyed the street—apparently just with his thoughts. A mutated walt.

I turned my stare on him and said, "Was it you? Did you try to kill us?"

"No," he replied firmly.

"Then who?" I demanded.

"Not here," he said. "Get in." He moved fast for the vehicle, and as he glanced back to see if I was following, his eyes shimmered silver blue, like the eyes of a nocturnal creature. "Come on!" he called. "Do you want to save your family or not?"

I ran to catch up with him. There was no choice in it.

The walt drove faster than I'd ever gone before. Dark had a lead foot, but this was a whole new level of speeding. Buildings literally blurred beside us. Every light we approached turned green so suddenly, so unnaturally, that cars coming in the opposite direction had to screech to a stop. All I could do was sit tight and hang on. The man drove in silence, his control never slipping, while my mind spun, trying to process everything that was happening. My thoughts jumped to Dark. If my family was covered, he would be the next person the assassins would target.

"My partner," I said to the walt.

"We've got people on him," he told me.

"What sort of people?"

"My people," was all he'd give me and it really wasn't enough when Dark and my family were concerned. I had to get control of the situation. I had to get my hands on this walt's phone and get behind the wheel, which meant somehow getting rid of him, but I had already seen what he was capable of. I'd have to take him by surprise. My eyes roamed around the interior of the car searching for something I could use, but the space was completely clear. So it would need to be a bare-knuckle blow to the side of his head, hard enough to knock him out.

I shot a glance at him, then looked away and back again, my eyes drawn to his face. He had combat scars and the signs of physical torture cut deeply into his skin. He had fingertips missing and long-healed rope and cigarette burns on his arms. Muscles cut taut lines across the scar tissue. He glanced my way with dark eyes both detached and scary sharp, which only comes from cheating death while others fall around you.

I knew a specialist soldier when I saw one.

Which, added to his being a walt, pretty much canceled out any hope of knocking him unconscious, but I still had to try. I clenched my fist.

The walt's jaw tightened almost imperceptibly and he took one hand off the wheel and rested his arm on the console between us. It felt like he was letting me know he was ready should I try anything. I looked down at his hand, trying to anticipate what he was going to do and spotted something that made the breath catch in my throat. On one of his wrists was a black sun split in half, identical to the tattoo of Omen, and to the victims.

"What is that?" I asked him. "What does it mean?"

"You'll see soon enough," he told me.

"I have to get to my family," I said, trying to keep control of my voice.

"This is their best chance, trust me," he said, the headlights of oncoming cars reflecting across his face, giving it an unnatural glow. Before I could say anything else, the stranger began to slow the vehicle and I looked out the passenger window, recognizing an outer-city suburb full of pre-war cottages and industrial estates. We pulled up outside a motel that had a distinct Norman Bates feel to it, a place that clearly did most of its business by the hour.

The man stopped the car and got out. I took a deep breath and followed. Lightning ripped the sky above and the rain pelted harder as we dashed across the parking lot to the motel building. The walt started climbing a set of stairs and I followed him up and along a walkway to room number thirteen. He unlocked the door, but I didn't see a key in his hand.

I followed him in, down a corridor that smelled of mildew and stale shower water, and into a room.

A group of about thirty people, men and women, sat around the cleared-out space. All eyes turned our way. A girl stepped out of the crowd to meet the stranger, and I heard her say his name—*Rocco*. She put a hand on his arm and shot a wary look my way, but my attention was focused else-where—on the front of the room, on a man. He was standing with his back to the group, typing on a laptop computer. Eventually he straightened and turned to face us. I stared into the black, inescapable eyes of the rogue agent, Omen.

"Silver," he said. "Won't you take a seat?"

17

Minus the disastrously unflattering uniform, the tragic eighties fringe and crippling teenage angst, I felt like the new kid at school all over again, shuffling awkwardly past cliques of people staring at me with anything from open hostility to unsettling fascination. I managed to edge onto the chair Omen was pointing to, which was positioned at the front of the group. The rogue agent crossed his arms and stood watching me. He stared for so long that it went from unnerving to disturbing and I went from shaken to angry.

"Agent DeLeon," I finally said.

The former agent flinched as if I'd slapped him awake. He stalked forward until he was standing right over me, and then he leaned closer still and said in a dangerous whisper, "My name is Omen."

He had two full sleeves of tattoos, and as he spoke their colors swirled and shifted and the pictures changed from relatively ordinary images to frightening ghoulish faces gnashing their teeth at me from his skin. I thought about arguing back, but that little voice inside my head that sometimes steps in and stops me from doing incredibly stupid things said, "Probably not the best time."

"Omen," I repeated to placate him, realizing I definitely needed to defuse the situation as quickly as possible. It didn't take a behavioral expert to see he was fractured and on edge. He was unshaven, bloodstained and stinking of sweat—and yet he had an alpha-dog magnetism to him that was undeniable. I'd noticed it when he was an agent, but now I felt it even more. I couldn't hold his stare.

I focused past him on the gathering of others and was struck then by the fact that although everyone there had such different features, they all seemed similar in a way I couldn't pinpoint—until I spotted the split-sun tattoo on one guy's wrist. I ran my eyes along the rest of the group. All the wrists I could see had the same mark. Among the faces I recognized the guy from the Bushel pantry. He was the youngest there, maybe even still a teenager, and he was sitting in the front row typing rapidly on a laptop balanced on his knees. He stopped and looked at me with the troubled eyes of someone who has grown up with trauma. His uncertainty turned to fear under my stare and that look unlocked my memory. I saw him running away from us. I saw the car pull up and Omen and Rocco step out. It was Omen who had lifted his hand and brought destruction down on our heads. Everything was starting to make sense.

"My partner almost died," I said with quiet fury.

Omen raised dark, arched eyebrows and said, "You remember. Interesting."

"No, it's really not," I shot back. "Dark is in hospital, my family are in danger. *Interesting* is not the word I'd use. Tell me why I'm here or move aside so I can leave!"

Omen's eyes lingered on mine as though he were searching for something, and in the darkness of his pupils I saw an image manifest. It was the form of a girl dressed in red, his partner: the Rose.

"They're saying you killed her and four other agents," I told him.

Grief, torture unmistakable, clouded Omen's expression, just for a second, then it was gone and he was blank, hollow. He smiled at me in a way that had nothing to do with humor and everything to do with insanity. It prickled the hairs on the back of my neck.

"Do you believe them?" he asked.

"I don't know what to believe," I told him. "Everyone is lying. Rocco said you would help my family. I need to know they're all right." My voice trembled slightly and I clenched my jaw down refusing to break.

"They're fine. For now." Omen said, his stare burning into me. "And you can go to them, but first you're going to tell me what you think we are."

"You're walts who have broken-thru with mutated symptoms," I said.

At my words, Omen's eyes darkened again, a storm spreading over the sky. "walts with mutated symptoms," he repeated to the group of people.

I felt the hostility in the room rising. It grew and intensified until it started to burn. I stood up, knocking my chair back. I had to shield my face. It felt as though I was standing too close to a fire. I gasped.

"Stop!" the young guy from the pantry cried out.

"Omen!" Rocco stepped in. "She's not the enemy."

His words worked like an extinguisher. The heat quickly subsided and Omen regained his control.

"Sit," he commanded me.

Without any foreseeable non-painful options, I retrieved the chair and sat down.

"Despite your unfortunate choice of words," Omen said, pacing behind me, "you are correct ... Did you ever think this was possible?"

"I don't know," I said. My hands were trembling. "I thought breaking-thru always causes massive instability."

"It does," Omen said. "But only temporarily." He stopped behind me and I could feel his eyes watching. "I know you've been questioning the Chapter ... for a long time. And you've always used non-lethal force during LIAs, am I right?"

"Zero fatalities," I murmured.

"You knew," he concluded. "You just didn't want to know."

Omen turned to his laptop and pressed a button and I watched as my conversation with the General at my house replayed before the whole group. I saw myself saying, *"Sir, how am I supposed to do nothing? I can't. They could have killed him, they could kill others—and I know for a fact that C11 doesn't care how many people die as long as their objectives are achieved. I can't be part of that any more—murdering innocent people—I didn't sign up for that! I won't do it! I want to fight against people like them—not be one of them!"*

Omen turned back to me and said, "They're not the only ones who can watch people, and we've been watching you."

"Why?"

"For the reasons I just said, Silver—try to keep up." Omen lips twitched.

I understood his contempt was more about his state of mind than anything to do with me, and that I needed to keep calm and tread very carefully not to set him off, but my heart was thudding fast and I could feel every second passing. What was happening to my family?

I glanced up at Rocco at the back of the room and saw he was watching me carefully. He gave me the slightest nod and I clenched my hands to stop the shaking and said, "How are they not watching us now?" Everyone in the room except me were walts, and should have been under constant surveillance.

Omen gestured to the young guy from the crime scene and said, "Marco, explain to Agent Silver—keep it simple."

My anger began to boil, but I kept my mouth shut.

Marco gulped, his eyes darting nervously. He stammered when he spoke. "We've been masking the ... the ... break-thrus with a corruption virus, then splicing old footage into their system so they don't realize it's happened ..." He swiveled his laptop so that I could see multiple screens of C11 footage. He was saying the walts had been breaking-thru and that he and Omen and the others had been making it look as though they hadn't, that the symptoms had spontaneously resolved. But I knew it would take some kind of unimagin-able genius to hack the Chapter's system ... someone more advanced than any of C11's technologists, who were a gather-ing of the most elite in the world. Marco looked like just any other baggy-pants, baseball cap teenager.

"It's been looking like spontaneous resolution of symp-toms," I said and Omen nodded. "But you're a ..." I didn't want to say walt again. "You're 'one' and if they're seeing old footage of you now, won't they realize what's happening?"

Omen smiled again and tapped the side of his head, "They can't see me at all—I've completely dropped off their grid."

"You can do that?" I asked.

"I can—yes," he responded.

I stared down at the carpet, trying to gather my thoughts. In a way this moment felt so stark and real—and inevit-able—but in another it felt like I was dreaming.

I looked back up to Omen, "Obviously they've just been telling us what they want us to believe. So what is the truth?"

"The truth?" He laughed at me, and I heard a few echoes from the others. "What is the truth—Silver?" He made my name sound like a joke.

"Clearly I don't know," I replied carefully. "But I want to."

Omen rubbed his face with both hands and laughed to the ceiling. "She wants to know." He took a second then glanced toward Rocco and said. "So tell her."

The former agent stepped back and Rocco moved to the front of the group. The two men stood in sharp contrast to each other: Omen disheveled, wild and raw, electrifying, terrifying; and Rocco cool and controlled, an ineluctable deadly force, frightening in a whole different way. Omen was volatile, but it made me think that maybe his emotions could be used to distract him, whereas Rocco's manner brought to mind a soldier who could hunt someone down with endless patience and undivided purpose—for as long as it took. Rocco started to speak to me. It sounded as if he were delivering a military briefing.

"Shaman syndrome is not a disorder, it is a chromosomal evolution of man. In layman's terms: caveman, human, Shaman. The original paper by Whitman explored this notion, but that was never released, and the discovery was handled by vested interests. We were the potentially powerful minority and we posed a threat. When other attempts to suppress our abilities failed, the coalition of governments conducted experiments and discovered that we could only be controlled by another Shaman with a stronger mind."

I shook my head. "I don't understand."

"How do you think people are being re-capped?" Omen spoke up. "How do you think they are capped in the first place as newborns?"

"I assumed it was a scientific formula or procedure," I said.

Omen curled his lips as though his body was about to physically reject my naivety like a seafood dinner gone wrong.

"I'm sorry," I said, my frustration breaking through. "You know what it's like being an agent. I haven't ever been past front desk on Medical Level."

"Newborns are capped and adults re-capped in the exact same way." Rocco stepped in. "A Shaman of a stronger mind takes power over them. It's not what you might think of as mind control—the person retains her will and logic, she just can't access her abilities. And when a Shaman breaks through it means they have evolved and surpassed the power of whoever capped them—they have moved up in the Order—the Shaman ranks. Capping is not an exact process. It's not natural for the structures of our brain. The closest comparison I can make is running high-voltage electricity through the mind. It can go wrong—and it does on a regular basis." Rocco handed me an envelope.

I opened it and took out a stack of photographs—dead babies, comatose children, adults in wheel chairs, institutionalized, bed-ridden, brain-dead. I saw a photograph of the young walt we'd taken in from the strip club. He was dead, eyes glazed, lips blue. I thrust the photos back at Rocco, trying to deny to myself that I'd seen them, but the images were burned into my brain. I tried to speak calmly.

"So within the Chapter, there are ... Shaman ... who are self-aware, and they're controlling the capping of all the others. But if the agency has let some Shaman out to work for them, then why don't they let everyone out?" I asked.

"Same reason they started trying to control Shaman in the first place," Rocco said. "They're afraid we'll try to take over the world."

"Who knows about this?" I asked. "Upper management? Does the General know?"

Rocco shook his head. "Some of them, such as the General, know that Shaman can break-thru without losing their minds and that some have enhanced skills other than strength, but no one knows the true extent except for the Shaman working for C11. They've been handpicked and are controlled by a person known as the Blood Horseman. He is the most powerful Shaman in the Order and he has embedded himself within the Chapter. He and his people control all the capping and re-capping of Shaman across the world. Only they know that there are Shaman working within C11, at least officially."

"The Blood Horseman," I repeated. "Who is he?"

"He's a ghost," Omen murmured, rubbing his face in a gesture of exhaustion.

"We don't know," Rocco said. "Each of us has skills, some stronger than others, but he is strong in everything. He keeps himself well hidden. Omen is a close second to him in skill and power—not close enough to detect who he is, but close enough to stay hidden from him. He keeps us all hidden."

"What do you mean skills and power?" I asked.

"Our senses are heightened beyond human capabilities," Rocco said.

"Show her," Omen instructed. "Seeing is believing—for humans."

Rocco paused, his eyes moving over my face. I saw he didn't trust me, but he still obeyed Omen.

"We have acute eyesight," he began. "X-ray vision." He glanced at a guy in a red T-shirt sitting close to me and said, "Axe."

"A hard drive, some paper and a switch blade," Axe recited, listing everything I had in my pockets.

"Nightvision," Rocco said. Someone at the back of the group turned off the lights and everyone's eyes glowed blue-silver in the darkness. The lights flickered back on.

"Extended range of hearing, infrasound, ultrasound—the ability to use sound as a weapon," Rocco continued, his tone still regimental. "Willow." He gestured to a girl with a crooked nose from an old break, and a long fringe of hair that almost covered her eyes. She seemed familiar to me, though I couldn't immediately place her. She hesitated, but Rocco kept his gaze on her until she lowered her head and closed her eyes. A wave of sickness swept over me and a tremor racked my body. It passed and the girl, Willow, looked up and mouthed, "Sorry."

"Frequencies below twenty hertz can cause nausea in humans," Rocco told me. "Useful in clearing a crowd. Go too low and it's lethal—also useful at times. We have a heightened sense of smell," he moved on. "We can detect pheromones and manipulate them to create emotions in others—anger, alarm, sexual arousal."

He pointed at a dark-skinned guy near the back. "Gallows." The guy stood up, breathed in deeply and released a long sigh. My heartbeats thudded faster and I found myself gripping the edges of the seat in fear.

"Enough," Rocco said and the guy sat down. The feeling eased, leaving a lingering tremor in my hands.

"Sense of touch. We can withstand pain," Rocco told me. A girl with bright orange hair stabbed a knife through her hand and pulled it back out without flinching. The guy beside her touched her hand and the wound sealed over. "Cold and hot," Rocco said. Another girl took a lighter and lit her fingertip, letting it burn. A pounding began behind my eyes. I wasn't sure how much more *seeing* I could take.

"We sense sub-fibers in all matter and can climb usually unclimbable surfaces. Exodus." He nodded to a blonde in the front row. She jumped up onto the wall and scuttled across it like a lizard.

"And these are just the basics that we're all capable of," Rocco said. "There are more complex skills such as rapid healing of ourselves and others, advances in the interoceptive senses—always landing on our feet when falling. Some of us can alter our appearance." A man in the group grew an instant beard and changed his hair from brown to blond, then became the same color as the wallpaper from head to toe. "Camouflage," Rocco said. "Contortionism." Several of them twisted into horribly uncomfortable-looking positions. "Some of us have a heightened sense of motion." The girl who had approached Rocco when we'd first arrived shot forward in a flash, slapped me hard across the face and darted back in a blur of color. She then held up her arms and her whole body hovered off the carpet. I rubbed my cheek and glared at her.

"We have genetic memories. We don't forget anything. And a few of us have extrasensory perception. We can use psychokinesis." Rocco himself gestured and lifted everyone and everything in the room off the ground several inches then placed us back down. "Some of us are telepathic, some have retrocognition, some of us precognition. Some of us can see others who inhabit different levels of this world. Some can—"

"Okay," I cut him off. "I get it."

"All of this the Horseman can do far better than any of us, except Omen—and he's building an army," Rocco said.

"An army for what?" I asked.

"For the annihilation of humankind. He's got delusions of godhood."

"Not hard to see why," I said.

I hadn't meant it as a joke, but heard a few chuckles and snorts of laughter, which Omen squashed with one savage glare.

"He wants to bring about a new era," Rocco said, his dark eyes fixed on mine. "The era of Shaman."

"Shouldn't you guys be happy about that?" I asked. "You are Shaman."

"Happy to be puppets at the mercy of a madman, forcing us to slaughter innocent people? Would you be happy about that just because your leader was a human?"

I got the point and shook my head.

"We're the resistance." Rocco held up the photographs again and I recognized in one picture the dead Bushels in their tidy lounge room.

"Your people?" I asked pointing to the victims.

"Yes—they *were*," Omen said.

"The Horseman executed them," Rocco said. "He and his soldiers are hunting us. My brother, Marco, was lucky to escape." He nodded to the nervous young man we'd almost shot.

"Okay ..." I said. "I understand, but why am *I* here?"

Rocco looked to Omen again. The leader nodded.

"We need you to locate the White List," Rocco stepped closer to me, "Chapter 11's record of every Shaman. We need to free as many as we can to join the fight against the Horseman before it's too late."

"What do you mean *free*?" My voice sounded distant to my ears.

"If we rank higher than the Shaman who capped them, we can break the capping and wake them up," Rocco said. "All our previous attempts to locate the list have failed. Every day he evolves further and gathers more power. Time is running out." Everyone in the room, except Rocco and Omen, shifted anxiously.

My mind was already working on the problem. In all my years as an agent I had never heard of the White List, but it made sense that something like that would have to exist; otherwise how would we know who to watch?

"Where would they even store something like that?" I asked. In the Chapter, as in most large organizations, information and orders dribbled down from the top. Omen had been more senior so it made sense he would know more. "In the Conference files?"

"That's where I looked first," Omen said. He shook his head. "Nothing. It may be somewhere more obvious; it may be somewhere more hidden."

"The Horseman dug Omen out before he had a chance to refine the search further," Rocco told me.

"Did the Horseman kill the other agents?" I asked. It was an important question for me. If Omen had killed the Rose, his partner and girlfriend, it changed things.

"Yes," Rocco said, and I detected a slight tightening of his expression, before he could stop it. "And framed Omen."

He fell silent and I noticed all the others had as well. No one was moving. I couldn't even hear breathing. I guessed Omen was verging on another breakdown. I dared a glance at him. He was completely frozen. He looked like a wax sculpture. It was one of the most eerie things I'd seen. Then he blinked, reanimating, and his focus went to me.

"His soldiers are everywhere in the Chapter. He himself will be there watching, waiting for another attempt on the List," he said.

"He's in Headquarters?" I said.

"Where did you think he was?" Omen sneered.

I had imagined he was elsewhere. Hoped, maybe.

"I don't want to point out the obvious," I said, "but if he uncovered you and you're almost as powerful as he is—what hope do I have—really?"

"Your hope is that he won't suspect you—you have a chance to fly under his radar."

"Won't he just be able to read my mind?" I asked.

"It's not that simple and there are ways to distract attention and hide thoughts and intentions—even for humans," Rocco said.

"But why me?" I asked. "I only have low-level clearance—wouldn't it make more sense to approach someone higher up—like the General? Don't you have anyone else on the inside?"

"No and we can't risk it," Rocco replied. "We've been watching you for almost a year. We knew you'd be sympathetic to the cause, but now that the agency has put a hit on you, we know for sure you aren't the Horseman or one of his people."

"They've put a hit on me," I repeated still struggling with the words. "So won't they get suspicious when I keep showing up alive? Won't they suspect I have outside help?"

"You're an agent. You have your own contacts. You have your skills and knowledge. They won't necessarily assume it has anything to do with us and we're going to keep creating scenes to try to keep the heat off you for as long as we can," Rocco said.

"And if I do this—you keep my family and Dark safe," I said.

"We need the names." Omen sounded as though he was tiring of the conversation. "Understand we're not asking you. For as long as you cooperate with us, we'll protect your family and your partner; as soon as you stop, we stop. We can't afford to waste resources on someone who is not one of us. Annrais Pope will be looking for any opening. She won't get paid until she has your head." Omen's words seemed logical, but it was a threat, and it was blackmail—there was no denying that.

"I'll find the names," I told him. "But first I want to see my family."

Omen nodded. "Go see them. Go tell them goodbye."

"I'm not saying goodbye to anyone," I said through gritted teeth.

He smiled faintly, in his predatory, mocking way.

"Rocco will be your shadow," he said. "He'll keep Pope's assassins off your back—for as long as you're one of us. Go." He dismissed me without so much as a gesture.

I stood up on weakened legs and started toward the door. Everyone in the group watched in silence. I paused before leaving to say, "I wanted to help people. I never wanted to hurt anyone. I still don't."

"To protect the people you love, you will do anything and everything," Omen said, his voice sounding hollow, and again an image came to mind of the Rose. His heart was broken, I understood that, but he had almost killed my partner: I wouldn't be forgetting that.

"God help you," Omen murmured.

He turned back to his computer and I followed Rocco out into the storm-black night.

Part 2

18

I was thinking about my grandfather, the violent psychopath. Unlike the photos of Dark's nonno, from which the love still beamed, the old black and whites of my mother's parents made me uncomfortable. I believed you could see the coldness in my grandfather's face, in his eyes—there was something missing. As we flew through the storm, jagged strikes of lightning slicing the starless sky, it was all I could think of—those eyes. The girl assassin, Annrais Pope—she'd had that same look, that void. I kept seeing her over and over and each time a sick fear pulsated inside me. If Pope had my family ... they were harmless ... helpless—just like all the Shaman Chapter 11 had abducted and killed. And I had been part of it. So maybe I deserved what was happening to me now. What do they say? You can't dance with the devil without getting burned?

But my family hadn't had any part in it—they were innocent—*and the innocent still suffer with the guilty.* Cold sweat prickled my skin, my jaws ached, my fingernails bit into my palms. I sat on the edge of the seat and focused on the dual heartbeats in my chest and in my head. Migraine pain split my skull, but it seemed entirely insignificant, welcome even—some physical manifestation of the emotions I felt. I thought I'd have to tell Rocco to pull over so I could be sick, but I managed to catch control by blanking out: Think of nothing, think of nothing …

It should have taken the best part of an hour to get from north Toran-R to my house. With Rocco at the wheel we made impossible time. We turned into my street. The neighborhood appeared unremarkable—the usual darkened yards and scattered night lights, the neon glow of televisions through loosely drawn curtains. I held my breath and looked past all the houses toward my home. The lights were on, but I didn't see any shadows of movement inside. Rocco swung his heavy vehicle into the driveway. I grabbed the door-latch, planning to jump and run, but found the door locked.

"Let me out," I demanded as he slowed to a stop in front of my house.

He turned off the headlights and we sat staring out into the darkness. His gaze moved left to right over the shadows, seeing what my blunt human eyes could not. What was out there? We sat in silence with the rain hammering the roof above us. I squinted through the windscreen streams, watching my house, searching for any signs of life. I still couldn't see any. My professional control snapped. I wrenched the latch backwards and forwards and slammed my shoulder against the door.

"Let me out!" I yelled.

Rocco sat unmoved, closed and unreadable.

"Hey!" I shouted and pushed him. It was like pushing a brick wall. He turned to me, his face half-shadows. A blast of lightning lit the night. Rocco's eyes glowed and I saw past him into the yard. Silhouettes of people stood everywhere, still, watching—waiting. A prickling weakness shot from my stomach to my knees.

"Are they yours or hers?" I murmured as the light died and the darkness swallowed the figures again.

"Some ours, some hers," Rocco said. "But now ..." he paused "... just ours."

I imagined the assassin corpses strew around the lawn among my father's palm trees and Mom's bird feeders. Not exactly an image for *Home Beautiful*.

"Let's go," Rocco said.

I grabbed for the door and this time it opened. My boots squelched down into the mud of the driveway. Cold rain pelted my face. Rocco kept me close by his side as we moved for the front door. I jumped at a sudden loud sound to our right. A crack of light appeared in the dark as the garage door lifted. Mom's little red car reversed out. I spotted her behind the wheel, peering out the window, trying to make sure she didn't hit anything as she backed.

"She needs to stay here." Rocco spoke beside me; his voice was steady and cool, but there was a sharpness to his words that made me react immediately.

"Mom!" I called out. I broke away from my Shaman guard and ran to the driver's side of the car. I half-jumped through the window to hug her, high with relief, laughing like a crazy.

Mom hugged me back even tighter.

"Thank goodness you're home!" she said. "I've been calling you all day!" She pulled back to look at my face.

"I know, I'm sorry," I said. "Mom, I'm sorry." Tears blurred my sight. "Are you okay? Are the others all right?"

"Don't worry, we're all fine," she said giving me a gentle smile. "They're just finishing dinner. Yours is in the oven. Go in and eat—I just have to pop down to the store—we're all out of cat food and parrot mix and milk and ..."

Rocco, standing so she couldn't see him, nudged me.

"It's a bit late, isn't it?" I cut in. "Wouldn't the store be closed?"

"I think they're open until ten on week nights, aren't they?" Mom asked.

"I don't think so … Are you sure?"

"Pretty sure," she said. "Do you need me to get you anything?"

"No—thanks—I think I'm okay … I ah …" My mind was a vacant lot, tangled with weeds.

Rocco nudged me again. He stepped into view and pointed between them—gesturing for an introduction.

"Mom, this is … a friend of mine—from work. Rocco …" I had no idea of his last name or if Rocco was even his actual name or a codename. "Rocco."

My newly acquired bodyguard leaned down. Mom's face flashed a micro-expression of shock and fear, which immediately smoothed into a smile. I felt a warm sense of reassurance and familiarity, and realized he was tampering with her pheromones or whatever it was they did. I seriously didn't like the idea of him diddling with my family's body chemicals.

"Rocco—this is my *mother*," I said pointedly.

"Pleasure to meet you," he said to her, all tall, dark and handsome with impeccable charm. "The roads are quite wet. Why don't you let us drive you to the store?"

"Oh." Mom beamed up at him; he had her at hello. "I'd love the company, but I'll drive."

"I really don't mind driving," Rocco said.

"No, no—I don't want you wasting your gas on me."

"It's just up the road. I insist," he said.

"So do I." Before he could stop her, Mom jumped out into the rain and pushed her seat forward so that we could get into the back. Rocco shot me a perplexed look that I would have found amusing at another time. I doubted he'd ever met anyone as stubbornly pleasant as my mother.

I climbed into the back seat, trampling random piles of trash and treasure. Rocco squeezed in beside me. With his height and muscle mass we were literally pressed shoulder to shoulder. We sat with our hands in our laps, not looking at each other. I felt like I was sixteen again and going to the movies with a boy for the first time. All that was lacking was my father's disgruntled face glaring out the window at us.

"What about the rest of my family?" I whispered to Rocco.

"They're covered for now," he replied.

Mom jumped back behind the wheel. She turned the key so that the dashboard lights flashed on, but not far enough to start the engine.

She tried to shift the gear into drive, but it wouldn't budge. She struggled for a minute then said, "I'm not sure why this isn't working."

"The engine's off," I told her.

"But I just turned it on," she said.

"It's definitely off," I said.

She turned the key again and the engine coughed to a start. Mom laughed and said, "Sorry, how embarrassing!"

"Happens to me all the time," Rocco said graciously. Somehow I didn't think so.

Mom turned down the Mozart blaring from the speakers, adjusted the heater, then reversed the car and headed down the driveway. Being a tiny three-door with rubber-band suspension, every bump and pothole jostled us together. It didn't help that Mom was driving with her headlights off. She was creative rather than muddled and forgetful, but driving admittedly wasn't her greatest strength any more than it was mine.

"Mom, headlights," I reminded her.

"Oh thanks," she said.

She turned them on and accidentally switched off the wipers. I waited to see if she would notice, but when we reached the end of the road and the windscreen was completely obscured with rain, I said, "Mom, wipers."

"Oh sorry—I don't know where my mind is tonight!" She turned them back on and bumped the indicator.

We drove straight for several minutes indicating left before I said, "Mom—you're indicating."

"Oops, sorry!" she said again. She looked back at us through the rear-vision mirror. "Do you know what the limit is here—I think it's fifty here and forty up ahead—do you remember?" she asked me.

"Not sure," I replied. Mom had a few obsessions—one of which was keeping exactly to the speed limit. In a cruel twist of irony she had, one night when I was a kid, been pulled over by the cops for going too slow. They probably thought she was stoned; it didn't help that she was driving a Kombi at the time.

We saw the forty sign ahead and Mom said, "Here we are." She took her foot off the accelerator and counted down, "forty-nine, forty-five, forty-three … I find Dad's car is easier to slow down in—this car's a lot speedier—don't you think?" she asked me.

It literally felt like we were crawling. The car behind us was almost tipping our bumper bar. I held my breath expecting to be slammed into or shot up at any second.

"Now I think it's fifty again," Mom said. "Do you remember?"

"I don't think it matters, Mom," I said, trying to keep calm.

The store came up on the left and we turned in. My mother drove up and down several lines—passing a number of free parking spaces.

"I find it easier parking on the left than the right," she explained to Rocco.

"Mom—just park anywhere—it's all the same," I said a little harshly.

She slowed and tried to turn, taking several attempts before maneuvering in. I could tell she was a little hurt and embarrassed, and guilt prickled me. She turned off the engine and I gripped her shoulder before she got out.

"Sorry," I said.

Mom smiled and patted my hand. I let her go and she climbed out. Rocco moved swiftly after her and I clambered behind.

We walked in a tight bunch to the store entrance, where other late-night shoppers were coming and going. Rain sparkled off the lamplights at the crossing. I scanned around us. Everything appeared normal, everything mundane ... maybe it was—or maybe it was the calm river surface with the crocodiles waiting beneath.

We entered the store and Mom grabbed a basket. "I'll just dash around and meet you at the front so I don't hold you up," she said, half jogging away.

"Wait!"

I started to run after her, but Rocco held me back and said, "We can follow her."

"What if there's a sniper?" I hissed, struggling out of his grasp.

He shook his head. "She's no use to them dead. They won't shoot her, but they will shoot you—stay close."

We pushed the pace to keep up with her. Mom was short but a fast walker. It had always frustrated me to go shopping with her. I liked a more leisurely pace and inevitably we ended up ten paces apart, calling out conversation to each other.

I thought about the fact that I could have lost her to-night and the guilt washed back in like a salty tide. "I don't usually snap like that—at my family ..." I tried to explain to Rocco.

"Yes you do," he said. "It's normal—human. People would die for their families, but they can't put up with their everyday imperfections."

His words made me feel ten times worse.

"What can I say?" I steadied my voice. "It's been a hard week—starting with you and your boss blowing us up."

He glanced at me—measuring, evaluating, not settling on a judgment but continually searching—a brilliant mind behind cold-blooded eyes. I wondered if what I saw was actually how he looked or if he could change his appearance like Omen.

A thought hit me. "You know my family are going to keep going out. They have work, appointments—life."

"I have that under control," he said. "We just have to get your mother back to your house."

We continued shadowing Mom around the shops, down the cat-food aisle to the birdseed, to the checkout and out. At the crossing, Rocco wrapped his arm around my shoulders and drew me close. The action made me immediately tense up and look around. I saw her then, Annrais Pope, leaning against the wall, watching us. She'd swapped her punk look for a schoolgirl outfit, her hair now blonde and pulled up in piggy tails. It changed her appearance but not her eyes. The same lunatic predator stared out from behind the blue. Her smug expression said she knew she would get me—it was just a matter of time. Rocco kept his eyes straight ahead, seeming to ignore her, but I stared straight into her face, sending her so much hatred that I felt it burning through me. She didn't flinch—just smiled and pulled up her shirt to show me my duty belt still strapped to her waist. Rocco led us to the car. He covered me while I got in and was then instantly at my side. As Mom reversed, he put his arm around me—shielding my head.

I didn't back-seat drive at all during the five-minute trip home—partially because of what Rocco had said and partially because my jaws were fused together with rage.

When we reached the house, Mom drove the car into the garage. As she opened the door, the sound hit me—a man screaming. The breath rushed from me in a gasp. I left Mom with Rocco and ran in through the laundry and out into the hallway. I rounded the corner into the lounge room and saw my Dad and my brother jumping up and down together in front of the television. My sister-in-law stood on the periphery holding her vomit bucket and looking stunned. I was shouting—"*What? What?*"

"Siamo vinto!" Dad yelled at me. "We won, we won! Ten million!"

He dragged me in and I found myself in a sweaty jumping group hug. Mom appeared and was also snatched in before she even knew what we were celebrating. We went around a few times, then I noticed Rocco standing in the shadows of the hallway, watching us, his arms crossed over his chest. I met his eyes and saw the truth. This was his doing.

He melted back into the darkness. I extracted myself from the celebrations and followed him. I found him waiting by the front door, but he wasn't alone. All eleven of our cats had congregated around him and were brushing up against his legs with a loud cacophony of purrs and friendly meows. I'd never seen them react like that to anyone before. He crouched down and patted them in turn, and I wondered about this paradox of a person. Soldier, mercenary, magician, cat whisperer, I thought.

Rocco looked up and maybe—*maybe*—there was an edge of humor to the cold black of his eyes. I got the distinct feeling then that he was seeing my thoughts. He had mentioned telepathy being one of the skills some of the Shaman had, but now wasn't the time to explore the notion. I just tried to clear everything from my thoughts, and ended up thinking of everything inappropriate and embarrassing. I rubbed my forehead and prickling eyes.

"You said you had a plan of how to get my family out of danger," I said.

He nodded, standing up, brushing fur off his hands. "You're going to convince them to go away," he said.

"What do you mean?"

He gave me a look that said he didn't like to explain himself when he thought it was clearly obvious. "If they stay here, they're at risk, especially if the Horseman attacks the resistance or steps up his plans. Omen will pull all our defenses into that, which will leave your family open. If they go away, I can send people with them."

"Where should they go?" I asked.

"As far as possible, as soon as possible. Tomorrow morning—first thing. I've given you the exit, you just have to make them walk through it."

"I don't know if I can. They have jobs, my sister-in-law is pregnant—"

Rocco narrowed his eyes. "You're a trained operative of the most covert organization in the world. You make a living from deception and manipulation. I'm sure you can manage to convince your family, now millionaires, to take a holiday. Perhaps pretend their lives depend on it."

His words were harsh but grounding. I had to get them out by whatever means, and once they were out of Pope's line of fire, I could figure out how to get them away from the Shaman as well. I didn't trust Omen any more than I trusted whoever was trying to kill me—if it wasn't Omen himself. I started thinking which of my overseas contacts I could call.

Rocco turned for the door and I said, "Are you leaving?"

"My people will stay surrounding the house. You'll be safe at least for tonight while Pope regroups, rehires ..."

"What was she doing at the shop just staring at us?" I asked.

"She's trying to intimidate you, to get inside your head.." He straightened as though someone had pinched him. "I have to go."

He opened the door and we saw a person standing right there on the doorstep. I reached automatically for my sidearm and grasped at the empty place where it should have been.

Then I recognized the girl as one of the Shaman—the one who had moved super fast and hit me in the face. She and Rocco shared a fleeting glance, as he stepped past her and vanished almost immediately into the darkness. I heard his car start up. The girl stayed where she was staring at me. She had a beautiful face and unstable, angry eyes.

"Can I help you?" I finally said.

"My name is Morningstar," she said.

"Congratulations." I wasn't in the mood for games.

The girl pursed her lips. "Do you know what a Morningstar is?" she asked.

I shrugged.

"It's a deadly weapon, with a deceptively pretty name." She stared directly into my eyes.

"Really? I thought Morningstar sounded more like a pony's name," I said.

"As opposed to Silver?" she spat back.

Fair point. "What do you want?" I asked.

"For you to remember your place—*human*."

I thought for a second, then finally put two and two together. She and Rocco obviously had some kind of close relationship—he had been assigned to spend his time watching me—now she was here with the third degree—two and two equals—one jealous girlfriend. Her approach seemed a little extreme considering I'd just met Rocco, and not exactly under romantic circumstances. "Calm down, Black Beauty—no one's after your man." I told her.

She snorted, not helping herself with the whole horse theme. "I can *see* everything you try to hide."

"I'm not hiding anything." I opened my Kevlar jacket. "Just use your mind tricks and take a look for yourself." I invited her into my brain then kicked myself for it—was inviting a Shaman into your mind like inviting a vampire into your house?

"I'm not permitted—*yet*. But if I was—it would be pathetically easy." She sneered at me, then turned and stalked away.

I shut the door and leaned against it, thinking. I could hear my family still celebrating, laughing and dancing. I had to use the moment. I had to convince them to leave and I had to get it right. Then I had to crack open my safe and get out every weapon I could find and guard my family through the night.

I checked my watch. Time was ticking.

19

With Dad still jumping up and down waving like a three-hundred-pound Sicilian schoolgirl and Mom beside him hyperventilating into a seasick bag, the giant cruise ship pulled away from the dock. No surprises. Dad was a traveller at heart—planes, trains, boats, cars—whatever, whenever—whereas Mom was an agoraphobic, scared speechless of flying and nauseated at the mere suggestion of sailing. But in a show of solidarity, she'd medicated up and agreed to fulfill one of Dad's dreams: taking a cruise together. An hour earlier we'd seen Benicio and Gemma off at the airport.

Dad had promised us all a cut of the money as soon as it cleared, so they'd taken leave from their jobs—with no intention of returning—and hopped a plane to my sister-in-law's native New Zealand to spend some time there before the baby was born. They'd even been talking about starting their own photography business. I honestly thought it would be a major effort to get everyone gone so fast—but it hadn't been. Some suggestions, some prompting, some light convincing—and within the space of fourteen hours my entire family were leaving the country. Money—it doesn't buy happiness—physical objects can't purchase subjective constructs—but it sure buys everything else. No one had wanted to leave me, but I'd promised I would join them as soon as I could. I'd told them I was going into work today to apply for leave—I'd even purchased a ticket to meet my parents in Hawaii just so they believed me. There was a possibility—a large one—that I wouldn't live out the day, but I had to chance it. I'd never dreamed that my ambitions to right some wrongs in life would endanger my family like this. Naive—I could see that now.

I kept waving as the ship shrank into the distance. The further it sailed, the worse I felt inside. Bad feelings mutated and multiplied. My parents hadn't left us much as kids, but I remembered one time we'd had to stay with relatives when they went to a funeral. I'd watched them drive off and I'd had the same feelings then as I did now—an empty ache in the pit of my stomach—a feeling that everything safe and right in my world was slowly vanishing. I'd run after their car on that day, and now I felt like jumping into the ocean. I wanted to tell them again that I loved them. How many times would be enough—if it were the last time you could say it?

I clenched my fists, channeling the bad feelings into anger. I wanted to know who had put the hit on me. There was a chance that Omen had hired Annrais himself to force me into this position, and if that was the case, I'd sent my family off "guarded" by people who could turn on them at any second. They were completely unarmed and unaware. During the night, I had called some international contacts and arranged for them to board the ship at the next port and to follow my brother and his wife from the airport in Auckland. Hopefully it wouldn't be blaringly obvious to the Shaman what I'd done, but if Rocco could read my mind, there was nowhere to hide anyway. Like I said, I had to chance it.

I gave a final wave at the horizon and checked the time: ten past ten. My mother's cousin should already be at the house picking up the animals. Like mom, this cousin was pet crazy—that and various other sorts of crazy ran in their family—and she'd agreed to care for the cats and others for a while. Mr Foofypants, Gypsy Rose, Frizzy, Sushi, Chirps-Bird and all the rest were part of the family too and I wasn't going to leave them there at the mercy of Pope and her psychos. If they could kill people at a whim, I doubted small and fuzzy creatures would mean anything at all to them. Rocco had left one of his people at the house to make sure no one snatched the cousin while she was there. After that, the place would be empty and unguarded and I wouldn't be returning. I'd taken enough clothes and supplies to last the week. If I survived longer than that, I'd figure something out.

I looked over my shoulder. Rocco stood leaning against the hood of his vehicle, his arms crossed over his chest, eyes hidden behind sunglasses—darkly handsome—except for his hair. The hair was tragic. It looked as if his grandmother had spit-gelled it to one side for him. Most people had a fatal flaw in life—I guessed morning hair was his.

I turned back to the water and took out the replacement cell phone I'd dug out of my home stash. I dialed the hospital. I'd rung them so many times in the last few days I knew their number better than I knew my own. The nurse who answered said Dark was awake, but that the doctor was with him. I'd spent a good part of the night thinking how to get him out and hidden. There were a few people unconnected to Chapter 11 who I could call—old buddies from our federal police days, among others—but if Annrais's assassins couldn't get to him past the Shaman, how would my contacts do it?

I wanted to talk to my partner so badly. I realized I was standing there with the phone pressed to the side of my head, the vacant tone bleeping in my ear. I needed to get in gear. I needed to get focused. Trouble was I couldn't remember a time when I didn't feel sick with tiredness. I took off my sunglasses and massaged the pain rebuilding behind my eyes. Stress had amped up the migraines, and the pills were in my duty belt, now in the possession of a psychopathic murderer … My hands started to tremble and I clenched them into fists.

"Get it together," I whispered. I replaced the sunglasses and turned around.

Rocco was standing right behind me. I took a quick step back.

"It's time to go," he said.

"Dark's awake," I told him. "Is there still someone on him—is he safe?"

"For now he's covered," Rocco gave his standard reply.

For now … at least he was honest about it.

"They're coming—we have to go," he told me.

I cursed under my breath. Pope was a hellhound. What would it take to send her back?

"I swear the next time she's in range, I'm taking her out," I told him as we strode back to the car. So much for my pacifistic ideals.

"Let us deal with her," Rocco said. "You'll draw too much attention if you start randomly shooting up buildings. You have to focus on the plan."

"Which is what?" I asked.

We got into the car and he started the engine. "You go to work and start looking for the White List."

He backed without looking. A few other cars were reversing at the same time and all of them stopped dead to let him go first. He drove to the exit, then took off, heading into Toran-R. I took his advice and started thinking about the task.

"I would have done what Omen did and started with the Conference." I spoke my thoughts aloud. "They're the ones who hold the reins. If they don't have access to the information, then who the hell would?"

"They hold the reins, yes, but they don't necessarily work at a functional level within the organization," Rocco told me. "In my way of thinking—it's the Head of Operational Services who assigns the field agents to their tasks—tells them which Shaman are about to break-thru."

"Okay." I processed what he was saying. "So you think maybe my boss, Twentyman, would have access?"

"Maybe not to the entire List, but possibly to individual names off it—and according to Marco individual portions of the List may have a digital location stamp, something to track it back to the originating system."

"So someone sends him the names of the ... individuals ... who are about to break-thru copied off the List—and these copies may lead us to the actual list."

"Maybe ... " he said.

I shook my head, my thoughts jumping ahead. "Even if I knew a hundred percent that Twentyman had stored the names on his computer, there's no way I'll be able to access his system—even under normal circumstances. And now they're hunting Omen, everything is locked down super tight."

"There's always a way," Rocco told me. "Use your knowledge, work your strengths and remember the people who trust you are your best asset."

"Spoken like a true mercenary soldier," I said.

Rocco glanced my way and said, "Yes and you'd better start thinking my way if you want to survive."

"If Omen is so powerful and was still caught, what hope do I have?" I repeated my question from the night before.

"Omen's position was compromised," Rocco said and I detected a definite tension to his words. His body changed as well—he sat more rigidly in his seat, clenched the wheel tighter. It was the first sign of discomfort I'd seen from him.

There was definitely something there, but I doubted he was a man who could be pushed into conversation. I looked out the passenger window at the city, at its people—everything was the same and everything looked different. The city I thought I knew so well had grown yet another face—a non-human face.

"What did you mean about the Order of Shaman?" I asked him, coming back to something I'd been thinking about the night before. "Like a pecking order?"

"Yes—if we were chickens," Rocco said, giving me a dark look.

"I didn't mean that in a bad way," I said, my words heavy with fatigue, and his expression softened slightly.

"It's related to power," he said. "As I was saying at the motel—the higher up the Order the more power. Worldwide—the Horseman is one, Omen is two."

"And who is three?" I asked.

"Me," Rocco said.

"And if you're higher in the Order than another Shaman, it means you could block his or her power and abilities?"

"Under certain circumstances—if they were incapacitated like they are when C11 caps them—then yes—but mainly it has to with number of skills, strength in using those skills in combat and the ability to sense each other. If I'm higher than you and I don't want you to know I'm a Shaman, I can block you from sensing it, but if you're lower you can't block me from seeing you—but—if you're under the protection of a Shaman stronger than me, then he or she can shield you as well."

"Sounds complicated," I said.

"It's really not," Rocco said, making me feel dense.

"There seem to be more Shaman breaking-thru than ever before," I said.

He nodded. "The more of us that wake, the more of us will wake. I can't explain it, but that's what's happening. Seems to be a domino effect of sorts."

"Everywhere?" I asked.

Rocco nodded. "The Horseman has his people in all the major C11 locations, all the capital cities around the world and many of the smaller facilities as well—and we have contacts everywhere too, but no one inside Headquarters as I said earlier."

"Does the White List include all wal—I mean Shaman—everywhere or just here?"

"Worldwide," he confirmed. "And the more people we have positioned across each continent and region the better chance we have. We don't know exactly how the Horseman will strike, but we know that when he does it will be global. That much is clear."

As he said that an idea came to me. "I know some countries have fewer resources for handling break-thrus. How are they dealing with the influx?"

"They're not," Rocco said. "The violence is escalating and maybe that's part of the Horseman's plan—we're not sure yet."

I jolted forward in my seat as he brought the big vehicle to a sudden stop right outside Headquarters, behind a car pulling into the only free parking space. The car's owner, a random suit, climbed out. He started to stride away then stopped, looked around scratching his head, then went back to the car, got in and drove away. I didn't doubt this strange behavior was the result of my new Shaman friend silently convincing the guy he was in the wrong place.

"There's heavy surveillance all around the building," I told him. "If they see us together, they'll check up on you."

"If anyone looks up my profile they'll find a perfectly legitimate person," he said. "Marco has made sure of it."

"Is he really capable?" I asked.

"More than capable," Rocco said. He glided into the space, then took a manila envelope out of his pocket and upturned it into his hand.

"Cell phone linked to my number—just press red." He handed me the device. "It also has the blueprint of C11 headquarters and security-camera locations. PIN is 3888. Don't get caught with it unlocked. Call me with updates."

"Call you?" I asked. "Can't you just see my thoughts?"

Rocco paused and I thought he wasn't going to answer, but then he said, "It's a lot more complicated than just seeing. There are many layers of thoughts and memories in a person's mind. Some people are very complex. I have to use facial expression, body cues, scent even to understand the simplest idea."

"Am I—complex?" I asked.

"No," he said.

I must have looked disappointed because he frowned and said, "It's not necessarily a good thing to be complex, and even if you're not, there are ways to make it more difficult for a Shaman to read you. You can think of other things to blanket what you want to hide, even silent counting or reciting the alphabet works, and thinking about sex always distracts people … "

"Don't say that or I'll start thinking about it and distract myself," I muttered.

Rocco almost smiled.

I rubbed my temples. Pure stress pulsated through my veins. I felt it peak and then start to ebb down, down, down until I felt calm: completely, unnaturally calm.

"Don't," I said to the Shaman. "Don't pheromone me or whatever it is you do. I have to feel what I feel; I have to be myself. I'm serious. Stop."

The calm flowed out and the pain rushed in, compounded by fatigue, fear and hunger. My hands went shaky and my vision fuzzed. The headache felt like knives behind my eyes, and the place where Pope had smashed me in the face throbbed horribly. I realized Rocco must have been blocking the pain since he first saved me at the warehouse.

"Okay—maybe pheromone me a little." I murmured. I couldn't work like this. I couldn't even walk.

The pain lifted to the point where I could see and steady myself.

"Time to go," Rocco said. "Wait for me." He opened his door and came around to my side, carefully positioning himself as cover while I climbed out. He hugged me close to his side as we walked to the entrance of the office. I could feel the tension in his body and scanned our surroundings, already knowing what I would see—who I would see. I looked back at the building across the street. It was a heritage-listed double-story structure with Romanesque balconies and stone gargoyle cats. Perched beside one of the statues, as still as a stone herself—Annrais Pope. She had a sniper rifle pointed at us.

"Psycho bitch," I murmured. "Why doesn't she just shoot?"

"She can't get a clear shot," Rocco said, weaving us in and out of the stampede of people crossing in front of Headquarters. We entered through the glass doors and Rocco relaxed his grip. All the transparent panels of the building were thick bulletproof glass. I glanced back to where Annrais had sat a few seconds ago and she was gone—like an illusion, a nightmare.

"She's not going to stop, is she?" I said.

"No," Rocco said.

"Why don't you stop her—like your people did with her assassins?"

"She's smarter than they were. She positions herself out of range or in public places. I'd have to use my abilities and I can't do that. We can't alert the person who has hired her that you are involved with us. We have to assume they are inside the company and that they may be connected to the Horseman."

I nodded. It made sense. A horrible, twisted, confused sense. I really *really* didn't want to go down to the office.

"Can you change your appearance to an agent and come with me?" I asked, as a last desperate idea.

"If we could do that, we wouldn't need you," Rocco reminded me, his voice calm and patient. "The Horseman would know. Pope won't risk hitting you in the office, but *he* is down there. Don't forget that."

A chill ran along my back. "Are we sure it's a he?"

Rocco shook his head. "It could be anyone—male or female."

Out of the corner of my eye, I saw Eric enter the building. His eyes went straight to us as though we were magnetic.

"My supervisor," I whispered.

I looked up at Rocco and found his face inches from mine. He kissed me on the lips.

It was just a Goodbye, Have a Good Day kiss—nothing pornographic, but still I felt slightly weak at the knees and couldn't help regretting that I hadn't brushed my teeth for the last two days. To pretend to be a couple as a cover made sense, I just hadn't been expecting it.

Rocco hugged me against him and whispered in my ear, "Get this right and we may still have a chance to stop the Horseman. Don't, and I'll be dead, you'll be dead, everyone you know and care about—dead. This world as it is will be gone. Find the List, Silver." He let me go and stepped back.

"No pressure or anything," I muttered.

I turned away, feeling Rocco's eyes on my back as I walked to the elevator. I couldn't bring myself to smile at Norm today, for which he seemed sincerely relieved.

I stepped into the elevator. On the outside I maintained my professional front, on the inside I was running around and around in circles screaming. I'd always wanted to feel like I was doing more of worth in my work and suddenly 'saving the world' was part of my job description. Be careful what you wish for.

20

Agents blurred around me—speeding up then slowing down. Faces leaped into focus for a moment's scrutiny then vanished. Everyone familiar now seemed sinister. I noted every twitch of their mouths, every shift of their eyes, every hair out of place—or not. They spoke to me but their words were lost. I just kept nodding, hoping I was giving the appropriate response. Hoping I wasn't blowing my cover in the first few seconds of the game. Any of them could be the Horseman or one of his soldiers. Trouble was we were all agents—all professional liars, to our friends, to our families, everyone around us—and we all looked suspicious to a certain extent. How could I differentiate between the normal shadiness and the unnatural kind? I reached my desk and sank into the chair. I avoided looking at the photographs of my family and Dark. An impromptu crying session wouldn't help anything now.

Jovic and Feng had photocopied yesterday's Op Services night-shift reports for me and put them in my in-tray. I snatched them up and read through. The executive summary—everyone was hunting for clues on Omen and no one was finding anything. Many of the agents from my division were out in the field investigating leads or working normal

walt cases; a few were on desk duty, sorting out incoming updates and compiling reports, like I was supposed to be doing.
For once I wasn't upset about being held back. Being stationed external to Headquarters would have made the search
for the List all the more difficult.

I glanced over toward Twentyman's office and saw Eric
skulking around outside the door. I wondered what, if anything, he'd had to do with the bounty on my head—had
it actually come from Twentyman or from someone beyond
him—maybe even the Horseman himself?

On the way down in the elevator, I'd resolved my decision
to start the search for the List in Twenty's office. The question
now was how was I going to get in and if, by some miracle, I
managed that, how was I going to get access to his computer
files? I'd have to know his password, plus somehow bypass
the Shake security. Both impossibilities—but one question at
a time—first—how to get in?

I took the cell phone Rocco had given me out of my
pocket and, keeping the screen half hidden beneath the pho-
tocopies, I opened the security blueprint of Headquarters. A
cluster of surveillance cameras was positioned right outside
Twentyman's office. Nothing inside though, which didn't surprise me. The man was so arrogant he would think everyone
else needed to be watched, but not him, or maybe there was
another reason he didn't want anyone keeping tabs on him—a
Horseman reason. Someone cleared their throat behind me
and I jumped out of my chair, reeling around. Byter stared at
me, his eyes wide, two cups of coffee held out in front of him
as though to fend off an attack.

"Sorry," I forced a laugh. "Just a little bit on edge here."

"No, I'm sorry." He gave an equally uncomfortable laugh.
"Shouldn't have snuck up on you."

I dropped back down into my chair, slipping the cell into
my pocket. It was still logged into the blueprint and sat like a

brick against my side. Byter perched on the edge of my desk and placed one of the coffee cups down in front of me.

"Thanks," I murmured. I looked up at my friend. He was wearing the same clothes as yesterday and had purple blotches under his eyes and crumbs of something in his beard—that tragic beard.

"We're in crisis and you still can't stop thinking about my beard," he said, a hint of a smile curving his lips. "It mesmerizes you, doesn't it?"

"Something like that," I replied.

His face grew serious again. "Any news on Dark? I keep ringing the hospital but they won't tell me squat because I'm not family."

"They said this morning that he's awake. I couldn't talk to him either because he was with the doctor."

"At least he's awake again." Byter's tired eyes brightened.

And I remembered what Rocco had said about the people who trusted me being my biggest asset. It gave me an idea. "Byter, I know you're crazy busy, but do you think you can help me?" I asked. "My Shake doesn't seem to be working." I prodded the security device on my desk.

"Oh." He picked it up and turned it over. "Sure, I'll just run a few tests and see what's up."

I watched him as closely as I could without being obvious as he took a device with five prongs out of his pocket. He inserted it into my Shake and the login box popped up; he typed in my name, codename and an override password. I watched his fingers as they moved across the keyboard—it looked like *4124squeakand-bubble*. My computer files appeared on the screen. He clicked on a few generic applications before logging out.

"Seems to be okay now," he said. "Might have just been a glitch."

He took the pronged device out of the Shake and said, "Try it now."

I did and went straight into my files.

"Thanks," I said, eyeing the device as he pushed it back into his jacket pocket.

"No problemo," Byter replied. "By the way I'm definitely still working on clearing the footage of the attack—I won't give up."

"Thanks, Byter, I really appreciate it."

"Anything for you," he said and punched my arm lightly. I noticed there was something a bit "close" about the way he was looking at me. Maybe I was dreaming it, but I was getting a vibe from him.

"How did you go with the other skipped footage?" he asked, breaking the moment.

"It just seemed completely random," I lied.

"That's what I thought too," he said. He looked up at the sound of approaching voices and smiled. Jovic and Feng were arguing their way toward us, and by Jovic's reddened face and strained neck veins, I guessed he was losing the debate. As soon as they saw us, the conversation was over.

Feng came over and gave my shoulders a quick massage and asked, "How is he?"

"Awake," I said.

"Told you he'd be fine." Jovic gave me a friendly nudge. "Man of steel. Just like me." He flexed a bulbous bicep. Feng scrunched up her face at him.

"You love it," he teased her.

"Not me," she replied. "I prefer my men more like Byter."

"Pleasingly trim," Byter said.

"Skinny like a girl," she said.

"Great—I'll just be in the bathroom—crying." Byter pretended to walk away and she laughed and dragged him back.

"Thanks for the copies," I told her, holding up the reports.

"It's nothing," she said, then leaned in so close I could smell her jasmine perfume. "Don't say anything to anyone yet, but guess who's about to move on up—Supervising Manager—Medical Division?"

I looked at her and raised my eyebrows and she nodded. A few days earlier and I would have just been happy for a friend, but now my skin prickled with unease—Medical Division was where the Horseman's soldiers re-capped all the walts—how could she become part of Medical if she wasn't herself a Shaman? The thought shook me. This wasn't some random person; this was one of my closest friends, I'd shared a desk with her for years—and maybe she was now reading my mind. I panicked and tried to think of something to block her. Instead of reciting the alphabet, I started to think about sex. Maybe it was normal human instinct to jump there, or maybe I just had a dirty mind? I glanced up at Feng. She was checking her phone messages.

"Well I'd better get going," Byter said, giving us a wave. "Us girly boys are in high demand."

"Stop sulking," Feng said. She sat down at her desk and opened her computer.

I took the opportunity to run after Byter. "Hey," I said, taking his shoulder. He turned and I hugged onto him, pulling him close.

"I just wanted to say thanks for everything." I squeezed him tight against my body with one hand while the other reached into his pocket and extracted the Shake override—distraction, misdirection—whatever—I had it. I slipped it into my pocket and stepped back, leaving him a little flushed.

He muttered, "Of course, anything for you." He gulped a bit and I felt like Judas—big time.

"See you soon," I said and went back to my chair.

Feng immediately leaned over and whispered, "What's going on?"

"Nothing," I replied.

She rolled her eyes. "We really have to get you a man. It's been way too long. I need some gossip here."

I faked a smile and glanced again at Twentyman's door. Now I had a way into his computer, but I still had to get into his office to get to the computer. A thought came to me. If the Shaman rebels could blur the C11 surveillance cameras around the city and splice in old footage to mask their comings and goings, maybe they could do the same with the cameras inside Headquarters as well—surely they'd already thought of that. I had to speak to Rocco. I massaged the ache behind my eyes and Feng said, "Have you *still* got a headache? Did you get a scan at the hospital after the attack?"

I shook my head.

"You should go get one—seriously," she said, her face creased with worry. "I knew a girl who fell off her horse, got a headache and died that night. You need to get scanned."

"I will, I promise," I said. "After. For now—I'll just grab some water. Back in a sec."

I headed for the bathroom, not the one closest to the office, the one further down the hall. It was always empty because no one could be bothered walking that far unless they wanted the extra privacy. I always went there. Being extremely smell sensitive, I would walk an extra mile to go to a clean bathroom. I walked in and did a check of the cubicles before choosing one and locking the door. I sat down on the closed toilet seat. There wasn't supposed to be surveillance in the bathrooms, but we weren't supposed to be torturing and murdering people either. I opted to keep the cover going. I pressed the red button on the cell phone Rocco had given me. He answered and I put on a New Relationship voice.

"Hey, how are you?"

He waited and I continued, "Yeah I'm okay ... but you know how I was going to go into that store and buy that present for my brother's birthday—well I just had a thought that maybe he'll see me if I go this afternoon, so I was just wondering if you could ... obscure his vision somehow?"

The message was so cryptic I doubted Rocco would get what I was talking about, but he answered straight away, "We can't interfere with surveillance inside Headquarters without attracting the Horseman's attention, but I can make a diversion that will get your boss to leave his office. You're talking about Twentyman, aren't you?"

"That's right," I said.

"So if you can get into his office, I can get him out—at least for a few minutes."

"What path do you think I could take to get in without my brother seeing me?" I asked.

"Have you thought about just making an appointment with him?"

No I hadn't, but I should have—I'd been having all kinds of visions of mission impossible break-ins, when I could just walk in.

"How will you know when to distract Benicio if I can't signal you?" I asked.

"You can—just press the red button as you're going into the office and that will signal me," he said.

"Great. Thank you—bye—love you," I said.

"Noted," Rocco replied. Something about his voice said he was smiling.

I hung up and left the bathroom, taking a direct path to the alcove beside Twentyman's office, where his fierce guard-dog PA, Agent Kenealy, sat behind her desk. She glanced up over her glasses as I approached, and a look of exasperation spread over her flabby-jowled face—as though I'd just farted on my hand and was trying to make her smell it. I didn't appreciate the look—in fact I felt like telling her to shove it. Her level of gruff unpleasantness was totally inappropriate, but I controlled myself. Kenealy was the gatekeeper to Twenty and getting in depended on her.

"Yes?" she demanded as I stopped in front of her desk.

"Good morning, Agent Kenealy." I used her last name instead of her codename, which was an unwritten way of paying respect to a senior operative—though I actually out-ranked her. "I have something very urgent to discuss with Agent Twentyman regarding … " I hadn't figured out what my cover story was. I swallowed and Kenealy narrowed her eyes. " … the Omen investigation."

Kenealy turned back to her computer and recited in a bored monotone, "He's in meetings all day. Send me an email and I'll forward it to him if I think it's relevant."

I reined in my rising anger. I felt like head-butting the woman. Instead I made my tone sugary sweet and used all my submissive body language cues. "I know it's last minute and I'm really sorry to be annoying. If there's any way you could squeeze me in anywhere I think the information would make a lot more sense if I explained it in person. I'm really sorry again."

Kenealy sighed heavily and pounded on her computer with big meaty man fingers. She spent several minutes fussing and sighing and finally said, "He can see you at eighteen hundred hours for four minutes only."

"Great—thank you so much," I groveled, and backed away from her desk. I checked my watch. Six hours to go. With a million things to do, I was sure the time would race. I spotted Jovic and Feng heading out of the office and felt a whisper of relief. At least I wouldn't have to spend the whole day thinking about sex or singing the alphabet song—although that didn't sound completely unlike some other work days I'd had.

21

First on the task list—I went back to the bathroom and used the cell phone from my personal stash to message my most reliable non-C11 contact in Toran-R to ask if he'd be willing to try to get Dark out. I explained about the bloodthirsty assassins hovering vulturously around the hospital, but omitted the part about the people with supernatural abilities who were also watching. He said he'd give it a shot—for the right money of course. I knew him to be one of the best retired tactical soldiers I'd met. I just had to hope and pray he was up to the task.

After that I messaged my overseas contacts minding my brother and parents—both reported to have them in their sights. *For now*—I repeated Rocco's words with agitation—*For now*. And then I rang the hospital. When the nurse who answered said she'd give the phone to Dark I felt the huge knot of anxiety in my stomach tighten. I needed to tell him as much as I could, while making it sound as though I wasn't telling him anything at all. I had to get it right. I pressed the phone hard against my ear and waited.

When I heard his voice on the line, sounding worn and distant. I almost broke down. I held my head trying to get composure and Dark said, "Please tell me you're not crying on the toilet."

I snorted out a strangled laugh.

"I can hear the echo," he said.

"I'm on the toilet but I'm not *on* the toilet," I finally managed.

"What's wrong?" he asked immediately.

"Well my partner's smashed up in hospital, there's that," I said.

"Apart from that ... something's wrong, I can hear it."

"It's just the echo," I told him, buying time, still trying to figure out what to say. "How are you feeling?"

"Awesome," he said, then grunted with pain as he tried to move.

"Seriously, how are you?" I pushed him.

"I have an infection in one of the wounds, but it's nothing to stress about, just means a bit more time in here."

I could hear by the gruffness that he was downplaying it and felt an extra twist of fear.

"Bos ... " I said. "I'm really glad you're getting out today ... I think the doctors are right—you'll have a much faster recovery in your own place. I asked my friend Tom Costigan to head in and drive you home—do you remember I said I'd call him? Just let him help you—don't be stubborn about it, there's no shame in it. You need help. Trust me."

Tom Costigan wasn't my contact's name—it was our unofficial code for "backup" based on an obscure book reference that only Dark and I understood, because it was one we'd had to study for school—or at least I'd studied it and he'd apparently sat behind me during the exam and cheated off my answers—which was why we'd ended up using it for backup.

My hand started shaking again and I swapped ears waiting for his response. After a pause he said,

"Tom ...? You must think I'm in a bad way ..."

"You are," I said.

"And you?" he shot back, his voice hard now. He had the phone close to his mouth.

"I'm fine, I'm at Headquarters," I said and I knew he'd hear the emptiness of the words. "Just take care—the medication you're on can give you hallucinations—you can see some crazy stuff—and it can feel very real at times ..." I tried to allude to the Shaman. "You can even feel paranoid, like there's people following you ..."

"Right," Dark said. I heard voices in the background and he added, "Doctor's here. Gotta go."

"Be okay," I told him, feeling strangled.

"Right," he said again, stiffly. "See you soon."

I hung up and sat for a minute reeling with fear. Then I kicked myself back into action and went to HR to report Dark's car stolen along with his and my duty belts. I knew by doing this, I was giving myself extra stress, having to fill out paperwork and explain the situation, but I didn't want Annrais Pope using our equipment to trap me with a frame up. Being arrested was the last thing I needed. Afterwards I went to the armory and picked up a new belt and accessories, including a new work phone and headed back to my desk to rehearse the story I'd be selling to Twentyman. Once that was in the bag, I turned my attention to my computer.

Since my situation had been so unstable post-attack, there were no tasks specifically assigned me, but I read the few incoming division reports so that I could at least give the impression of keeping up to speed and then I went into research mode. I brought up Omen's profile, released after his defection. Since it was a general overview available to all levels of clearance the information was sparse and generic. How many years he'd served as an agent, his expertise, training history ... nothing that would give me an advantage over the Shaman leader. And at this stage, I seriously needed an advantage. He had me on all accounts. I tried to access more information, but everything was shut down tight.

I ended up sitting staring at his photograph on the screen. If I hadn't known who he was and someone had told me this was a photo of a serial killer, I would have taken one look at those eyes and said, "Yeah I can see that." I think it would have been a completely different story if he were smiling. He was one of those people a genuine smile could change from frightening to attractive. But with the girl he loved dead and the weight of the world on his shoulders, I understood he had very little to smile about. I ran a search for the Rose, Evelyn Drake's, profile but found it removed. The Chapter had a way of doing that. If an agent died they just erased all history of them—as though they never existed. But I had a clear picture in my mind of the woman in red. No one could erase that.

I ran another search—this time using the name *Rocco,* even though I was quite sure it was a codename and that Rocco had never been a part of C11. The Shaman rebels seemed to be using codes as well. As expected the search turned nothing up, so I went into the Lexicon—the C11 database of all the law enforcement, military and Special Forces personnel in the country. I searched again for Rocco and again—nothing.

I sat back in my seat and an idea came to me—I accessed the surveillance archives and ran a place and time match for that morning in the Headquarters' lobby. I found un-corrupted footage of me and Rocco standing there talking. I focused in on him and freeze-framed around his face, then directed a search for his features. The search program rapidly flicked through hundreds of different faces before settling on a driver's license shot of him. I leaned in and read the name—Adam Best—with a legitimate address and other details.

I pressed further into his file and found all the right doc-uments that would convince anyone that this was, in fact,

Adam Best. He hadn't been kidding about Marco being capable. Rocco was officially anonymous. I could always just ask him who he was—but he didn't seem the type to open up and I really needed to know who I was dealing with if I was to have any chance of outsmarting them and getting me and all of mine out of this alive.

My thoughts returned to Dark. I took out my cell phone and signed into the tracking application we were trialing for Byter. I watched the locator signal closing in over the city, then focusing in more and more until it found the hospital and then his room within it. So he was still there—and I hoped he wasn't doing anything crazy and impulsive to get out because he thought I was in trouble.

I worried for a moment that the application could be used by the Horseman against us. Byter had assured us only he knew about the microchips and their function, and I'd always trusted our friend completely, but now I wasn't sure about anything anymore. I considered removing the app, cutting the microchip out of my arm, but right now it was the only way for Dark and I to track each other and I couldn't risk shutting that down. I rubbed my forearm nervously and second-guessed the decision, but let it ride.

I glanced up at the office clock and saw with a jolt that it was almost time to see Twenty. I pushed back from my desk and moved fast for his office. Kenealy waved me through with one hand, the other still typing, and I found myself walking down the corridor to Twentyman's office—pressing the red button of Rocco's cell hidden in my pocket, signaling him the plan was a go. I breathed deeply to steady myself. My boss was in a familiar position, reading papers at his desk. Even he looked haggard and unbathed. As usual he made me wait while he finished the document. When he did look up, his expression was brutal, so I decided to launch straight in.

"Agent Twentyman. I've been reviewing the details of Omen's infiltration of the C11 computer systems and I noted that he hacked a large amount of data from Conference files. It occurred to me that he might have been trawling for something significant to use against the Chapter, maybe even something related to the location and identity of walts—possibly for blackmailing purposes or for something even worse ..."

I rattled on for a while longer, sticking as closely to the truth as I dared for authenticity, knowing full well I could be talking to the Horseman himself, and when I was done Twentyman leaned back in his chair. I could see from his eyes that he was thinking hard. He opened his mouth—

Agent Kenealy was heard running down the hall, her matron shoes clopping even on the plush carpet. When she opened the door and leaned into the room, her face was flushed in blotches.

"It's him!" she hissed to Twentyman. "Omen—line 1."

Twentyman sat bolt upright. He swallowed to compose himself then picked up the phone. He spoke for a few minutes, mostly saying, "I understand. Yes, I understand," then he was on his feet, yelling orders at Kenealy as they ran out. Whatever Rocco had told them had worked. I was alone in the office. I jumped into action.

I rushed around the desk and sat in Twenty's chair. I hoped he'd left his computer on so that I wouldn't need the override device I'd stolen from Byter, but the screen was black. Cursing quietly, I booted up, inserting the device into Twentyman's Shake and typing in his names and Byter's code. Twentyman's computer files came up. I ran a search for the White List, which came back with zero files. Then I skimmed all his folders, files and emails searching for any sign of names from the List. There was plenty of confidential information, but not what I was looking for. I glanced up at the door, my legs jittering and hands shaking. I couldn't linger. Who knew when Twentyman would get back? I ran one final search and the results were the same—nothing. I grabbed the override out of the Shake, and stood up—as I did a piece of paper on Twentyman's desk caught my attention. It was sticking out from a half concealed book and I could just see the word *Blood*.

I pulled the paper free and stared down at the words written in red. *I am the Blood Horseman.*

I blinked, shocked—it seemed so clear that it had to be a mistake or a joke—or something. Why would he have just left this here? Was Twenty actually the Horseman—could it be that simple? I put the paper on the desk and took a photo with my phone. A door slammed beyond the office and I jolted. I'd been there way too long.

I placed the paper back inside the book and positioned the chair exactly as it had been, then left the office, keeping my head down and walking straight to my desk.

Feng was back in the office, standing beside her chair looking around. Groups of others were also huddled talking and watching the door.

"What's happened?" I asked Feng as I reached our pod.

"Someone said Omen's in the building and he's requested a one on one with Twentyman," she told me, raising thin, shaped eyebrows.

Jovic came through the door and headed in our direction. "False alarm," he announced and a general muttering broke out.

"Why would he prank Twenty?" Feng asked as Jovic joined us.

"Because he's a nutjob," her partner said, sitting down at his desk. "I mean he shot his partner. He's just taunting us."

"Did you ever meet him—when he was an agent?" I asked them.

"Omen?" Jovic said. "Few times. The guy was stuck up."

"I thought he was hot," Feng said.

Jovic gave her an annoyed sideways glance. "You think everyone's hot."

"Except you," she said.

"Except me," he muttered and something about his voice made me wonder if I'd missed something there as well. So much for being a secret agent with expert skills of observation and behavioral decoding. I was missing things right in front of my face. But now wasn't the time for a self-esteem crisis. The doors from the foyer parted and Twentyman entered looking even more fierce and ticked-off than usual.

Eric sidelined him as he walked in and they exchanged a few words. They glanced my way, then headed back out, and I saw their silhouettes through the frosted glass doors turning left, toward the auditoriums. I may have missed a few office crushes, but that was suspicious behavior if ever I saw it. Had Eric seen me coming out of Twentyman's office? Maybe he was a Shaman too and he'd read my mind? My chest felt so tight I could barely breathe. I couldn't just wait for them to come for me. I had to strike first.

Jovic looked busy on his computer and Feng was talking on the phone so I left them, slipping away without drawing their attention. I exited the office and paused beside the wall, seeing the Twenty and Eric in the distance, turning into one of the lecture rooms. I crept after them, trying not to look like I was creeping: even though the corridor was deserted, the cameras were still watching. I came to the room they'd vanished into, and with painstaking care turned the door handle and peeked inside. It was a smaller training auditorium, just fifteen or so rows down to the stage below. My boss and Eric were standing near the front with their backs to me. They were talking, but I couldn't hear what they were saying.

I crouched down and slipped through the door, crawling through the dimly lit auditorium to the stairs and inching down until I could just make out their words. I just hoped surveillance wasn't on me, but the chances it wasn't were slim. I made a half-hearted attempt to make it look as though I was searching for something underneath the seats while straining to hear Twenty and Eric's conversation. It became easier when they raised their voices.

Twenty was saying, "No. No! It's a massive waste of resources. I told you. She's been under the spotlight for over eighteen months now with no result. She's borderline, but she hasn't turned."

"And I told you," Eric said, with a sharp tone that I'd never heard him use with our boss before, "it's only a matter of time."

"She has the backing of the General. If something happens to her, he will bring the full force of his inquiry down on us. He's watching. He knows," Twenty barked.

I peeked above the seat. It sounded as though they were talking about me, but they hadn't used my name.

"And *that* is all thanks to you!" Twentyman continued. "I said to step back from her or he'd notice—and you didn't—and he did!"

"I was trying to force her to expose herself!"

"By giving her more paperwork!" Twenty gave a harsh laugh. "You just exposed *yourself* as being incompetent—and what's more, you didn't realize, but I've been keeping a close eye on you as well and I've noticed a few things that you better start explaining right now—or it's you that's going to be relocated—permanently!"

Eric started laughing then, a forced, annoying cackle. I stared at him with loathing that sharply snapped to shock as he whipped out a knife and slashed it across Twentyman's throat. Blood spurted everywhere. My boss gasped, gurgled and collapsed. I clutched the seat beside me, frozen with shock. I thought the door would burst open and agents would rush in, that the cameras would have picked up everything, but the auditorium fell to silence as Twentyman's gasps failed. Eric stood over the body, calmly cleaning the knife on a handkerchief. I'd thought Twentyman was the Horseman, but clearly I'd been wrong. And I'd thought Eric was an annoying prick, but ultimately harmless—and I'd been wrong again. So who was he? Could Eric be the Horseman?

I felt my work phone vibrate in my pocket and grabbed at it, afraid it was about to ring, but it was turned to silent. I checked the ID and saw it was the General. I rejected the call, then peeked back above the seat, jolting to see Eric was now looking my way, squinting through the darkness. He started toward me then stopped, taking out his own phone and answering it, "Yes."

His expression widened to surprise. "Oh—it's you—I'm so sorry—I didn't recognize the number. Yes. Yes. I understand, but he made me. He knew. Yes, I know but I ... I know, I'm sorry. I am. I know ... Horseman ... please. Yes—I understand. I will do it now."

Looking shaken, Eric grabbed Twentyman and, as I watched, the body seemed to shrink further and further and cave in until only a pile of ash was left. Eric swept what remained into a corner with his foot. Then he straightened his jacket and jogged up the stairs on the other side of the auditorium, vanishing through the door. I exhaled and stood on shaky legs. I stared down at the few crumbs that were left of Twenty. There wasn't even any blood left. A sharp pain stabbed through my head and I gripped it. This was crazy. I had to get out of there. I barged out the door, then pressed back against the wall. Eric still stood talking on the phone at the other end of the corridor, near the doors leading into the office. Was he still talking to the Horseman? I didn't know, but being backstabbed in the office had just taken on a whole new meaning.

I kept close to the wall and hoped I could move past without him noticing, but just as I reached Eric, my phone vibrated again and he looked up from his conversation and spotted me. I tried not to run—or scream—grabbing my phone out of my pocket so that I had a reason not to look at him. It was the General again—and I needed to talk to him desperately—but not here. I hurried to my desk and grabbed my jacket. My shift had officially ended fifteen minutes back and conveniently being on reduced duties meant I didn't have to do doubles. What I did have to do was to talk to the General about Eric, about Omen, about my family and Dark—things had gone way over my head and I needed his help.

22

When I stepped out into the lobby, I saw Rocco waiting for me. He was leaning against one wall beside a fake hibiscus in an oversized terracotta pot. I pushed through the surge of suits escaping work. Rush hour. Dark hated the term. He'd always argued it wasn't one hour, it was several, so why don't they change it to Rush Hours? Probably for the same reason they don't change Morning Sickness to Pregnancy Sickness, even though some girls are hanging over the bowl from dawn to dusk and beyond. Rocco and I met in the center and kissed. This time it was slightly more lingering, long enough at least for me to notice the warmth of his lips. Something I shouldn't be noticing given the current dire circumstances.

He put his arm around me and we walked to the glass doors and out to his black SUV parked in front of the building. Night lights softened the sharp edges and hid the grimy corners of Toran-R. The city, all business by day, took on a whole new persona at night. It became a wonderland of possibility, of magic and excitement. The darkness also obscured my view of the surrounding buildings, so I couldn't see her, but I assumed Pope was there, lurking in the shadows, staring at us through telescopic sights. Rocco covered me as I climbed into the car.

"Is she out there?" I asked as he got behind the wheel and started up.

"It would be smart to assume so," he said. The relentless traffic stream beside us came to a sudden stop and Rocco pulled out, heading down the main strip toward the freeway.

"What's happened?" he asked, looking over at me.

At first I couldn't form words, and then I told him everything all at once—ending with my intention to speak with the General and tell him everything. I probably should have withheld the last part, but it had just rushed out with the rest.

Rocco took everything in then said, "You can't tell him anything. You can't trust that he's not affiliated with the Horseman."

"No ... " I said. "He can't be. Twentyman said that the General was looking out for me, and Eric didn't argue that. If somehow the General was involved wouldn't Eric have said something ..."

"Not necessarily," Rocco said, taking a sharp right turn.

"It's not him," I insisted. "If it was—he'd never call himself 'the Horseman'. He was bitten by a horse when he was younger and he has a phobia of them."

I closed my eyes and massaged my head.

"Even if you feel sure, you still can't tell him anything. If Omen thinks you're not working with us, he'll see you as our enemy. He'll withdraw all protection from your partner. And that's the best case scenario."

"Meaning what?" I demanded.

"Meaning Omen is unpredictable. If you anger him, he may hurt Dark."

His words hit a very raw nerve inside me and I struggled not to start yelling at him, instead I said, "I still have to talk to the General. He's rung me twice. If I don't ring back he'll think something's wrong."

"So call him," Rocco said. "Tell him Twentyman is dead and how it happened, but do not say anything about Omen, the List or Pope." He gave me a warning look as I dragged my personal cell out of my pocket.

I rang the General and heard his cheery voice asking me to leave a message. I hung up and dialed his home number. His wife picked up after several rings.

"Hello. It's Silvia. I'm sorry to disturb you," I said. "I just—really need to talk to Jack."

The wife didn't know his codename; she certainly didn't know where he really worked. She thought I was one of his secretaries. They'd been married for more than forty years. I could hear their grandkids playing in the background.

"He's not here I'm afraid, dear," Mrs Marshall said in a soft voice. "But I can tell you where he is. He's at the City Club having a drink with some old friends. Boys, hey?" She laughed.

I forced a chuckle. "Yeah, boys. Thank you. Hopefully we can catch up soon."

"Lovely—you must come over for dinner."

She'd said it every time we spoke for the last five years, maybe knowing, like I did, that it would never happen.

I thanked her again and we hung up.

"I need to see him," I said to Rocco.

"As I said—see him—"

"But don't say anything, I heard." I cut him off.

Rocco changed direction, heading back into central Toran-R, where the City Club was located in a large high-fashion arcade.

I massaged my aching head—trying to get my thoughts together. "I feel like I'm losing it," I murmured to Rocco.

"You're okay," he assured me. "You have to keep going. As I said, Omen won't tolerate any breakdowns."

"Except for his own," I said bitterly. "Everyone else has to be made of stone and he gets to lose it every five seconds?"

Rocco's eyes flickered toward me and he said, "Be careful, Silver." After a pause, he added in a stilted kind of way that made it sound as if he wasn't used to giving encouragement, "You're doing fine. Most people would have broken by now."

"It's hard to have to suspect everyone you know," I said. "It's a bad feeling."

"Better a bad feeling than a bad ending."

"Do you know how the Horseman plans to use his army? Are they just going to attack humans in straight-out war?" I asked.

"I highly doubt that, but we don't know," Rocco said. "Omen has something he's looking into." He swooped the car into a space near the arcade. "Are you ready?"

I nodded—another lie. If I kept it up I might actually start believing it myself. And then what?

We moved through the exclusive shopping arcade, past designer fashion and shoe shops, a specialist paper maker, a jeweler that didn't have its prices in the window—because if you had to ask apparently you were in the wrong place.

"Go in first," Rocco told me as we approached the club entrance. "I'll be right behind you."

I nodded. The City Club was actually a men's club, but women had recently been allowed in certain areas. Perhaps the City's board were only just now receiving news of the sexual revolution, several decades behind everyone else. I entered through the automated swinging doors. With its gold trim, designer décor and subtle classical music, the reception area said "exclusive". Unfortunately, the desk staff had interpreted that to mean snooty and condescending. The two desk boys looked me over in an unfriendly way as I approached. Look, I had to say, I'd definitely had enough of getting that look today. I remembered something the General had told me—act like prey and you'll get treated like prey, act like a lion and you'll get treated like a lion. At the time, I'd imagined a gazelle wearing a fake mane, but I'd understood what he meant.

I walked the last few steps to the desk with authority. I pulled out my federal badge and said, "I want to speak to Mr Jack Marshall."

"Do you have an appointment to see him?" one of the guys said.

"No I don't. Page Mr Marshall—now." I stared him down until he cracked. I'd inherited the Sicilian Death Stare from my father—I made a note to use it more often.

The guy picked up the phone and spoke to someone. Behind me, Rocco entered the club. Immediately the faces of the desk staff transformed from disgruntled to almost adoring. It was such a rapid shift that it put my teeth on edge. Up against the Shaman skills, humans were like robots with buttons to press on and off. Rocco stopped at the desk and placed scarred hands down on the oak.

"I'd like some information on joining," he said smoothly.

The receptionists jumped into action, tripping over themselves and each other to provide him brochures and information sheets. Several minutes into their groveling session, an internal sliding door opened and the General stepped out. He had a business-like look on his face that dissolved into surprise as soon as he saw me.

"Silvia!" He walked over. "Sorry for the delay, I didn't realize it was you."

"No, I'm sorry, sir. I didn't mean to disturb you, I just really need to speak with you. I tried calling you back but it didn't go through."

He took his phone out and squinted at it. "It's turned itself off again." He said with annoyance. "I really hate this thing." He patted down his tie and looked around the reception area. "Let's go in there, shall we?" he said, pointing to a smaller room closed off from the main area by a glass door. I followed him in and he shut the door behind us. He took out a checking device and swept the room for bugs and tags. I sat down on one of the lounge chairs. A selection of the day's newspapers and business magazines was arranged on the coffee table in front of the chair. The room smelled like businessmen—coffee, newspaper and cologne. I saw a flash in my mind of Eric cutting Twentyman's throat and held my head, in pain.

The General settled down in the opposite lounge and fixed me with his incisive eyes. "You look very pale, my dear. Tell me everything that's on your mind."

For a second, I almost broke down. I wanted to tell him everything, for him to step in and save me, but I caught myself. I couldn't risk it. Instead I did what Rocco had told me, and what I'd been practicing all day: I pushed the whole truth behind other thoughts and started in. I told him that I'd witnessed Eric kill Twentyman and dispose of his body.

At the end of it, the General looked pale himself. He swallowed slowly and ran a hand through his hair, thinking.

"You need to leave this with me," he finally said. "It's all part of what I've been looking into."

He shifted on the couch and I noticed he seemed to be moving with pain.

"Are you all right, sir?" I asked.

"Honestly?" he said.

"Yes honesty would make a good change—I don't mean from you," I said to clarify. "Just in general."

He smiled and said, "Of course ... last night as I was walking to my car someone shot me."

A prickling sensation washed over me. "What?"

"It just grazed my side, but still it wasn't pleasant. It appears I've become a target. But don't worry," he assured me. "I'm handling it. I know what's happening and I'm not in any way defenseless." He smiled and the sides of his eyes crinkled.

"What should I do?" I asked, my throat dry.

"Keep going as though you haven't seen or heard anything, but don't go anywhere isolated or alone. Is there someone, other than your family, who you can stay with?"

"Yes …" I managed to say. "I'm seeing someone."

"Good," the General said. "But watch out for him too. If I'm a target they may come after my close associates as well. You haven't noticed anyone following you or anything unusual in that respect?" he asked watching me closely. I shook my head numbly. He leaned forward and gave my shoulder a squeeze. "Don't worry. I know it all seems very frightening, but I've been through many of these situations in my life, when the tables seem to be turning against us, but you've got the training. You've got the skill. You'll get through this. Just think with your mind and not your heart. All right? We'll beat them."

"It would help if I knew who 'them' was," I said.

"Indeed it would," the General agreed. "Which is why I'm here now."

I realized I was busting in on him working and quickly stood up saying, "I'm sorry."

"Don't be! But I better get back to it." The General stood as well and I followed him to the door and out. Rocco was still there quizzing the staff. The external doors parted and the General said, "Stay safe."

"You too," I said.

He smiled and turned away and I left, heading at a gradual pace toward the car. Soon Rocco appeared beside me.

"What's the story?" he asked as we got into the car.

"I told him about Twentyman and he said he'd handle it."

Before he could answer, Rocco twitched as though he'd been stung by something. "Omen is calling us in," he said and by the look in his dark eyes I guessed that wasn't a good thing.

23

I expected to return to the same northside fleabag, but Rocco sped southward instead into a suburb of gated-off estates. We turned into one of these exclusive communities and drove through streets of houses that made a normal four-bedroom double-brick look like an impoverished shack. If it had been a different time, a different situation, I would have enjoyed looking at the mini-palaces, imagining, dreaming. As it was, I just saw a blur of imposing gates and manicured lawns glowing under white spotlights, while sickness sat heavy in the pit of my stomach. After Omen's call, Rocco had completely shut down. He hadn't spoken a word or reacted to my questions and he was clenching his jaws so tightly there were ridges on the sides of his face. I didn't need to read minds to know something was seriously wrong.

He swung into a cul-de-sac and pulled up outside a house. A path of lights led to a fortress-like front door.

"New meeting place?" I stated the obvious, still trying to break the silence.

"We change all the time," Rocco finally responded. His voice sounded hollow and official. "For safety." He opened his door. Then his eyes went back to mine and he said, "Stay behind me."

The tone of his voice didn't fill me with confidence. My hand went to the gun in my duty belt. It was potentially useless against Omen, but it had to be better than nothing.

We left the car and approached the front gate. It slid open automatically and we walked along the path in silence. Every instinct I had was telling me to run, but every thought in my mind was about Dark so I followed Rocco into the house. We passed through an entrance hall, immaculately elegant but so cold. I guessed people who could withstand freezing and burning didn't generally need climate control. We took a left into a lounge room. It was full of rebel Shaman. Even though it was a completely different place, they were seated in the exact same order. The Order. Everyone turned to watch us enter—except Omen. He stood at the front of the pack with his back to us, working on his laptop. Marco was sitting at the same table, typing on his computer. He glanced up at us and his eyes betrayed his fear. He quickly looked back at his screen.

Morningstar also stood near the front. She didn't seem to even notice me: she just stared at Rocco, her face tight with tension. Rocco gestured to me to stop at the door and continued on toward the Shaman leader. He stopped several paces from Omen's back.

Eventually Omen straightened and turned around. He hadn't shaved since the day before and looked even more unstable and wild. There was a look of starvation to his face and eyes, as though his grief was consuming him from the inside out. He smiled and it sent a shiver through me. The smile faded fast until there was nothing but fury in his stare. The tattoos of his arms started to move and snarl. Without sound or warning, Rocco dropped to his knees, shaking as though he was being electrocuted. I stared in shock.

"Stop it!" Marco leaped up, his chair smashing to the ground. "You're killing him!" He tried to run to his brother, but hit an invisible barrier and staggered back. He burst into sobbing tears. Morningstar hid her face in her hands. Some of the other Shaman turned away, some just watched on impassive. I thought, Screw this, I'm not going to stand here and watch this psycho kill the man who has been protecting me. I grabbed for my gun.

Omen's eyes flicked up to mine. He gestured and I flew sideways through the air, smashing against the wall and sliding to the ground. Sharp pains ran through my chest. Omen gestured again and Rocco stopped shaking. He let out a low groan and slumped to one side. He lay still for some time, before struggling up to his hands and knees. After another minute, he stood, swaying, blood trickling out of one ear. Omen squared up to him, their faces inches apart.

"If it wasn't for your sister ..." Omen whispered, almost inaudibly. He held the stare for a heartbeat longer and then he was coming toward me. I used the wall to drag myself up, and watched him come, like a fin cutting through the sea. I grabbed for my gun, but it was gone, maybe knocked out of my hands when I hit the wall.

Marco tried to get between us, trying to protect me.

"You—move." Omen flicked his hand and threw the younger man to one side.

The Shaman leader came right up to me, right into my personal space. I did what Rocco had told me and pushed everything in my mind to the back and brought the first song I could think of to the front as a blanket—*two thousand bottles of beer on the wall—two thousand bottles of beer*. I met Omen's eyes and his face registered surprise, then he smiled. He broke into chatty conversation, which didn't quite read as authentic since his eyes remained crazy and threatening.

"Say—I heard your family are off on a trip."

Weakness ran through me at the mention of my family.

"It was kind of Rocco to get them out of the line of fire—wouldn't you say?"

I wasn't about to say anything till I figured out where he was going with this.

"I would say it was pretty kind—and pretty stupid," his voice turned to a snarl. "To jeopardize everything for four inconsequential humans. To tie up resources that *we* need and to try to hide it *from me*." He shot Rocco a savage stare. My Shaman companion was now standing steadily, watching us, his expression carefully blank. He had gone against Omen's orders to keep my family safe. I hadn't realized.

"Luckily for him he wasn't the one who tried to remove your partner from the hospital."

I cringed. Obviously my contact had failed. What did that mean for Dark?

"Is he all right?" I whispered.

"He's dead," Omen said and I felt as though the floor had just dropped out of the room.

"Your contact," Omen clarified a few seconds later, but with a look in his eyes that said he knew how I had taken it.

I struggled to breathe around the heart pounding in my throat. Finally I recovered, met Omen's stare and said, "Do you blame me for trying?"

"Of course not," Omen said. "I understand completely, which was part of the reason I was trying to help you, why I was offering protection for your family in return for you joining us. I opened my arms to you. Your actions, however, make it quite clear to me that you have mistaken my kind understanding for weakness and that you are *really* not paying your task the attention that it deserves—that *it needs*. So ..."

He clicked his fingers and the flat screen at the front of the room flashed on—showing surveillance of Dark's hospital room and the hall outside it. My partner lay vulnerable on the bed, still hooked up to the machines and bags of liquids.

"See those two there?" Omen pointed to two people dressed as police officers standing just outside the room. "They're my people. See those two?" He pointed to another couple sitting on plastic chairs just along the hall. "They're Pope's assassins."

He narrowed his eyes. His lips didn't move, but he obviously sent a message. The two Shaman stepped away from the doorway. They started down the hall away from Pope's people. The assassins reacted immediately. They got up and made a direct line for Dark's room.

My panic flared and I said to Omen, "I will pay full attention to the task."

"Will you now?" he said, his expression mocking.

"Yes I will—I promise."

"You promise." He laughed.

"I'll go back to the office now—I'll find the List," I said.

"Well there's a little something called a cover, Silver, which you blow when you start acting out of character. You can't go back until your next shift starts, which means you wasted a whole day and now a whole night. While the Horseman continues to build strength, we're sitting here in the dark!" His voice rose to a yell and I felt like I was hurtling through the air on a rollercoaster.

Rocco moved in closer behind him. The Shaman boss spun around and shouted, "You—back!"

He sent Rocco hurtling across the room, but he managed to stop himself before he smashed out through the window. The whole house trembled and I was reminded of the devastation Omen had caused at the Bushels' house. I had a feeling that was nothing. Technically I had spent all day searching for the List, but I didn't think arguing back was going to get me anywhere—except dead.

Omen whipped back around and physically shoved me against the wall. He moved in so close that all I could see was the bloodshot lines of his eyes. "You—listen to me," he snarled through gritted teeth, while I cowered into the corner. "People have died for this—my people. My ... my partner." He almost lost it, but regained himself. "You get your priorities straight. You get this job done by tomorrow or this will not end well for you or Dark."

He strode back to his computer and Rocco moved in and dragged me to my feet. As he led me out of the room, I looked back at the screen and saw the two Shaman who were guarding Dark returning to their post. The assassins backed away.

Rocco took me through the house into the kitchen. He pushed me down onto a bar stool as Marco and Morningstar entered behind us, Marco clutching his laptop.

Rocco's girlfriend marched straight to him and demanded, "I need to talk to you, right now!"

The two of them went into the room beside the kitchen and closed the door. Raised voices carried through the wood—well, raised voice. She was yelling and he wasn't saying a word. I'd learned that was never a good sign in a relationship.

"Are you okay?" Marco spoke softly beside me.

I turned to him and decided to try the truth for a change. "Not really. Are you?"

He didn't answer, but judging by how badly his hands were shaking, I guessed he was feeling even worse than I was. I got up and searched the cupboards for glasses. I filled two cups with water from the tap and put one down in front of him. The glass clicked on the granite and Marco stared down at it. He gripped the bench top. He looked as if he was teetering on the edge of a major meltdown.

"Where are the family who live here?" I asked to distract him.

"No one lives here," he managed to say. "It's one of Omen's houses. We make it seem like a family owns it to throw the Horseman off our tracks." He hesitated then said,

"I'm sorry for what's happening to you. I feel like it's my fault. If I hadn't been at that house … If I hadn't run …"

He stared at me with earnest dark eyes. He had lovely eyes like Rocco—but while Rocco's were hard, I could see everything Marco was feeling—fear, confusion, anger, sadness, guilt. For a reason I couldn't have explained, I felt an immediate liking for the guy. He was one of the good ones.

"It's not your fault at all," I told him. "You're caught up in this as well."

He lowered his voice and said, "I hate this feeling. Like I'm in a cage." He clenched his fists.

"I understand." I wanted to tell him things would get better, but I didn't. I had the feeling he'd lived too hard to be consoled by empty hopes.

The argument or tirade from the other room had died down and now I could only hear murmurs. I glanced toward the door, feeling bad for Rocco. First Omen punishes him and then his girlfriend shreds him as well, both pretty squarely my fault.

"She's Omen's sister," Marco told me.

I looked back to him. "Morningstar?"

He nodded.

"Is that what Omen meant with the sister comment?"

"No," Marco looked away. "He meant our sister—mine and Rocco's. She was his partner."

"The Rose?" I said, surprised. "I mean, Evelyn?"

Marco nodded.

"I'm so sorry," I said. "I had no idea."

"We didn't really know her that well," Marco admitted. "We didn't grow up together—none of us. We had the same mother, but she … she wasn't around."

"So you met Rocco later on?" I said.

"I'd just woken up when he found me," Marco said. He sat down on a bar stool beside the bench and I copied his movements.

"Woken up—like in the morning?" I asked. It seemed like a strange thing to say.

"No, no, sorry, I forgot I was talking to a human," he said, then hesitated, uncertain, as though I may take offense to the word, but I didn't—I was what I was. He continued, "Waking up is what you call breaking-thru. We call it waking up because it's like you've been asleep, living in a dream, and then wake up to reality."

"Is it as bad as it seems?" I asked. I'd seen enough walts going green to know it must be pretty rugged.

"Yes," he admitted. "Worse. For me it took a long time and I ended up in a ..." he hesitated and flinched a little at the words "... psychiatric hospital. Rocco came and got me out."

I nodded. It wasn't uncommon for walts to be institutionalized, even several times, before completely breaking-thru, and agents weren't sent in until they were right on the edge of going green. If a walt was re-capped prematurely the effectiveness of the process was compromised. At least that was the story the Chapter had sold us.

"Had Rocco already ..." I tried the new terminology "... woken up by then as well?"

"That's how he found me," he said. "We'd never seen each other. We never even knew, but when we woke up we could *hear* each other. The doctors thought I was schizophrenic—hearing voices, having paranoid fantasies and everything. That's how we found Omen—Evelyn can hear us too ... or she could ..."

He looked down at his hands and I tried to change the subject.

"It must have been such a relief to find out the truth, to see your brother," I said, feeling a sudden sharp longing to see my own.

He smiled faintly. "It was like he took everything horrible that had happened and threw it away." He massaged the split-sun tattoo on his wrist.

"What does it mean?" I asked, pointing to the tat.

"It's the two births." A quiet, nervous voice spoke behind us and I turned to see a girl standing at the door. I recognized her from the motel. She was the one with the long dark hair and badly broken nose, who had used pheromones to make me feel fear. Rocco had called her Willow, and she'd been the only one of the Shaman to seem even remotely uneasy about demonstrating her skills on me. Willow moved toward us, her steps uncertain, eyes submissive. I noticed her nails were bitten down to the blood on most of her fingers. Again, I felt like I had seen her before.

"Two births?" I repeated.

"One into this world and one into this life," Marco said.

Willow came close beside me at the counter. "Don't worry," she said quietly, a tremor to her voice. "You'll find the List. You're very strong. I can see. Where you walk—the path clears, like you're carrying a light in the darkness." She looked up at me and I was surprised to see admiration in her eyes. I had absolutely no idea what she meant about the path clearing, but it was nice to know someone thought I stood a chance.

Both Willow and Marco flinched.

"Omen wants us," she said, wringing her hands and biting her lip.

"You should stay here," Marco told me.

I nodded. I had zero intentions of going anywhere near their crazy leader.

As they left the kitchen, the door behind me opened and Morningstar and Rocco emerged. Morningstar gave me a foul look on her way out and I saw it now—the resemblance to her brother—the same tempestuous eyes. I kept my face blank. I'd nearly gotten her boyfriend killed. I'd hate me too.

I turned to my Shaman companion and the calm of his eyes was comforting. I wondered if there was anything that actually shook him.

"I'm sorry. I really am," I said.

"Don't be," Rocco said. He removed his jacket. There were sweat marks and bloodstains on his shirt. "It was my choice."

"To help my family and put yourself at risk?"

"There's a reason why I'm with Omen and not the Horseman," he said. "I made a decision in life that I wasn't going to hurt innocent people—no matter who ordered me to."

His words brought unexpected tears to my eyes. They reminded me of the conviction I'd once held then lost somewhere in the unforgivingly secretive, corporate atmosphere of C11. Once all I'd wanted was justice for the innocent lost. I said something along the lines to Rocco and as the words came out of my mouth I realized how naive I had been—there would never be any justice for the little boy from my neighborhood, no peace for his mother, or any other parents whose child was taken—just life in continuation. You kept running or you fell down dead, while predators picked off the sick, the weak, the young ...

I wiped my eyes, feeling stupid, crying in front of him. I forced a laugh. "The General said I'm too emotional to succeed as an agent. I can see his point."

"He's wrong," Rocco said and his tone didn't leave room for argument. "Your emotions—your heart—is you; lose that and you're just a machine ... like me." His voice held an edge of frustration and regret.

"You're not a machine," I argued, even though there were actually times when he seemed very robotic. "You've shown emotions to your brother, your girlfriend—even to me."

He considered my words. "It isn't easy to show anything," he said. "I wish I were a warm person, but I'm not capable."

"That's not true. You've been very comforting to me. Besides it's kind of difficult to be all warm and fuzzy when people are trying to kill you from every angle."

He jolted and I assumed Omen was calling again.

He pointed to the darkened lounge room through the doorway beside us.

"You should lie down and try to sleep. You'll be safe here."

I nodded and moved into the room. Rocco stood at the doorway and watched as I sat down on the sofa. He looked as though he was going to come closer, but didn't. He gave me a final nod and left. I stretched out on the couch, so wound up with stress and bad feelings, so cold, I thought I'd never sleep, and I didn't want to either. I wanted to stay awake and plan my next step—but then I was out like magic, or, should I say, like Shaman influence.

24

I woke in the half-light of dawn, disoriented in time and space, unsure why the images around me weren't connecting the way I thought they should. Then, as the different parts of my brain checked in, reality happened—like a bucket of cold water. I sat up and groaned. My body ached head to toe. My stomach snarled, a savage starved beast. I staggered up and limped to the mirror on the wall. *Mirror, mirror, on the wall* ... The person who looked back was haggard with blotchy skin, frizzy hair and black smudges of mascara smeared under her bloodshot eyes. Bad hair day, bad face day, bad life day.

My mouth tasted like a stinkbug had crawled up into it and suffered a violent end. I tried to smooth down my hair and winced from a sharp pain in my shoulder. I pulled my collar to one side and inspected the damage where Omen had put his hands on me the night before. A purple and black bruise had blossomed over the skin. I touched the discoloration and flinched—it hurt. What had I expected?

It reminded me—Dark had an annoying habit of pressing my bruises. I thought of my partner and felt ill. If I didn't locate the List today ... Omen hadn't threatened me directly, but after last night I wasn't left with any questions of what he was capable of when he was angry.

But what were the chances of finding the List in one day? I could search for years and not find it. I considered that maybe now was not the time for obedience, maybe now was the time to get the most fierce automatic weapon I could find and try to blast Dark out and make a run for it. Would a gun hold up against Omen and his Shaman rebels? Unlikely, but if today went badly, it might be the only option I had. I didn't like the way I'd handled things with Omen yesterday. I'd let myself be led around—be pushed and forced. I had to find a way of getting control of the situation. I crossed the room to the window and peered out past the curtain into the waking neighborhood. If I ran now, how far would I get? Would I even make it to the car to get my bag? I shivered from the morning chill and wrapped my arms around myself.

Someone cleared her throat behind me. I turned to see the girl, Willow, standing in the doorway, holding a pile of clothes. Her eyes flickered to mine then away; she breathed unsteadily, still nervous.

She had no reason to fear me, so I guessed it was disposition.

I nodded to her and she came forward. She held the clothes out to me and said, "I thought you might need some. I think we're the same size."

Beneath loose-fitting clothes the girl's frame was painfully skinny—and I definitely wasn't—so either she had a complex or I did.

"Thanks." I took the outfit. I had extra clothes in the car, but more wouldn't go astray. Especially if I ended up on the run.

Willow turned away and studied the pictures on the walls as I started to change. Ideally I should have showered first. It had been a few days and I felt stale, but, according to Dark's school of hygiene, it was nothing a good blast of deodorant wouldn't fix. I pulled my Kevlar jacket over the top of the outfit and felt my cell phone buzz in the pocket. I took it out and read the text message from work—the password for the day was *Hangman*. I didn't like the sound of it. I held the phone in my hands, contemplating ringing the hospital. After the previous night's scene, I decided not to chance it. Instead I checked my partner's location. According to the app, he was still in hospital.

I noticed then that the Shaman girl was still in the room, looking at different objects, but standing quite close, as though she was waiting to talk to me. I put the phone away and turned to her.

She immediately looked at me and said, "I don't mean to … invade your space." She swallowed awkwardly. "I just … I guess I was just wondering if you remembered me."

I said, "You are familiar, but …" There was an uncomfortable pause where I tried to think of how to tactfully say no.

"It's okay." She guessed the answer, or saw it in my thoughts. "I know you've met a lot of us."

Met—a nice way of saying captured and imprisoned.

"I took you in?" I asked.

She nodded. "When I was younger—before I woke up for good." She moved closer—searching for the right words. "I was scared—and you made me feel better. I always wanted to find you and say thank you—and then when I saw you at the motel …" She trailed off. "So, thank you. Really."

I studied her face more closely and remembered. She'd looked quite different when I'd met her. She'd had short blonde hair and a terribly bruised-up face. She'd been a too-young girl in a bad relationship—confused and beaten down. When she'd started to go green, she'd attacked back with the supernatural strength walts got when breaking-thru. She'd damaged the guy significantly, maybe even killed him, I couldn't quite remember.

I also couldn't remember being that comforting. Maybe I'd sat with her and talked to her while the sedatives worked, but that would have been about it. Not really enough to warrant sincere gratitude. Obviously it had been for her, though.

She gave a laugh that hid a cry and said, "I always said I was going to have a different life from my mother, and I ended up being her—exactly."

I nodded. People started out with hopes and dreams and good intentions only to be betrayed by genetics and learned habits burned into their brains from when they could barely comprehend life—abnormal becomes normal and healthy feels wrong.

Rocco entered the room and stood by the door waiting. Our eyes met. It was time. I wished I had something profound to say to Willow about life and things working out in the end, but I didn't. Profound utterings weren't my strong point. My mother, on the other hand, had an insightful phrase, saying, quote or cliché for all and every occasion. She'd even covered the bathroom walls at our place with paper and written all her favorites. I felt a surge of fear for them—maybe I should have told them what was happening, but then they would have never left me. I had to believe I'd done the right thing.

I zipped up my jacket, gave Willow a final nod and followed Rocco down the hall. As we approached the lounge where the Shaman had gathered the night before, my stomach turned to concrete inside me. I *really* did not want to see Omen. Thankfully, the room was dark and empty. I breathed a sigh of relief. We turned the corner to the front door and I stopped short.

The rebel leader stood beside the door, wearing a stripy bathrobe and eating a bowl of cereal. He fixed me with those piercing eyes and gave one of his smiles that wasn't really a smile. His arms were completely bare of tattoos and for some reason I found that more disturbing than when the images were coming to life and snarling at me. It felt as though Omen's anchors to himself were dropping away.

"Hoping to sneak out?" he asked me. He put a spoon of the cereal in his mouth and crunched. I noticed they were Fruit Loops and thought, At least he's eating a mental-state-appropriate breakfast.

Omen's chewing froze. He looked up at me and tilted his head. I thought, Shit! It sucked to be around a mind reader.

He put the cereal down on the pedestal beside the door and walked toward us. He sidestepped Rocco without even half a glance and brushed past me saying, "Remember the dead-line." He emphasized the 'dead' and I gritted my teeth, biting back what I wanted to say to him.

Rocco opened the front door and we walked out to his car. I shivered, exhaling mist and rubbing my frozen hands to-gether. I climbed up into the car and crossed my arms over my body. A voice behind us called out to Rocco. Morningstar came running along the path. He moved back toward her. I watched through the car window as they hugged and kissed each other. They looked into each other's eyes and whispered something between them. I turned away, feeling a twist of bitter something. I knew he was just pretending with me, keeping up a cover, but I'd still developed some kind of feel-ings for him. Exactly what I wasn't sure. Maybe this was what Stockholm syndrome felt like—the love of the captor—but he hadn't actually captured me, Omen had, and I definitely felt no love there. So what were these feelings for Rocco? Maybe just the normal human need to attach to someone, especially heightened in times of stress, threat or crisis. Maybe it was something more.

The pair parted and Rocco climbed behind the wheel. Morningstar waved him away from the curb. I noticed, behind her, sitting all along the front wall, a large gathering of cats, presumably looking for Rocco. I wondered why they were attracted to him: was he emitting some kind of ultrasonic impulse they found irresistible? I found something especially appealing about a man who liked animals—and not in the culinary sense like Dark. One of my partner's favorite, frequently retold jokes, which I found highly annoying, was *I like animals, especially beside the peas and potato on my plate.*

Rocco and I didn't have the long stretching history or easy banter that I had with Dark. Rocco was a difficult person to understand, closed and emotionally locked up, carrying demons on his back and dangerous without a doubt, and then there was the whole thing about us being a different species of person, but there was still something strong and unshakeable about him that I couldn't help but be drawn to—like one of the cats. I shook my head—why was I even thinking about this now? Maybe my mind was just trying to avoid facing reality, but I really couldn't afford not to. Things had never been more real than they were now.

I looked out my window as we drove and sniffed quietly—the cool and the sudden emotion had made my nose run. I felt Rocco looking over at me. There was a loaded pause as if he was going to speak, but he didn't. Several more minutes passed before he said, "Today has to be it."

"Can I just ask you a question?" I burst out in anger. "How the hell is killing my partner going to help your cause?"

Rocco shook his head. "Omen is angry and he's in pain. And his power is growing. And the more powerful he gets, the more unstable he is."

"Is that how it works?" I asked. "The more power the less control."

"It seems to be for some Shaman, but not all. I feel as though the more strength I've gained the more clarity I have." He looked over at me and said, "I will do everything I can to keep your partner safe—from everyone—but as you saw, I can't match Omen."

"I think you could," I said.

"Omen is second only to Horseman," Rocco reminded me.

"And you're second to him," I argued.

"Second to second is third, Silver, and I'm a long way behind either of them—trust me," he said.

I felt bad for pushing him, he'd already risked everything for me and I was virtually a stranger to him. "I'm sorry, I didn't mean to yell at you," I said. "I appreciate what you've done for me—more than I can say."

I thought he might say something like 'I'd do it for anyone' or 'It's what I believe in' but instead he nodded and said, "I know."

Something about the way he said it made me think he meant—*I understand.*

"Your brother told me about your sister," I said.

Rocco clenched his jaw and I thought that would be the end of that conversation, but then he spoke, or forced himself to speak. "I can't talk about it."

"I just wanted to say I'm sorry. I can't imagine ..." I said, then I started to imagine what if it was my brother and I felt pain—a terrible cutting pain.

"They're safe," Rocco said.

"That's how selfish I am," I said. "You're the one suffering and I can only think of myself." I shivered, emotionally spent.

"It's normal," Rocco said quietly.

"Don't you mean *it's human?*" I said, a little bitterly.

"Not just human," he said.

After another stretch of silence, I said, "Your brother—he seems like a good guy."

Rocco nodded. "He had a rough upbringing, but he has a good heart. And as I said to you, that's what matters." He leaned in and turned up the heater, even though he was obviously not feeling the cold. This man, I thought, just keeps making it more and more difficult not to like him.

We took the exit onto the freeway, which ran straight over the river into Toran-R. At this early hour, the traffic was still fairly thin, so Rocco put his foot down and we sped toward work. I wouldn't have minded if it took longer.

"Do you have a plan for today?" he asked me.

The words triggered a memory and I said, "There's something I forgot." I dragged Rocco's cell out of my pocket and opened up the gallery looking for the picture I took of the paper from Twentyman's desk. I searched for several minutes without finding it.

"I took a photo yesterday," I said. "In Twentyman's office. He had a piece of paper that had *I am the Blood Horseman* written on it. I can't find the picture."

Rocco's eyes sharpened. Driving with one hand, he took the phone and looked through it.

He shook his head. "Gone."

"How?"

"I don't know, but it means he must have written it."

"The Horseman? Why would it be on Twenty's desk then? Obviously he wasn't the Horseman."

"He's taunting them," Rocco said, his voice tight. "He's getting sick of the game. He's ready to strike."

My stomach clenched uncomfortably.

"Today has to be it." He glanced at me.

"So everyone keeps saying."

"What's your plan?"

"Good question," I said. Did I have a plan for today? It would have been great if the answer had been yes, but the truth was I did not have a plan. I didn't even have a clue. Where would be the next most logical place to search for the List? I thought maybe in the Surveillance and Technical Operations databases, but while Surveillance kept visual track of the Shaman, they didn't necessarily decide *who* to track. So where did the orders of who to track come from? I thought most likely from Medical Division, where they actually re-capped the walts, where the Horseman's people worked. It made sense that his soldiers would be in charge of knowing exactly who was a Shaman in this world.

So my current thinking was that the Medical Division computer systems might be the next place to look for the List. But really that was just a guess. I had no real intel or notion that it would actually be there, plus I didn't have clearance for Medical level. As I'd told Omen, I hadn't even been past the front counter before. I did still have Byter's Shake override, though, so if I could get past the counter and into one of the laboratories, I could get into the computer system and check. I had to assume that the laboratories where they re-capped the walts weren't monitored by surveillance, otherwise everyone would see what the Shaman were actually doing.

So the question was—how could I get into Medical Division without clearance? My mind went to the obvious. The only time Op Services agents were granted temporary passes for Medical was when we were bringing in a walt, so if I could get myself re-assigned to active duty and pick up a walt, then I'd have a legitimate reason to be there. The other option was Feng. She had told me the day before that she was going to be made Manager of Medical, but involving her would be seriously risky, especially since there was a high chance she was a Shaman soldier. I would have to make up a story about why I needed to be down there and I'd have to assume she couldn't read my mind and see the truth—big assumption given what was at risk here ...

I translated my thoughts to Rocco and at the end he said, "You're right. It is a possibility that your friend is a Shaman or even the Horseman, but there's also a chance that she's not, and it's preferable to risk using her than to go out into the field. Given Pope's failed attempts, she'll be getting desperate by now."

We flew past a police car. I expected the sirens to blare with flashing blue and red—but nothing happened.

"Did you block their minds?" I asked.

"No," he replied. "Just distracted their sight away from us."

"Do you have to—say something—like I don't know—a magic word ..."

Rocco looked at me and raised an eyebrow. "You mean like abracadabra," he said, a dry smile behind his voice.

"I don't know." I shrugged. "Do you?"

He shook his head. "It's natural to us, like seeing, tasting, touching is for you. As with everything else, our skills can be strengthened and refined with practice, but really they're just an extension of the normal, everyday ones. We're just an evolution of what is already natural."

"Supernatural," I said. "You're the next model up—and humans become obsolete." I said the last bit feeling a whole lot of impending doom.

"It's more complicated than that," Rocco told me. "More power is not necessarily always a good thing. Private thoughts provide people time to filter emotions and ideas, to inwardly contemplate. We don't say everything we think for a reason."

"Are all Shaman telepaths?" I asked.

"Not all," he said.

"What are your particular skills?" I said. "Or skills you don't have, for that matter?"

He pressed his lips together. He didn't like the question, but he gave me an answer, or at least a partial one, "I'm not a healer ... and there are other things."

We hit the city and I looked up at the huge digital clock planted on top of a central building—4:59. The streets were still somewhat deserted, but there was a scattering of early starters, wearing suits and scarfs, clutching cups of coffee and hurrying to get out of the wind. It was blowing straight off the glacial river, where city ferries were already cruising up and down and crisscrossing to various stops. We drove over the bridge, heading along the last stretch to work, and cruised in toward a red light. Rocco turned it to green as we approached, but the car in front of us didn't move. The couple inside were distracted, kissing and laughing. I thought if they were in such a good mood so early in the morning, the relationship had to be going well.

Rocco turned to me to say something, but his words became a sharp intake of breath. He raised his hand as though he was going to hit me, and everything seemed to slide into slow motion. I flinched and turned my face to the window, just in time to see an object pause inches away from the glass. It hovered there, stuck. I could see the air streams out behind it from where Rocco had brought its forward propulsion to a sudden halt.

He moved his hand and the object shifted, flowing sideways, striking the car in front of us. I saw the impact start to tear the vehicle apart and felt Rocco's hand close over my arm. He ripped me out through the driver's-side door and ran with superhuman speed away from the exploding cars. The sudden acceleration knocked the air out of my lungs and blurred our surroundings. I could hear screams echoing behind us, more and more distant, until Rocco suddenly stopped. He put me down onto the cold concrete ground of an undercover parking lot, behind a row of cars. I kept my eyes scrunched shut, trying to get my breathing under control and to stabilize my spinning head. When I'd managed it, I looked up at him. He was crouched, completely still, watching the entrance to the parking lot.

"What the hell was that?" I whispered.

"An anti-tank missile," he replied, his voice cold, military.

"A missile," I repeated. "For me?"

It seemed just slightly excessive. A hit like that would cause massive collateral damage. Pope could have blown away half a city block. "I thought her reputation depended on her subtlety," I said.

"She must have got a major shove from whoever hired her. I think it must be him," Rocco said.

"The Horseman?" I said. "Why doesn't he just send his soldiers?"

"Same reason we can't attack outright yet. He can't afford to be discovered until he's ready," Rocco said. His eyes shifted in thought. "There is C11 surveillance everywhere along that street. I didn't manipulate the footage. All my concentration went to the missile."

"So the Horseman will see exactly what happened? He'll see us ..." I said.

"We may have moved too fast for the technology, but regardless, it's now too dangerous for you to go into the office."

"I have to go. If I don't find the List, Omen might kill Dark."

"You can't save your partner if you're dead," he said.

"What are my choices? Will Omen listen to reason?"

Rocco looked at me—the answer was no.

"Then I have to go in, unless I try to bust Dark out and run." I took the risk by putting the idea out there.

"With both Omen *and* the Horseman on your back ...?" Rocco shook his head. "No chance. Suicide."

"I'm stuck then," I said.

Rocco thought for a second in silence, then he said, "Okay, it's now only a matter of time before the Horseman comes after you inside Headquarters. But he still has to be subtle. If you keep to the populated areas you might be okay. I'll work on a way to get Dark clear. It's really the only option."

I swallowed my fear and nodded. Rocco stood and opened the passenger door of the car closest to us. He gestured and I dragged myself up and climbed in. He got behind the wheel and started the engine, without the key, without doing anything visible. We drove out of the parking garage. Siren screams rang through the air and Rocco navigated through the back streets to avoid the roadblocks that would be starting to go up all around the explosion site. We swooped into a back alley behind Headquarters, and Rocco handed me back my gun, which I'd dropped the night before. We went on foot around to the front entrance. Rocco held me close to his side, and scanned the tops of the buildings around us.

"Is she there?" I asked.

He shook his head. "She must think she took us out."

We entered the lobby and paused. Rocco hugged me and said into my ear, "Good luck. Keep me updated."

I nodded. He kissed me goodbye.

His lips were as cold as mine.

25

As the elevator lowered me toward the office, I couldn't help feeling like I was descending into hell itself, that the doors would open into the inferno and I'd see the devil waiting at front desk, curling his tail innocently around one hand. He'd say something like "Welcome home" or "I've been waiting for you"—or maybe even "Trying to sneak out?" He might even be eating a bowl of Fruit Loops.

The elevator doors parted and I winced, but there was no fire, no unfathomable pit, no smoothly smug devil, just the opulent entrance hall and Marissa sitting anxiously behind her computer. The look on her face as I stepped out said she'd been waiting for me. She watched me walk the distance to front desk, asking as soon as I was within range, "How is he? I keep ringing the hospital, but they wouldn't give me any details."

"Everyone's been saying that," I told her, trying to keep my voice conversational. "I haven't been able to call this morning. I'll let you know as soon as I find out."

She looked a bit deflated but said, "Thanks."

She unlocked the door into the office. As I walked through she called out, with a breathless sort of urgency, "Silver! I was thinking, when Dark has recovered—I might ask him out for a coffee or something." Her eyes were wide and bright. "Do you think I should?"

The normalcy of the question in such an abnormal time threw me for a second. She was thinking coffee; I was thinking how the hell are we getting out of this alive.

"Why not," I said. "You never know." Why should I crush her hope? Life would do that well enough. She gave me a big smile and I turned and entered the office. I walked toward my desk, trying to draw as little attention as possible. Luckily, everyone seemed occupied, but being back in was a fast reminder of where I'd left things yesterday. The night before and this morning had been so intense that it hadn't been in my mind, but the situation remained—Eric was one of the Horseman's soldiers. He'd killed Twentyman and there was a big chance that today he'd be coming after me.

As I crossed the floor, I scanned around, checking all the places where Eric usually lurked, but he wasn't there. Was it too much to hope that the General had dealt with him last night?

I shot a glance toward Twentyman's office. It was still in darkness and Agent Kenealy was not at her desk. It made me think of Twentyman dying. I hadn't even tried to step in to help him. I'd been shocked, but that wasn't an excuse. I should have done something. I sat down at my desk. Feng and Jovic weren't there yet, but I knew they were on morning shift as well. I needed Feng for my plan to access Medical, but I was also afraid to see her, so I was torn between relief and agitation. I leaned over and called out to an agent codenamed Yellow in the next pod, "Hey—do you know where Feng is?"

"Yeah," he said. "She came in before and just left. They're working in Greenborough today."

My hopes sunk. Greenborough was another C11 facility across town. So that was Plan A down. I'd have to go with

Plan B—get back to active duty. But that would mean going out into the field, and after this morning that seemed like a *very* bad idea. Maybe just getting my limited duties lifted would give me a reason to go to Medical, without having to go out.

I dialed my contact in HR and was relieved when she picked up. We did the "How are you?"/ "How is Dark?" chat for a few minutes before I said, "Anyway, I was wondering if there was a way you could change my limited duties status so I can go out into the field. It's hard to be stuck at my desk just thinking about Dark all day."

"Sure, shouldn't be a problem," she said. I heard her typing and then a pause. "Actually," she said. "It will be a problem. Your Division Manager, Agent Twentyman, is out on sick leave and I need his signature to transfer you off the assigned duties."

"Can another Division Manager sign me out?" I asked.

"Usually, yes, but because of the Omen situation all the orders are from the top and we need Division Manager clearance. I'm really sorry, Silver."

"Thanks anyway," I said calmly, cursing inside.

We hung up and I massaged my aching head. So that was Plan B gone as well. On the up side I still had the Shake override.

"Silver." A familiar voice called my name from across the office. I looked up and saw Byter heading toward my desk. He was walking faster than usual. "Hey," he said when he was close enough. "Have you seen my override?"

It was official—God hated me.

"Yes, I have actually." I managed to keep casual. "I found it under my desk yesterday. I should have given it to you straight away—"

"Except you were too busy breaking into Twentyman's computer," Byter said without too much subtlety; luckily his beard stifled some of the volume. His cheeks flushed an angry red.

My mind snuffed out on me like a rat jumping a sinking ship. I just stared at him wordless, witless.

"I know you're trying to find out who hurt Dark, but stealing from a friend is not the way to go. Dude, the amount of time I've spent trying to help you. You could have got me fired, or arrested. I covered for you, but this is the last time. Consider us—un-friended." There was an awkward pause and then he stomped off.

I watched him leave and instead of mourning a friendship lost all I could think was it was lucky he had forgotten to take the override. Byter reappeared a second later and marched back toward me. I dragged the device out of my pocket and put it into his outstretched hand. He stormed away again and I decided now was as good a time as any to eat the emergency chocolates. After all, I didn't have to worry about putting on weight—being a decomposing corpse would take care of that.

I sat there compulsively stuffing my face with chocolate while I stared at my blank computer screen. This went on for a while before a little voice inside spoke up and reminded me of something Rocco had said: "You're a trained operative of the most covert organization in the world. You make a living from deception and manipulation."

He was right. I was trained for this—I had to stop feeling sorry for myself and take control.

I shoved the remaining chocolates back into the drawer. I needed to go to Medical Division and access their system. I had no idea how without the Shake override, but I'd have to figure that out along the way. I stood up and headed back toward Marissa at front desk.

She was on the phone, but smiled brightly at me as though we were now best friends, which I thought might work to my advantage. She hung up from the call and leaned forward.

"I need to go down to Medical for a few minutes," I told her. "Are you able to give me a temporary clearance?"

Usually we'd need to explain why we needed a clearance, but when trying to lie convincingly the fewer details the better.

"Sure," she said easily, her French nails clicking on her keyboard. "Until ten-thirty am okay?"

I checked my watch—six-fifteen—plenty of time.

I nodded.

She handed me the temporary pass and I headed for the internal elevators. The doors parted, I entered, swiped the pass and pressed eight for Medical. A few other agents bustled in before the doors could close. They all wore white coats which meant they were Medical Division operatives and more likely than not Shaman soldiers. Rocco's warning to keep to populated areas replayed loudly in my mind.

I pressed myself into the corner, trying to make myself invisible while images of the elevator becoming a human-sized microwave haunted my thoughts. Thankfully the others didn't seem to even notice me and we reached level eight without incident. I followed the group out of the elevator and just kept following them, past the check-in desk, where the attending agent stood occupied by a walt drop-off, and into the halls. My heart thudded heavily in my chest. I trailed them past the closed laboratory doorways and a chill ran over my skin. I'd always found Medical level creepy, but now that I knew what was happening there it wasn't creepy, it was horrifying. I felt cameras watching and recording me from all angles. I had to get this right. I saw my chance as one guy broke away from the group and turned to unlock an office door.

I stopped beside him and said, "Excuse me." I gave what I hoped was a warm and open smile. "I feel so stupid, but I was supposed to bring a file down to your manager, and I realized I didn't actually transfer it to my USB." I held up the small device from my pocket. "It's stored on the intranet. Any chance I could use your computer to grab it—save me the embarrassment of going back up?"

As soon as I said it, I realized that if it were stored on the intranet the manager's computer would have access to it. I silently kicked myself. I'd blown it. The guy looked a little confused as well, but then his face smoothed and he smiled, showing very straight white teeth.

"Sure—sure—come in," he said. "I've done that before."

I figured if he was a Shaman, he mustn't be a telepath—either that or he was inviting me in to kill me. I paused in the open doorway, then forced myself to walk in. His office was cluttered and disorganized with precarious towers of papers and books everywhere. Frosted glass doors led from the office space into a laboratory.

The guy booted up his computer, shook in, then gestured to his chair. "Help yourself," he said, giving me another wide smile.

"Thanks," I replied, noticing he was giving me a lot of eye contact. I hoped it was just male interest.

He went to the other side of the office and started pushing books back onto the jumbled shelf. I sat down, pushed the USB into the port and opened up the intranet. On top of that screen, I opened his files and ran a search for the List. After a few minutes, the guy glanced back at me. I smiled at him over the top of his computer. He smiled back. Several more minutes in and the search came back with nothing. I gnawed the inside of my mouth in frustration. I had to face the possibility that the List wasn't actually kept on any accessible system, that maybe just one person, possibly even the Horseman himself, kept the List. Maybe it was even a hard copy. I was searching for a ghost. I knew I couldn't take any more time without arousing suspicion.

"Thanks." I stood up and pushed his chair back in.

"Not a problem," he said, stepping toward me, flashing another dazzling smile. He looked like a spray-tanned shark.

"Well, have a good day," I said and made a speedy exit from the office.

I moved back toward the elevators, keeping my head down. Halfway there, I glanced back and saw the guy coming out of his office. He looked one way and then the other, saw me, and headed quickly my way. My heart bucked. He knew what I was doing. I was in trouble. I sped up the pace and reached the elevator. I thumped on the buttons loud enough to make the desk attendant look up, but the elevator seemed stuck way up on level one. I sensed the guy closing in behind me and broke for the stairs.

I barged through the door and sprinted upward as fast as I could move. I heard the guy enter behind me and the thud of his boots on the concrete steps. However fast I was going, he was much faster. I reached the landing of the seventh level and saw the exit doorway. I didn't have clearance to enter, but made a split second decision to try to break in. I had zero chance of actually getting through, considering it was made of reinforced steel, but at least the effort would bring security running.

I leaped toward the door and Rocco's mobile device dropped out of my pocket. I scrambled to grab it and tripped on the step. I dropped to my hands and knees and a shadow fell over me. I reached for my gun and looked up expecting to see the guy leering down at me, but he wasn't leering, he was just smiling—not a crazy I'm Gonna Enjoy Killing You smile either—a normal smile. He held out my USB stick and I realized I'd left it in his computer. He was chasing me to give it back. I took the memory stick and forced a smile onto my face.

"Thanks," I said, feeling weak from the sudden rush, as well as dumb, really dumb.

"Getting some exercise?" he said.

I nodded and used the rail to help myself stand. I slipped the device into my pocket. "As you can see, I need it."

He shrugged graciously and started to say something, then jolted the way the rebels did whenever Omen called them through their minds. But this guy was probably not a rebel—which meant it wasn't Omen calling—it was the Horseman.

"I'd better go. Thanks again," I said. The agent didn't respond, just remained frozen in motion. I really didn't want to be there when he came back to reality.

I knew I couldn't get through to level seven, no matter how long I stood there kicking the door, so instead I took off, sprinting up three more flights to level four—Surveillance and Technical Operations. I swiped my hand across the security panel and pushed the door open. I dared a glance over the railing back down the stairwell. The guy was still standing where I'd left him. Whatever the Horseman was telling him was lengthy. I went through the door and headed fast to the elevator. I took it up to level one.

I practically ran to my desk and slumped down low in my chair, shaking and sweating like an animal. I couldn't believe I'd tripped over. Amateur. I'd put myself at serious risk and I still hadn't found the List. An idea occurred to me then, one so simple that I had no clue why I hadn't thought of it sooner.

I picked up my work phone and dialed the General. This time he answered after a few rings.

"Silvia, how are you?" he said, his tone carefully neutral.

"Good—thank you, sir," I said, framing my words in case we were being listened to. "I'm just working an angle on the Omen case ... the brief says that he broke into Conference files and stole a lot of data. I was worried that that information could include walt identities—that he might be planning some kind of exposure ..."

The General thought then said, "I understand your concerns and I'm glad you're considering his motivations, but as I understand it, Omen didn't get to anything too serious. All the highly confidential information is kept under the watchful eye of our Head of Security and his report wasn't troubling."

"Oh—okay," I said. "Well that's—that's good—not so good with tracking him, but good it's safe ... thank you, sir."

"You're thinking along the right lines," the General said. "Keep going. Keep working on it and so will I." It sounded like encouragement, but I heard the meaning behind the words, keep acting normal—but whatever that was I had no idea any more.

"Goodbye, sir," I said and we hung up.

I went into my computer and clicked into the shared work files for Op Services and brought up the company's organizational chart—or at least the one they made common knowledge to agents. I ran my finger over the screen searching through the divisions and titles until I found it—Head of Security.

"Agent Mikembe Masekela," I read it out.

Here was the man I needed to talk to. I jumped up, and with a quick check around for Eric, I headed back out to Marissa. I asked if she could ring Security to make an appointment for me with Masekela. She told me that he didn't take appointments to meet with agents at my level, but added in a hushed whisper that if I really needed to talk to him, I could try to catch him as he left the building to go home. She gave me a roundabout time of when he usually passed through and I slunk back to my desk. I thought if I sat there all day, in the office full of other agents, maybe I'd be all right—maybe. I took out my phone and checked Dark's location. It came back with the hospital—he was still there—we still had a chance, but I had to get this right.

26

It was a good thing that the boyhood Mikembe Masekela had dreamed of becoming a secret agent and not a stand-up comedian. The man had zero sense of humor and even less sociability. I'd had better-flowing conversations with pieces of furniture. Despite me trying every trick in the book to melt him, Masekela (Codename: Goliath) remained a slab of steel. He stood with his arms crossed over a mountainous expanse of chest while I babbled on and on and on, feeling increasingly shrunken under his hard stare.

I'd spent the remainder of the day hiding at my desk, researching his profile, while I awaited my chance to question him. Finally two hours after my shift had officially ended and eight minutes to eight, the man had emerged from level six and I'd just managed to corner him beside the water cooler in the entrance hall. According to my research, C11's Head of Security, who stood just over seven foot, was a forerunning expert on both ground and cyber tactical protection, had a black belt in just about every martial art possible and was a member of QN7—a highly select group of people with the most impressive IQs in the world—which made him scary smart as well as just plain scary. It didn't help matters much.

Something else that didn't help—I'd been too scared to go to the bathroom the entire day and now I desperately needed to go, and there was a guy at the water cooler who had been filling up his bottle for what felt like the last hour.

"So ..." I said for the fifth time in a row, trying to block out the tinkling in the background while racking my brain for something to say. There was only so long my monologue about the weather was going to hold up. "So ..." I swallowed. "I was wondering if you were free, and if we could go for dinner ... together." I mentally kicked myself. That had come out sounding a lot more suggestive than I'd intended. I think I'd even raised an eyebrow.

"I'm married." Goliath spoke for the first time, his voice a very deep bass.

"Oh, I know, I'm sorry. I didn't mean like that, I meant as colleagues," I tried to explain.

"I make it a rule not to associate with colleagues outside of work," he told me.

"Right." I swallowed again. "What about just a coffee then?"

"I don't consume caffeine."

"Scotch on the rocks?"

"I don't consume alcohol."

"How about a Cuban?"

"Good day, Agent Silver." Goliath stepped around me and strode toward the external elevator. I followed him and entered the elevator with a group of other agents going up to the lobby. There was no reason for me to return to my desk and I needed to get something, anything, out of Masekela before the chance passed. The security chief positioned himself as far away from me as possible and I didn't really blame him. My approach had sucked. What was I thinking? No further opportunity to speak presented itself in the ten-second ride up.

Rocco was waiting for me again beside the hibiscus. He eyed Goliath as the big man cleared the lobby in a few strides and left the building, briefcase in hand. Rocco and I met up in the middle of the lobby and did the routine greeting—hug, kiss, whatever, whatever—and then we left the building. Rocco was careful to keep us close to the wall and behind groups of other people as we made our way around the building. At this later time, the rush-hour crowd was home and the dinner crowd had arrived. Dressed up or dressed down, their mood was a whole lot lighter.

"Any changes with getting Dark out?" I asked Rocco, as soon as we were clear of Headquarters.

He shook his head, his expression grim. "I've sent two people I can trust to watch Omen's people and the assassins. I've told them to intercede if anything happens. It's the best we can do. Omen doesn't trust me. He's starting to suspect everyone." He led the way into a side street where he'd parked a replacement vehicle. He opened the door for me and I felt a flash of fear as my thoughts returned to the morning's attack. Having been almost blown up in a car wasn't going to help my whole driving phobia. I could see intensive therapy in my future—a lot of it—if I survived. I gritted my teeth and forced myself to climb in.

"And you? Any luck with Masekela?" Rocco asked as he slid behind the wheel. I'd sent him a cryptic message during the day, which he'd obviously deciphered.

"The guy is a seven-foot vault," I told him. "A happily married, teetotal, non-coffee drinking, smoke-free vault."

"I guessed that," Rocco said. "His mind is the same—locked down—no spaces in."

"Is he Shaman?" I asked.

"No, just a higher-level human."

"Awesome," I muttered. What even did that mean? Humans have levels? My head was pounding. "What am I going to do?" I felt like laughing, not a good sign considering nothing was funny in the least. "I can't go back to Omen empty handed."

"No you can't," Rocco said. Even he looked tired and worn, with darkness shadowing his eyes.

"There's only one other thing we can do," I said and he waited for me to continue. "Break into Masekela's house and hack his system."

Rocco gave a nod and said, "Funny you should say that—it's exactly what I was thinking. I did a drive past his residence today. He's got major firewalls and premium surveillance in place. We have to assume that means he takes his work home with him."

I felt a flash of hope that was quickly dissolved by the reality of what we were planning.

"Okay," I said. "So we're going to break into the house of the Head of Security of the most highly protected intelligence agency in the world and steal highly confidential information which he's made it his life's work to protect."

Some things are less daunting when you say them aloud. That wasn't.

"You're forgetting something," Rocco said.

I looked up at him.

"He's human. I'm not." The headlights from a passing car crossed his face and his eyes shimmered silver-blue. I saw his point.

"Are you ready?" he asked me.

"No—I have to go to the bathroom," I told him.

"You'll have to hold it," he said.

"I have been holding it—for about six hours. I *have* to go. Right now."

Rocco glanced out his window, then gestured. "Behind the car."

I didn't like the idea, but at this stage it was either behind the car or inside the car.

We both got out. Rocco hovered at the front keeping guard and I went to the back—into the alleyway. Goodbye dignity.

Once we were both back in the car he turned to me and said, "All right?"

I gave him a look that said, What part of this could possibly be all right? He left it at that.

Rocco swung the car out of the alley and headed west. The further we drove the smaller the buildings became until the city scrapers had shrunk down to residential houses. Being so close to the city, these places were the oldest: the original houses built when Toran-R was first established, when it was little more than a large town with dirt roads. Many of the houses had been revamped and rejuvenated; some had been knocked down and rebuilt into modern designs. Rocco handed me a parcel—a sandwich, drink and chocolate bar. My empty stomach growled in anticipation.

"It's all I could get quickly," Rocco said.

"No, this is great," I said, ripping off the wrapping. "Totally. Thank you."

I started devouring the sandwich, then noticed he wasn't eating anything. "Do you want some?" I held it up to him.

He shook his head.

"Do Shaman eat?" I asked. He raised his eyebrow at me and I said, "Well, I haven't seen any of you eating."

"We eat," he said. "In fact we need a higher intake of food than humans. This is the suburb ... " He turned the conversation back to the task at hand.

"How did you find his house?" I asked as we drove.

"We traced his wife and found it through her."

"Really?" I said, surprised. "You'd think being who he was, he would have hidden their tracks better than that."

"No offense," Rocco said, "but in my opinion C11 agents, even those who rank highly, are little more than glorified office personnel. None of you have ever seen any kind of real combat, and I mean battle, not just surveillance and pick-ups."

"I guess it depends on your definition of battle," I said, feeling slightly insulted. "I'm guessing you've seen some pretty serious action, judging by your scars. What were you?"

He glanced at me, his eyes evaluating, analyzing, maybe deciding if he could really trust me, then he said, "I trained with various ..." he chose the word "... groups and ended up in a special operations taskforce."

All of which gave me exactly no information about him. "What sort of things did you do?" I asked.

He shrugged. "Whatever we were ordered. Everything that couldn't go on record."

"Like what?" I pressed him. "Just an example."

He narrowed his eyes. I was asking him to give out classified information. I expected him not to talk, but he surprised me.

"Have you heard of the Stasi Romeos?"

I shook my head.

"When East and West Germany were divided, the state security service of the East sent men known as *romeo agents* to develop relationships with, sometimes even marry, West German women, who they used to gain access to government information. I was involved in a similar operation in the Middle East."

"You were married to someone?" I asked.

He shook his head. "Not me personally, but I was part of the general operation."

"Didn't you feel sorry for the girls—thinking they'd found the love of their lives only to be—deceived?"

"The targets weren't women this time," he said. "The targets were males and the operatives were females."

"So it was men getting used?" I said.

He nodded. "Does that make it any less offensive?"

"Not really," I said. "I still feel sorry for the men if they thought they were in love."

"Maybe some of them were in love," he said. "Maybe some of them weren't. Not everyone marries out of love. Sometimes it's more complicated—calculated."

"No doubt," I said. "Not that I'd really know. I've never been married. According to Dark I'm not marriage material."

Rocco glanced over at me. "Sounds like he's afraid to lose you."

"Maybe—but he's a pretty literal guy. It's more likely that he actually thinks I'm not marriage material."

"Whether you are or not would depend on who you were marrying."

"Have you ever been married?" I asked him.

He shook his head. "On duty I moved around all the time. I never had the chance to form any long-term relationships. I don't think I wanted to."

His words brought a question to my mind.

"You're a Shaman," I said. "C11 would have had you registered. How did you avoid surveillance and break-thru without them knowing? Your brother said Omen hid all the others, but you weren't already in contact with Omen when it happened to you, were you?"

"No I wasn't," Rocco replied. He was silent for some time before he said, "I was pronounced dead."

"What happened?" I asked.

Again he took a while to respond. "I had a disagreement with my commanding officer. I'd done unacceptable things in the past, but the closer I came to waking up, the more I realized who I was—and who I wasn't. I couldn't do what he ordered any more, but you can't resign from a job like that, so ... They thought they'd killed me. I would have looked dead. C11 registered me deceased, closed my file and pulled surveillance. In the morgue, I woke up and regenerated. I stayed low." He turned into a well-lit suburban street and said, "Passing Masekela residence on the left."

I looked out his window and saw the house—a white, two-story split-level design squashed in on a narrow block. We did the neighborhood circuit, then doubled back and parked across the street.

Rocco narrowed his eyes at the building as he said, "He's got surveillance everywhere in the house, except his office, and the bathrooms."

"Well, I can't imagine his family would agree to being filmed in there," I said. It made me think of the walts, about their privacy stripped down to the most primary function.

"How could I have ever thought it was all right—what we were doing?" I asked Rocco.

"You thought you were doing it for their sakes, and if it makes you feel any better, Chapter 11 monitors all their agents as well—twenty-four/seven—everywhere in every way. Marco has been splicing in old feeds of your house since the night you joined us."

A wave of disquiet washed over me. "No chance. I swept my house for bugs almost every day and I never found anything."

Rocco gave me a look. "How do you think they maintain such strict secrecy?"

I just sat there for quite a few minutes. He must be right. I'd been such an idiot. I'd thought I was so smart, keeping my secret life so tidy. And all the time I was the one being deceived. "No—it doesn't make me feel any better," I said, feeling dizzy and remembering some sincerely embarrassing moments in life I really hoped hadn't been recorded.

Rocco took out a small laptop and opened it between us. He tapped the keyboard and brought up a house floorplan in one half of the screen; and in the other he opened up live surveillance footage of inside the house.

"He's got almost everything covered, but Marco has identified a blind spot in the rotational scope of the cameras. If we time our movements to coincide with that, we can go unseen."

"But why don't you just get Marco to cut in old footage here as well?" I asked.

"I will if it's completely necessary, but the less interference the less suspicion we raise. Ideally we don't want him knowing he's been hacked. If he checks his security, which we have to assume he will, and sees himself doing something he didn't do tonight—it's a problem. There's a difference between monitoring millions of people and one person."

Rocco pressed the keyboard, flicking from one room to the next. We saw Masekela's wife was in the kitchen, his teenage daughter watching TV in the living room, his son playing video games in the media room. Rocco raised the footage to the second floor of the house and then to the third, searching for Goliath himself. He jumped down toward a closed door—the footage stopped there.

"I'm guessing he's in his office," Rocco said. He squinted up at the house and added, "Yes, he's in there."

"How can you …?" And then I remembered, Shaman had X-ray vision. I supposed it worked in a similar way to the halo-vision installed in Dark's car. The car Pope now had, along with everything in it. If we survived this, Dark was going to kill me for sure.

I studied the open blueprint on the laptop and said, "We'll have to enter through one of the bathrooms."

"I'm thinking here," Rocco pointed. "We can go through the garden, in through this bathroom window—move along the hall, up the stairs and into the office. We'll upload his entire hard drive to this," Rocco held up an external drive.

"You're prepared," I said to Rocco. "You knew I wouldn't get anything, didn't you?"

"I wouldn't be working with you if I thought you couldn't do this," he said to me. "Every operation needs a contingency plan—always." He glanced back to the house. "He's left his study—we're moving now."

Rocco opened his door.

And before I'd had the time to fully comprehend the insanity of the mission, it had already begun.

27

We stayed low and kept to the shadows as we crossed the road and headed toward the front fence of the Masekela house. I started to slow as we neared, but Rocco sped up. He grabbed my arm and leaped. We cleared the twelve-foot stone wall without a scrape and thudded down on Goliath's premium lawn.

A snarl ripped from the shadows beside us and a Doberman Pinscher, with its mouth curled up around a jawful of sharp teeth, rushed us. I cringed back, but Rocco stood his ground. The guard dog's growl softened into a whimper and a wag. It dropped down, crawled on low haunches to Rocco's shoes, and rolled over on its belly for a scratch. He patted it and said, "Good girl, Biscuit—stay here."

"Biscuit?" I whispered to him as we crept around the side of the house. He gave a faint smile. We stopped halfway down the side path and Rocco pointed up to our point of entry, the bathroom window. When he'd said we were entering there, I'd assumed it was on the first floor, but the window sat at a high second level. We had no rope or any kind of grappling hook. I was about to ask the obvious when Rocco grabbed me again, slung me half over his back and started to scale the sheer vertical wall.

He climbed it unaided, like Spiderman, though obviously without the costume or the hero complex. I felt uncomfortable being held like a sack of potatoes over his shoulder, so as soon as we made it to the window, I scrambled up onto the sill while Rocco grabbed hold of the security bars. Without much perceptible effort, he dragged the whole frame out of the window and pushed up the glass. I slid in onto cool tiles beside the toilet and Rocco followed, using one arm to maneuver in while keeping grip of the security frame with the other. Once in, he pressed the bars back in place and I glanced around the room, lit by the streetlamp outside. It was immaculate and floral fragranced, and there was even an elaborate crystal chandelier. Rocco turned the handle and inched open the door. He peered out, keeping very still, waiting for the cameras to shift their focus. Eventually he gave me the nod and pushed the door wider. We slipped out and I followed him along the hall toward the staircase to the third floor, toward Masekela's study. We passed a door with light spilling out from underneath and Rocco pointed to it and mouthed, "Goliath. Bedroom."

My nerves twanged, but we made it past and to the stairs. There Rocco stopped us again—waiting. I clenched my hands into fists to stop them from shaking. We were in a vulnerable position—in full view. If Masekela came out, he'd see us immediately. I could hear the television sounds and the clink of plates downstairs.

Rocco finally gestured again and we continued moving, all the way up to the third level and along the landing to the office. Rocco knelt in front of the closed door doing something while I stood guard. When he was finished, the door clicked and swung open and we entered the room. The rest of the house was pleasantly warm, but the office was running a few degrees below even the chilly outside temperature. That suggested to me there was major electrical equipment in here that he was keeping deliberately cooled, though I couldn't see anything much through the darkness except for shadowy shapes.

I heard Rocco crossing the room.

Light shone onto his face as he powered up the computer. He plugged in his storage device and started the transfer. I peered back out the door, keeping watch on the hall and stairs. We sat in silence until Rocco whispered, "Silver, he's coming."

"What?" I hissed. There was no one there. Then I heard a door open and close on the bedroom level and seconds later saw Goliath wearing boxer shorts and nothing else heading up the stairs.

My heart seized up. I spun back to Rocco to find him directly behind me.

"Geez!" I hissed.

"Shhh." He pressed his hand over my mouth. "Listen—I'm going to change you into his wife. You need to distract him."

"What?" I asked.

Then I felt the strangest sensation, like cold water inching its way down my entire body, followed by an uncomfortable cramping and pushing on my skin from all sides. Momentarily, I couldn't breathe, but then it was over and I felt nothing. Except completely, utterly uncoordinated, as if I could barely stand on my own two feet.

"Go, distract him," Rocco said to me. He pushed me out the door before I could say anything.

I used the wall to steady my walk as I crossed the landing toward the stairs. Seriously, I felt like I was walking in roller skates on ice. My whole body felt out of proportion and unattached. My breath stuck in my throat as I reached the staircase and saw Goliath, paused a few steps down, reading from a newspaper. He sensed me there and looked up. I smiled and to my sincere relief he smiled back. It was a genuine smile, an expression that completely transformed his entire face. He went from scary to boyish—perhaps even cheeky cute. I held the railing and moved down to where he stood. He put his arms around me and hugged me close against his body, completely enveloping me in dark muscle. I tried to remain in the hug while I figured out what the hell I was doing, but Goliath pulled back. He kept his arms linked loosely behind my back.

"Let me look at you, my love," he said tenderly. "I need to see you and memorize your beauty. All the hours we're parted have starved me."

Now why hadn't any of the guys I'd dated said that to me?

Goliath kissed me and I tried to respond as a wife would—seriously difficult considering I wasn't his wife or anyone else's. I started to feel suffocated and had to pull away. I stumbled a bit on my new legs.

"Are you all right, my love?" Goliath's face creased with concern.

"Yes," I said, my voice foreign to my ears. "Just a little warm." I smiled at him. "Do you mind if I get a drink?"

"Of course—I will get it for you," he said.

"No, no, no," I said. "Let *me* get one for *you*. You can wait for me—in the bedroom."

A smile spread over Goliath's face. I led him to the second level and made sure he went into the room. Then I hurried down the stairs toward the kitchen. I entered their lounge room and stood just outside the entrance to the kitchen where the real Mrs Masekela stood talking on the phone. She was a tall and curvy woman with perfect dark skin. Without Rocco's supernatural insight, I had no idea where the surveillance was located down here: I could have been standing in full view of the cameras. No other options, though—it was stay here and risk the cameras or move and be seen by one of the family.

The minutes ticked by. I wondered how much longer Goliath would wait and how much longer Rocco would take.

Desperation was starting to set in when I saw my Shaman companion crouched in the doorway on the other side of the kitchen. He beckoned me urgently. To get to him I'd have to cross over behind the wife and I wasn't sure I could do that. Then I heard heavy footsteps on the stairs and I decided I could. I bent low and made the dash, behind the central counter, across the open and to Rocco. Goliath entered the kitchen from where I'd been standing. He saw his wife on the phone and paused. They smiled at each other. He went to the fridge and poured them each a glass of cranberry juice, then turned his back on where we were hiding.

Rocco tugged my arm. He led me fast through the house to the front door. We paused as he silently disarmed the security and then we were out in the fresh air. We ran across the yard and jumped the fence, Biscuit watching us the whole way.

As we got to the car I said, still in the wife's voice, "Was it there? Do we have the List?"

Rocco smiled and nodded.

I felt like screaming yahoooooooo, but I held it inside. Rocco touched me and I felt the same strange feeling in reverse and then I was back in my own skin. I breathed a sigh of relief.

"How do you feel?" Rocco asked me.

"Pumped," I said. He raised a questioning eyebrow and I clarified, "As in adrenalin rushing through my veins—not—anything else. I can't believe we did it," I said.

Rocco nodded and I couldn't help but grin. I had to say, I felt very pleased with our little team of two. It felt as if we'd achieved the impossible.

Suddenly Rocco was lunging at me. I heard a dulled thudding sound and then white hot pain burned up my legs: we were being peppered with bullets. Rocco hauled me behind the side of the car. He started to open the door. We heard a whistling sound and he grabbed me again and ran. The car exploded. We were way too close. Rocco turned and lifted his hands, repelling the flaming debris back toward the assassins shooting at us through the smoke haze. They ducked for cover, and without Rocco holding me up, I tumbled into the gutter. My legs weren't working, so I dragged myself hand-over-hand toward a parked car as the shooting continued. Rocco grabbed my arm and hauled me up over his shoulder, then took off.

I gripped onto his jacket and struggled not to black out. It had suddenly gone very quiet inside my head. Rocco sped down the street, moving faster than the human assassins could track. He scaled a fence and leaped up onto the roof of a house. He slowed, probably thinking as I was that we were out of range, but then figures materialized from the air around us: four masked Shaman soldiers attacking simultaneously. Rocco had to throw me off his shoulder onto the roof tiles to free up his hands to fight back.

The Shamans' movements were so fast, all I saw was a blur of grayish black as they hit each other with everything they had. I managed to drag myself back to the chimney and prop myself up against it enough to get my gun out. I aimed it at the fight, but didn't shoot, afraid I'd hit Rocco by accident. Waves of terrible feelings, strange sounds and disorienting senses swept over me. I saw one of the soldiers stretch himself to gigantic proportions. Rocco gestured, and threw the giant onto his back.

The fight continued for several more minutes that felt like hours before Rocco burst out of the disorder and snatched me up. He leaped from that rooftop toward the next. He swung around mid-air and raised a hand, exploding the entire roof off the house where we had stood. The explosion sent three of the soldiers crashing off onto the ground. We hit down on the neighboring house and the fourth assassin was right on top of us. He was super fast, contorting and camouflaging his body to avoid Rocco's blows. Finally Rocco managed to get in a powerful strike, but in the process he almost dropped me off the side of the roof. He clamped a hand over my leg, right over one of the bullet wounds. I cried out, but kept my senses, managing to get a hand hold on the guttering and push myself backwards. The Shaman assassin had his arm around Rocco's neck and was squeezing mercilessly. The arm actually looked more like the body of snake. I found I was still holding my gun and raised it. I aimed it at the Shaman's head and fired point blank. He jolted back and collapsed, releasing Rocco.

He coughed and gasped, holding his neck. The sound of running boots came from behind us and Rocco rasped, "Quick."

He grabbed my arm and leaped over the edge of the roof.

28

According to the Greco-Frey Measure, I had an above-average level of pain tolerance. I'd always felt pretty smug about that. As Rocco dug the third bullet out of my leg, I screamed a scream that ruptured several blood vessels in my left eyeball. Zero self-congratulation at this point in time. Unfortunately Rocco wasn't a healing Shaman and his pain blocking influences were currently hindered by his need to self-regenerate and the extent of my injuries, so we were doing it the old-fashioned way—alcohol as an antiseptic and a pillow to muffle the screams. On the upside, the pain was so insanely intense that the discomfort of all my other minor injuries vanished in comparison. On the downside, I wanted to curl into a ball and die. Rocco was, no surprises, mechanical, swift and thorough. I was bracing for more pain when he dragged the strips of my cut jeans down and said, "Done."

I attempted to sit up but the room spun like a nightmare carnival ride and I slumped back down.

Tears trickled from the corners of my eyes as I stared up at the ceiling of someone's lounge room. We'd broken into a neighboring house to hide. I started to shake and couldn't stop. Rocco put his hand on my shoulder and a sense of calm stilled the tremors. The pain remained, but it was dulled. I felt distanced from it. My legs were a mess, but I knew the situation would have been much much grimmer if I hadn't been wearing the Kevlar jacket and body armor—both of which were now ripped up, dented in and lying on the floor beside me. Even with the armor, if it hadn't been for Rocco I would have been dead.

I looked up at his face in the moonlight, shaded with shadows and shimmers of light.

He lifted off his shirt. His chest was riddled with bullet wounds, the injuries so gruesome they made my toes curl up in my boots.

I watched as he turned his skills on himself—using psychokinesis to draw the bullets and frags out of his body. Some of the wounds had started to close over and he had to rip them open with his fingers to access the bullets. He didn't even flinch, but I did enough wincing and shivering for the both of us. When it was finally over, he pulled his shirt back on and cleared away the implements we'd used.

"At least we know for sure now," he finally spoke.

"Know what?" I asked.

"The Horseman is the person who wants you dead. He sent both Pope and the Shaman after us."

"Could it have just been a coincidence?" I said, hoping it could be.

"Not the way it went down. They were working together—if the assassins didn't get us, then the Shaman soldiers would."

I thought about the fight and about the future—Shaman against human. Humans wouldn't stand a chance. It was a completely different league of fighting. As Rocco had said in the beginning, they were a whole new race or model of person.

With that thought, I remembered why we'd been in Masekela's house in the first place. "The drive?" I asked.

"Shot up," Rocco said.

My heart sank down into the acid pit of my gut.

"I did quickly glance the List as it was copying," Rocco said. "The telepaths may still be able to extract it from my short-term memory before it degrades, if we hurry."

"I'm ready," I said, which was a complete lie. I couldn't even walk.

Headlights drifted across the window above us. Rocco pushed me flat to the ground and dived down beside me. We lay there, staring at each other. Voices sounded outside the house, footsteps clomped on the sidewalk. I held my breath. Shadowy silhouettes appeared behind the curtain. We watched them pass and vanish. The steps faded. The voices grew silent. I started breathing again. Rocco narrowed his eyes at the wall, seeing through to the outside. He rolled over onto his stomach but kept low.

"How come they couldn't see us?" I whispered.

"I blocked them." He gestured to his head. "But they're still out there—we have to wait for them to leave the vicinity."

We fell silent, waiting. Rocco lay close, his side warm against mine.

"What was it like for you?" I murmured, my head resting on the carpet. "Waking up?"

Rocco was quiet for so long I didn't think he was going to reply, but then he said, "I felt ..." he struggled for the words "... confused, disoriented."

"Probably didn't help waking up in the morgue," I said.

"No it didn't."

After another stretch of silence I whispered, "When I was talking to your brother he said you and he and your sister didn't grow up together."

Rocco shook his head. "We were all separated. Our sister had a stable adopted family. Marco went through many places."

"Where did you grow up?" I asked.

Rocco paused as he always did when I asked for personal information. "I was born in Barbados," he eventually said.

"Really?" I said. "I would never have guessed that." He definitely didn't have a Caribbean accent. In fact, he didn't have any discernible accent. "Was your mother living there?"

"When my mother was pregnant with me, she was arrested there trying to smuggle drugs out of the country. They jailed her for six years."

"Did you ... stay there with her?" I asked, imagining a child behind bars.

He shook his head. "No one in her family would come to get me after I was born, so when I was three months old, they took me from my mother and put me into a state orphanage. I ran away early on ..."

"And your mother just kept on having children," I said.

"Children she didn't want and wasn't psychologically capable of caring for." He glanced at me with dark eyes. "She was a damaged individual."

"From capping?" I asked. I was assuming she was a Shaman too, since it was genetic and all her children had it.

"From her upbringing more than anything," he said. "I have genetic memories so I know exactly what happened to her. It explains some things, but it doesn't make anything better."

"I guess it wouldn't," I said. "Some things—nothing can make better."

I felt Rocco studying me. When he spoke, his tone was careful, "I've been thinking about what you said, that you entered law enforcement to help people. I can see part of you does want to save, but I can see another part of you is driven by a different motivation—a desire to punish and destroy. They're dark feelings, but they can be used for the right purposes."

"Isn't everyone like that though?" I asked, his words making me feel uncomfortable. "Good and bad?"

"Potentially many people have the feelings, but not everyone could act on them—rationally."

"We were given an open directive to take out any walts that couldn't be brought in safely. I made a personal decision to ignore that directive. If I hadn't a lot of innocent people would be dead, ostensibly in order to protect others. Where does it say one life is more important than another?"

"I know," he conceded. "Often it's gray, but sometimes it's not. Sometimes it's very clear who is the enemy."

"Speaking of the enemy," I said. "Even if we do recover the List and the rebels wake other Shaman, what's to say they won't turn to the Horseman and join him in exterminating humans?"

"Some may," Rocco said, "but I believe most won't."

"Why?" I asked.

"Because most of them have relationships with humans. Most of them have humans who they love."

"Is there a human you love?" I said.

Rocco considered the question, and I watched him in the shadows. He was definitely a person who used his face like a mask, but occasionally the mask lifted and I saw a glimpse of the real person underneath. "I want to love ... but I'm not sure if I can," he said.

"What about your girlfriend?" I asked, aware it was the kind of question a person asks when they are actually interested in someone.

Rocco started to answer, then he glanced sharply up at the window. "They're leaving," he said.

"Then let's go," I said.

He stood and lifted me, carrying me through the house to the garage, where we found a handy car. Rocco opened the doors and started the engine. The garage door lifted up in front of us and he drove out into the street. As we picked up speed, my personal cell phone buzzed in my pocket. I dragged it out and checked the ID. It said Dark. I almost dropped the phone in my rush to answer.

"Bos!"

"It's me—is the line secure?" he whispered.

Tears filled my eyes. "Under normal circumstance it would be," I told him, trying to keep composed. "But shit's gone crazy."

"Tell me about it," he murmured, and from the way he was breathing I could hear he was in pain. A machine was beeping somewhere in the background. He was still in the hospital.

I made a quick decision and spoke fast, "Bos, you're being watched by two separate groups. Assassins and walts who have harnessed their mutations. They have supernatural skills. Some of the walts are allies, some are not ..."

My phone cut dead. I tried to switch it back on but couldn't. The screen remained blank. I checked my work phone and the one Rocco had given me as well, but they were also blacked out.

I glanced at Rocco and said, "You?"

He shook his head. So that left Omen.

"We have to go get Dark. He's incapacitated and unarmed. He doesn't stand a chance against them," I said.

Rocco didn't answer; instead he grimaced with pain as Omen mentally called him in—loudly.

"We can't. We have to answer the call—now," he said. He clenched his jaw and sped up, flying through the suburban streets.

"I have to help my partner!" I told him. "Let me out. Rocco—please!"

"You can't risk it, Silver!" He raised his voice. "You won't get to the hospital in time, you can't even walk. You have to stay with me. You have to see this through—trust me." He looked into my eyes.

My mind spun—and all I could hear was my instincts telling me to get to my partner, but if Rocco was right and Omen would order Dark killed for retribution then if I did anything but comply I could be condemning him.

"We're almost there," Rocco said quietly.

Within minutes we were pulling up at an elementary school, its buildings square shapes in the darkness. Rocco came around to my side and lifted me out. He carried me through the grounds to the school hall. He pushed open the door and we saw the rebel Shaman gathered in the center of the space. Omen stood at the head of the group—waiting.

Part 3

29

Rocco sat with his eyes closed, wires running from his head to a laptop computer, as the resistance's strongest telepaths and others Willow told me were called retrocogs scoured his memory, trying to piece together captured fragments of the List. Omen paced the floor beside the group. Morningstar and Marco stood close by. The rebel's best healer, a man known as the Surgeon, happily agreed to fix my legs. They went from shredded and useless to completely healed, no marks, no scars, in a matter of seconds. The pain lingered for a few extra minutes as my brain struggled to catch up and then that vanished too.

I thanked the Surgeon. He had pungent garlic breath and spoke to me at length about various healing properties of the earth. The guy was an encyclopedia and at another time I would have been interested to listen, but as it was, I couldn't escape fast enough. I just wanted to sit somewhere by myself and try to get my phones working and locate Dark. When I was finally able to disentangle, I found a quiet corner of the hall and pulled out all three cell phones—they were all back on, full reception. I spent a minute agonizing over whether I should phone Dark or if a sudden call might give him away if he was now trying to escape and finally I decided he would have known to turn the sound to silent. I tried to call him, but it rang into voicemail. With bad feelings wrenching my insides, I used the tracker app to check where he was. The application searched for longer than usual and then brought up an error. I tried another three times with the same result. Something, or someone, was interfering with the signal and I was pretty sure I knew who that someone was.

I didn't dare a glance toward Omen, afraid to do anything that might send him into another crazy fit that would end with Dark getting killed. Instead I checked my email in case my partner had written. There was nothing from Dark, but Mom and Dad had sent a letter. I skimmed it briefly to make sure all was okay. It sounded like my father was having the time of his life and Mom was—managing. They'd attached a photo of Dad looking rather sloshed, wearing a captain's hat, saluting with one hand and squeezing Mom against his side with the other. She had a long-suffering, frazzled expression on her face. It brought tears to my eyes.

There was nothing from my brother, which wasn't surprising, but there were several from my mom's cousin who was taking care of the cats and the other pets. She'd written a daily diary entry for each cat in their own individual voices, significant work considering how many of them there were—and Dark had accused *me* of being a crazy cat lady. I shut it down. If I lived through this I'd give the diary the attention it deserved, but at this stage I didn't want to spend the last hours of my life reading about special fish dinners and escapades in the sand box.

I put the phones back in my pockets and glanced up at the Shaman gathered around Rocco. Images from his mind were flashing up on the computer screen. Many of them were images of me, only I looked a lot more glamorous than in reality. Um. Wow. I noticed Morningstar glaring in my direction and an uncomfortable heat rose around me. If looks could kill … Actually, hers probably could, so I decided to go sit somewhere out of range.

I found a bathroom at the far end of the hall. It was a typical school bathroom block, dank with dripping taps, the lingering smell of deodorant, a random sports uniform forgotten on one of the wooden benches. I went to the sink and splashed cold water over my face. It brought my senses to sharp attention. A cold breeze ran up my leg from the ripped jeans. I looked into the mirror and jolted. Morningstar stood right behind me with her arms crossed over her chest and a very Omen look on her face—all dark arched eyebrows and killer eyes. I turned to face her.

"They can't find the List," she said. "Just a thousand angles of *your face*."

"What do you expect?" I said. "My face is all he's been seeing for days."

She narrowed her eyes at me and stepped closer, right into my personal space, just like her brother did. "I told you to remember your place. I warned you."

I seriously wanted to hit her, crazy psycho bitch, but instead I said coldly, "It's his mind: maybe you should be discussing this with him."

"Oh I will be," she said, and I felt sorry for Rocco and maybe just slightly sorry for her as well. Experience had taught me that it was never helpful for couples to interrogate each other about whether or not either found other people attractive. Let's face it, the real answer was always *Yes*. That was only natural. It was what people did with those feelings that mattered, and Rocco hadn't done anything inappropriate—unfortunately for me.

I knew I should probably keep my mouth shut, but I ended up saying, "Good for you." I turned my back on her, which was like turning my back on a snarling dog.

She grabbed me by the neck and slammed my head into the mirror, shattering the glass. I turned to take a swing at her, but she moved superfast and kicked me in the knee with her steel caps. My leg buckled from underneath me and I crashed to my side. Morningstar raised a hand to strike again. I covered my head.

"Hey!" Someone spoke from the doorway. I looked up and saw Willow. Her usual nervousness was gone, now she just looked angry—and scary. The two Shaman girls stared at each other and I sensed a silent battle of minds, which ended in Morningstar storming out of the bathroom.

Willow came in and kneeled down beside me.

"Are you okay?" she asked and I nodded, massaging my forehead. "Try to avoid her," Willow said. "She's intense beyond normal. She was like that even before she woke up."

"Did you know her before?" I asked.

"I knew the family," she said, and there was something in her tone.

"Why would a guy like Rocco be with a person like that?" I asked, still burning with anger.

Willow shook her head and I recognized the emotion in her eyes was sadness. I considered the possibility that Willow herself was interested in Rocco. As I thought it, she gave a small laugh and said, "No, I'm not—it's even worse."

I wondered what was worse than liking a taken man, then I realized. "Omen?"

She looked away, as her eyes misted with tears. "For years now," she confessed. "But he doesn't even see me."

I understood how she felt—it sucked loving someone who had zero interest in you—and it was hard to move on if they were always around. Add in that they can read your thoughts and it would be a complete nightmare. "I'm so sorry," I said to her.

She gave a shaky smile and wiped her eyes. "Sometimes I feel like I'm still in high school."

She flinched and I guessed we were getting the call from the man himself. Time to face the music. Willow helped me up and we left the bathroom and walked back toward the Shaman gathering near the center of the hall. I noticed then that there seemed to be even more rebels than before. Good news, I supposed. I stopped at the back of the group beside Marco. Willow pressed further in, taking up her place. Rocco stood at the front with Omen. I avoided eye contact with him. I didn't want any more trouble with Morningstar. A catfight over a boy was the last thing I needed

Omen starting speaking—his voice loud in the silence, drenched in mocking sarcasm as always, "Unfortunately even though our good friend Agent Silver managed to locate the List, we have been unable to recover the data."

I shut my eyes and yelled a curse in my mind.

"However," he continued. "We did find a marking stamp that ran throughout the document, and we've determined that this stamp gives location coordinates—the place of original production. It tells us where to go to recover the List where it is primarily stored. It is a C11 facility on Dunbar Road. Do you know this place, Silver?" Omen spoke to me and everyone turned to stare.

"As far as I know it's a low level storage facility," I said.

"Low level?" Omen raised his eyebrows. He stepped to one side and pointed to his laptop screen. It showed footage from surveillance outside the Dunbar facility. A high fence encircled the entire perimeter of the building with a boom gate to allow entry and exit. Considering it was C11, this level of security wasn't surprising, but there were also armed guards stationed all around the grounds.

"Shaman?" I whispered to Marco.

"Human." Omen was the one to answer. "But hardly low level. The List is here," he spoke again to the group. "And we're going to get it by—"

A sharp beeping sound came from Omen's open laptop. The Shaman leader moved quickly in front of his machine. He tapped on the keyboard and the sound cut off. The group stood in complete silence as Omen typed for several minutes. There was a strong sense of anticipation among the rebels, but I didn't know what we were waiting for. Finally Omen announced, "The Horseman is ready to attack. The time for hiding and covert action is over. We need to move now—first on the facility to gain the List, and then immediately into the field. The more Shaman we can safely wake up and recruit before the Horseman's first strike, the better chance we have," Omen said. He turned to Rocco, who took the floor. He went into military mode, giving terse, direct orders on who was to do what during the break in at the facility.

"First strike?" I asked Marco. "What does he mean?"

"Omen thinks the Horseman is going to make humans turn against each other," he whispered back.

"How?"

"Pheromones and directed ultrasound," Marco said. "You can't see it, or even feel it. They'll have no idea what's happening to them."

A chill ran over my skin. This was biological warfare of a whole new kind.

Under Rocco's instructions, everyone started breaking up into groups and leaving the building. I cut through the crowd, and headed straight for Omen, who was packing up his laptop.

"Omen," I said behind him. "I did what you asked. Now I need to get my partner clear of the hospital and somewhere safe."

"Your partner?" Omen said glancing over his shoulder as if it was the first he'd heard of it.

"Dark," I said, trying to keep my fury and frustration from volcanoing.

Omen narrowed his eyes in thought, leaving me hanging. I gritted my teeth.

"Actually," Omen said. "We still don't have the List. After we do I'll let you know about Dark. I suggest you don't run away—as yet."

He snapped his briefcase shut and sidestepped me. He headed for the door, where Rocco stood directing people. He and Omen left together. I saw Marco glance back at me, then he was gone as well. I looked around for Willow and couldn't spot her.

What was I supposed to do? What had Omen meant? Did I have to go with them? Did I have to stay here?

"Silver." Someone touched me lightly on the arm.

I turned to find Morningstar standing in front of me. Her face was flushed and she looked slightly embarrassed.

"Listen," she said. "I'm sorry about before. I cleared things up with Rocco and everything's okay."

"Good," I said, cautiously.

"So—he asked me to drive you to the Dunbar Road facility. He and Omen are busy leading. My car is around the side …" She gave me a reassuring smile.

And I should have realized what was happening when I felt suddenly drawn to her, my guard dropping, but whether it was exhaustion or confusion, I didn't pick up on it.

Right then, to me, she seemed genuinely sorry and I didn't seem to have directions from anyone else.

We got into her car and she drove through the streets, with the top 40s playing on the radio and her window down, the cold night air blowing around our hair. We didn't speak until she slowed outside a closed pizza store on the outskirts of the city.

"This is one of our safe houses," she explained. "Omen wants me to pick up something. Just wait here. I'll be back in a second."

She left the car and I grabbed out my cell to check Dark's location. The tracker signal was still corrupted.

The door opened again, sooner than I'd expected. I looked up. A strange man scooped in to sit behind the wheel. The barrel of a gun pressed against the back of my head. I looked into the rear-vision mirror, into Annrais Pope's dead eyes. Another girl sat beside her, also with a gun trained on my back.

"Drive," Pope said to the guy.

He started the engine and took off.

Morningstar stood on the pavement, waving us off.

30

Few will argue—there is something irretrievably creepy about a person singing nursery rhymes when there aren't any actual children around. I guess it didn't help in this case that the singer was also sorting through torture implements and that I was strapped into an old-fashioned dentist's chair in a dank and dimly lit basement with a steel reinforced door and soundproofed walls.

While Annrais Pope started in on the fourth round of the psycho's rendition of "Incy Wincy Spider", I lay immobilized, watching the light globe above me swinging on its wire, blown by the gusting air duct in the wall behind it. I'd completed a fair few resistance and interrogation exercises while I was in training to become an agent, but I'd never actually been tortured before. As I understood it, the contract had been to kill me, but I guessed I'd pissed Pope off big time by refusing to die.

My thoughts turned to the Shaman rebels. They would probably be closing in on the Dunbar facility about now. It was hard to know how that would go with someone as unstable as Omen in the lead, but one thing was for sure—I'd served my purpose as far as they were concerned and there was no one coming for me. So unless I could channel Houdini in the next few seconds, I was in major trouble. I struggled against the ankle and wrist restraints and searched the room for anything I could use—or anyone.

A scattering of Pope's groupies lounged around the area. I doubted if any of them were genuine Undertakers like she was. Probably just lost souls on the wrong track. One of them was staring at me transfixed, another seemed to be praying, three were making out. It reminded me of something the General had told me—he'd said one of the biggest mistakes we can make in this life is assuming other people are thinking basically the same way we are. It's the quickest path to getting hurt in a variety of ways. In reality, there are some seriously messed-up individuals wandering this world.

Speaking of which: Pope turned toward me. She was wearing a heavy-duty butcher's apron and held a cordless drill in one hand. Her hair and make-up were Cleopatra style and her zombie eyes stared into mine. Yes—I was in big trouble.

"Before you start," I said, my voice a little shaky shrill, but not that bad considering. "Can you tell me who hired you?"

"The Devil," Annrais said in her dead monotone.

"Great," I said dryly. "Should have known it was that guy."

She sneered and started coming toward me.

"Whatever he's paying you I can double it if you let me go," I said.

"I seriously doubt that," she smirked. "I've seen where you live—with Mommy and Daddy."

Just to add insult to injury.

"Well you of all people should understand not to judge a book by its cover. How do you think I've been able to afford so much protection?"

Annrais paused—the mercenary in her forcing her to consider. "No," she said. "I'd do you for free."

"Fuck you, you twisted bitch." I swore at her some more, struggling hard against the restraints. Enraging the psycho—not one of my finest ideas.

Pope closed the distance between us fast. She pushed the drill to my hand and I screamed as metal tore my flesh to the bone and left me gasping. She laughed.

White lights danced across my sight and my head lolled to one side. She grabbed my face and said, "No sleeping, Princess—we have a *long* way to go." She revved the drill in my face.

I shut my eyes, opened my mouth and let out a scream—louder and longer than I'd ever screamed before or thought was physically possible. It just seemed to go on and on; and as the sound blared around me, I saw a sudden flash of white light before my eyes. With a huge rush of adrenaline, I ripped out of my restraints and smashed Pope across the face. It was a massive hit that took her completely by surprise. Before I fully registered what I was doing, I'd leaped to my feet, standing on the chair, and grabbed the light cord above my head, using it to swing across to the air vent. I hit the metal with so much force it buckled in and I crashed into the pipe, skidding along it until I collided with a wall.

I managed to scramble around and crawl forward through the duct until I found another vent. I kicked it out and pushed myself through, falling into a room of the house. Footsteps echoed around me in the darkness and just as I was struggling to my feet, the door to the room smashed open, light spilling in. I lunged behind the couch as one of Pope's assassins opened fire. Bullets peppered the couch and through to where I lay with my hands pressed over my head. They thudded into the wall behind me, narrowly missing my body. Another round and I wasn't going to be so lucky. As soon as the firing stopped, I jumped up and charged the assassin, crashing into him as he was trying to reload. Somehow I managed to wrench the gun from his hand and slammed it into his face, knocking him out. More footsteps were thudding along the corridor and behind them I could hear Pope shouting, "I want her alive!"

I cursed and looked around the room, spotting a window. I ran to it and dragged it up, climbing out just as more assassins charged into the room. A spikey hedge broke my fall as I threw myself clear of the window and into the backyard of the house. I started moving, but then something hard struck me across the back of the head, jarring my senses. Pope's steel-cap boot came down on my back and she dragged my arms backward painfully and I felt shackles closing around my wrists. I convulsed against her, trying to break free, but she was unnaturally strong and locked me down.

"Nice try, sister," she hissed in my ear. "But I'm not done with you yet."

She flipped me over onto my back so that I was staring up at her face. She had a gruesome injury from where I'd struck her. I pulled against the restraints, determined that she was not going to drag me back down there. I was not dying here.

"Pope!" one of her people standing on the porch behind us suddenly called out. "Look! Pope!"

"What?" Annrais yelled, turning toward him.

"There's something there—at the side of the house."

The guy was pointing into the shadows.

"There's something there," another of her assassins echoed.

"It's just the wind stirring the trees, you idiots," Pope said. I squinted toward where they were pointing and caught sight of a shimmer of silver-blue, then something taking shape out of the shadows—a huge dark shape. A savage, rumbling growl reverberated around us.

Everyone froze as a creature that looked like a dog but bigger, much bigger, with jet-black fur and sabre-like teeth, slid into the light cast by the streetlamps behind the house. Gigantic paws padded silently on the ground. I'd never seen a canine that big in my life and I'd seen some pretty huge mountain dogs in Eastern Europe during agency training.

"What-the-fuck-is-that?" Annrais pronounced every word.

The hulking beast leaped without warning up onto the porch of the house, scattering Pope's assassins. Some of them started shooting at the creature. I took the chance and kicked Pope's legs out from underneath her. She reacted immediately and scrambled up and onto me before I could make a move. She grabbed a handful of my hair and shoved her gun against my forehead.

"Lights out," she whispered and started to pull the trigger, but then her face contorted with pain and her hand involuntarily lifted the gun away from me. Then her whole body rose and flew across the yard, slamming into the house.

Rocco broke out of the shadows and hauled me to my feet. The shackles fell off my wrists. We locked eyes then the huge dog leaped down behind us, morphing as it did from beast to man—to Rocco's brother, Marco.

He came forward and took my other arm. "Are you okay?" he asked.

"I'll tell you when my heart starts beating again," I said.

He smiled a very canine smile, then bullets started skimming over our heads from assassins firing from inside the house. We ducked low and the two brothers helped me run to the side of the house and along a path to the front where Willow stood fending off another group of Pope's people. I felt rushes of fear and pain, hot and cold and nausea as she messed with everyone's pheromones, and sent out signals below human hearing. Some of the assassins dropped their weapons and ran—others kept coming, firing shots. One hit Willow in the shoulder. She reeled back, but kept her feet. The moon shadows crossed her face and I saw it change and stretch. A strange script appeared all over her skin.

I became aware that the yard was full of other figures: inhuman shapes, creatures of dreams and night terrors, with long, drawn faces, translucent white skin, blood-red eyes and fangs. The remaining assassins completely lost it and started firing on the creatures. They seemed completely impervious to the bullets. Rocco urged me forward and we ran to his car parked down on the street. I slid into the back seat with Marco, while Rocco and Willow jumped in the front. Pope burst out through the front door of the house and hoisted a rocket launcher onto her shoulder. Rocco gestured toward her and with a massive explosion of glass, shrieking metal and snapping wood, the entire house collapsed in on itself, forcing Pope to abandon her weapon and leap clear. She rolled across the lawn, but I didn't see if she managed to escape the falling debris or not. Rocco was already driving, speeding us away. I stared out the back window and saw the strange creatures Willow had summoned vanishing into the mist.

"What were those things?" I breathed.

"Other beings," Willow said from the front seat.

"As in ...?" I prompted.

"Non-humans."

I stared at her in shock.

Rocco looked back in the rear vision. "I told you some of us can see those who inhabit different levels of this world."

'Yeah—but I thought you meant different levels of this earth—like they could see—I don't know—earthworms or something—not ... whatever they were ..." I could hear myself freaking out a bit so I took a deep breath and calmed my voice. "I didn't think you'd come."

"You thought we'd just leave you to die," Rocco said, his eyes meeting mine again in the mirror, guarded emotion in his stare.

"I didn't think you'd even know I was gone," I said.

"Willow read her," Marco said. "Morningstar."

Rocco clenched his jaw. Willow reached back and took my hand. She touched the injury. It didn't heal it completely, but the wound shrank a little.

The three Shaman jolted violently—enough to make Rocco swerve.

"He's waiting," Willow said. She started biting her nails.

Rocco pressed his foot down on the accelerator and we flew toward Dunbar Road.

31

We pulled into the empty parking lot where the Shaman rebels had assembled in the night shadows. As soon as we got out, Omen was right there in Rocco's face, with eyes of knives and a teeth-bared snarl. His voice was a savage whisper. "What part of *I order—you obey* is not completely clear to you?"

Rocco handled the abuse with his usual controlled silence and I noticed he wasn't even looking at Omen: he was staring past him to Morningstar. She stood among the gathered rebels. Obviously I couldn't read their minds, but the hard anger of his eyes and the devastation on her face made things pretty clear. I thought I felt a twitch of pity for her. Who knows what might have happened in her life to cause her personality to malfunction the way it had? But then I realized the twitch was actually blood running out of the drill hole in my hand and any notion of pity was gone. The psycho bitch had almost got me tortured to death; getting dumped seemed like light punishment. Omen noticed Rocco's diverted attention as well and turned to stare at his sister.

After a second of assessing the situation, he said, "I told you she was not to be touched until after we had the List."

I assumed "she" was me.

Morningstar tried to speak but Omen snapped his hand shut, snapping her mouth shut with the same gesture.

"No excuses," he snarled. He lifted a hand and threw her across the parking lot. She flipped mid air and landed on her feet. She looked to Rocco for support, but he said nothing. No one else from the group offered her any help. Her eyes misted over. She turned and ran into the shadows.

Then the breaking moment was over and Rocco turned his eyes to Omen and said with complete control, "I'm here *with* you not *because* of you. Take that for the truth it is or kill me now!"

It felt as if everyone in the group inhaled sharply and held it. The rage in Omen's face stayed for a second longer and then evaporated into his more usual expression of silent derision. He stepped back from Rocco and made an overly emphasized After You gesture.

Rocco took charge, addressing the rebels: "The standing guard changes at zero two hundred hours. That is in five minutes' time. We'll hit the new shift right as they're starting. Remember: disable—don't kill. We get the List and we get out."

Omen nodded in approval of the plan.

"Move out," Rocco instructed.

We left the lot and moved as a tight mass down the deserted road, the longest industrial stretch within the city limits. I walked beside Marco at the back of the pack. In contrast to all other times I'd seen him, Rocco's younger brother now seemed calm. The fear and anger were gone from his eyes. It'd seemed like it should be the opposite, considering we were just about to attack a C11 facility and basically announce to the Horseman 'Here we are—come kill us' but, as they say, action is the antidote to despair. He, and probably all the others, were tired of hiding and planning to do something—now they were actually doing it.

They were ready, but I felt anything but. I had the shakes and couldn't stop, which I guessed could be delayed shock, maybe from the torture—maybe from everything. All I could think was: Where is Dark? I could see Omen walking at the front with Rocco and I really wanted to run up and kick him in the back, bash the hell out of him until he told me that my partner was all right—but of course I wouldn't even get close to him, let alone touch him. As I thought these thoughts, Omen glanced back and caught my eye—he gave me a nod as if to say, Learning, are we? I returned a look that said, Kiss my ass. He smirked.

Rocco pulled the group up with the facility in sight. It was a low, rectangular building surrounded by a high fence topped with a roll of razor wire. We watched as a stream of cars exited through the boom gate and turned in various directions down the strip, their headlights flashing bright then vanishing into the darkness. The shift had turned. I heard Rocco speak, voice quiet but urgent, "Now."

Without further instruction the rebels separated into four groups, each closing in on the facility from different sides like a hunting pack. I stayed beside Marco, and we headed, dead on, toward the boom gate. We came so close that the C11 Security agent posted in the boom gatehouse saw us. I thought he might call for backup or even open fire, but he only had time to narrow his eyes, and then he fell silently and didn't rise again. Marco grabbed my arm and I found myself flying through the air beside him, up and over the fence, into the enclosed concrete square. All the rebels were leaping over and thudding down from every angle. This brought the new guards running—yelling instructions—"Hands up!"; "Get down!"—and so on.

Poor bastards didn't stand a whisker of a chance.

The Shaman hit them with a barrage of supernatural strengths and, like the boom gate's guard, they all just fell with hardly a sound. When Omen had announced they were moving on the facility, my mind immediately began devising elaborate plans to get in—stealing guards' uniforms, forging passes—but why would the Shaman bother with that when a confrontation was so effortless for them? Again I was reminded of the fragility and helplessness of humans against Shaman. How could we fight an enemy that could directly affect our minds? Rocco had ordered the rebels to disable not kill, but some of the guards looked extremely still. I understood the anger of the group against the Chapter, but I assumed most of these guards were like me, agents who didn't have a clue what was really happening—but we should have.

The mob marched on, a hungry and desperate beast. We burst through the front door of the facility, meeting more guards: they fell just as fast with not a shot fired. I assumed Omen was taking out the security surveillance as we went, since no alarms were sounding, and no backup arriving.

Apart from the guards, the building was largely empty at this hour, unlike Headquarters, which was always bustling. We passed hallways of offices, conference halls, tearooms, pushing further into the building. Omen and Rocco led the pack. They seemed to be following a location device, which I guessed held the coordinates for the server hosting the White List. We left the main building and approached a large warehouse-style building behind the facility. It was locked down with high-level security, which Marco disabled in seconds. Omen opened up the doors with a flick of his hand and we entered. The inside was nothing like I'd expected. I'd imagined lines of massive steel shelving and towering server stacks, but instead it was a huge office-like space with long rows of computers on benches for as far as I could see.

"The hub," I heard Omen say. "This is where they control the List. I knew this place must exist, I just couldn't find it.

It was like a mirage: everywhere I went it wasn't." He gave a bitter laugh, then led the group into the area.

"Everyone boot up and get a copy of the List," he ordered. "No mistakes this time."

The rebels scattered around the room, each of them going to stand in front of a computer. I copied them, sitting at a desk halfway down the stretch of building. I couldn't help but notice the photographs beside the computer screen, pictures of smiling kids, a shaggy dog ... There was a small calendar with marked dates–*Angie's birthday—speech night—Brett's Final.* I turned my attention back to the task. I didn't have my USB, I'd left it in the office, but there was the option of just taking the whole hard drive. It wasn't like the rebels were being subtle any more. I rummaged around in the agent's pens and equipment and found a steel nail file that I used to unscrew the computer box cover and prize out the hard drive. I pushed it into my jacket pocket and glanced up at the rest of the group.

Everyone was concentrated on the task—except Marco. He was standing in front of a door at the side of the building. I left the desk and went over to stand beside him. He didn't even register I was there. His face was frozen like a store-window manikin. I'd seen Omen and Rocco lock up with the same unnatural stillness, as well as that Medical officer at Headquarters, and it made my skin crawl every time. It was a sharp reminder that Shaman were not human, even though most of the time they looked the same as us.

"Are you all right?" I asked Marco.

He blinked and turned my way.

"There's something behind this door," he said, his face pale white. "I can hear—something."

"Something like ...?" I pressed.

"I don't know," he said. He glanced over his shoulder toward Omen and Rocco. Then he went to the security code board beside the door and pressed his hand against it. The locking mechanism clicked open. Marco took the door handle and slid the heavy door across. We stepped into the room through a gust of freezing air billowing out from just above the door. The mist cleared and I looked around.

It was an equally large warehouse space, but there were no desks here. It took a second to understand what I was actually seeing, and as I did, it felt like the ground was being ripped from under my feet like a trick carpet. The entire hangar was packed full of prison-like cells with gurneys and smaller cages inside, with people hooked up to bags and machines, restrained and chained in various degrees of sedation and damage. Experiments. On living people.

Everywhere I looked horrors burned into my mind. My whole face was pricking and my vision started to go white. I saw children there, bruised and frail. I thought I was going to be sick or even pass out, and realized I'd started to back out of the room without knowing I was moving. I looked at Marco. He had tears running down his face.

I leaped as a hand closed over my arm. I turned to Rocco.

His dark eyes were empty of emotion. "We have to go. The Horseman's soldiers are coming," he told me.

"Are you seeing this?" My voice came out loud and harsh.

"We knew the Horseman was conducting experiments on Shaman, just not where ..."

"And now you know where," I said. "We have to get them out."

"There's no time," Rocco said.

"Bullshit!" Marco broke out. "They're our people! We're not leaving them!"

He started to run into the room, but Rocco gestured and his legs just buckled and he started to fall. Rocco scooped up his brother before he hit the ground and slung him over one shoulder.

"He's too young. He doesn't understand. He can't help anyone if he's dead. We have to run now so that we can live to come back." He looked deeply into my eyes. "We will come back. They're almost here."

I couldn't move, so he grabbed my arm and dragged me out of the room. We broke into a run, joining the last of the rebels fleeing the facility. We sprinted around the side of the grounds and leaped over the fence. I could hear many voices at the front of the building. A car pulled up beside us. I shied away from the headlights, but Rocco pressed forward. He opened the front door and pushed me in. Willow sat behind the wheel.

"Okay?" she asked me.

I couldn't reply. I felt like my face was frozen and my body was a hollowed-out shell.

"Go!" Rocco said from the back, and Willow slammed her foot down, taking us away from that nightmare place—leaving the helpless to the mercy of demons.

32

The place of rendezvous was an eerie returning. It was the same colonial-style house in Bank Terrace in the inner out-skirts of Toran-R, where Dark and I had attended the Bushels' murder, where we had first encountered Omen's power. The house was the same, minus the bloodied bodies, but I was changed, so everything looked different. I couldn't stop think-ing about what I'd witnessed. How could I ever stop thinking about it? How could anyone do that to another person? It was true, atrocities such as these and worse had been perpetrated throughout all the history of humankind, but we were largely sheltered from it in our safe little part of the world. We read horrors in books, in newspapers, online, but never really saw it—and Omen was right—we needed to see it to really feel it.

I sat on a couch in the darkened living room of the house, wrestling with my mind, which now seemed to belong to someone else, someone angrier, colder, smarter and more driv-en than me. My whole body shook with the headache from hell. My thoughts strayed to what Rocco had said to me about who I was—dark in places—and I'd asked, weren't we all? I didn't know the real answer to that. I didn't feel like I was in a position to analyze humanity as a whole. I didn't even know who *I* was any more. Was I the person who felt heartbroken by tragedy, who went to pick up the pieces when all was said and done, or was I a person who could fight the source—stop it from happening again? That's who I'd wanted to be; but I'd forgotten myself somewhere along the way. Or maybe I'd just grown up and found out life wasn't that simple. Rocco had said at times it was. Maybe he was right. I felt so much hate right now toward whoever was torturing those people: if I met them who knows what I would do? Maybe I'd fight them, maybe I'd collapse into a crying heap on the ground. I'd never been in this situation before. Nothing had ever been so real and raw.

I could hear the Shaman resistance in the dining room, feel their excitement as they examined the List, the names of all the Shaman still 'sleeping', who they could wake to fight the Horseman—to stop his plans. Would they be in time? Only one thing was certain—the world was about to change forever. We were on the verge of war, one that may see the extinction of humans. It sounded impossible, but who would have thought creatures as huge and powerful as the dinosaurs could be one day reduced to fossilized bones, to dust and dreams?

I had to find Dark; I had to get my family together. I had to try to take them somewhere safe before the war broke out—if such a place existed. Dawn light threw shades of gray through the darkness. I knew what I had to do, but I felt like I could barely move. I fought back the exhaustion and dragged my phone out of my pocket. I startled as it buzzed in my hand from an incoming call. My heart thudded faster. I thought it might be Dark, but it was the General's number. I hesitated then answered.

"Silvia?" My mentor sounded uncharacteristically aged and nervous.

I had no idea what to say to him.

"Silvia, are you there?" he asked.

"I'm here … I'm sorry …" I finally found my words.

"Dark called me. He's worried about you. He said you're in trouble."

I felt a rush of emotion. If Dark had called the General it could be that he'd gotten out.

"When did he call you?" I asked. "Was it from the hospital?"

"I'm not sure where he was," the General said. "Silvia—tell me what's happening."

I considered lying, that's what I'd been doing my whole life, that's what felt comfortable, but I decided then, no more—let there be truth. "I found something out. Something terrible about the Chapter."

"Tell me," the General prompted.

"The agency—it's not what we thought it was—it's just a cover up—someone inside C11 is controlling everything— they're going to use the walts to try to destroy the world."

The General paused and then he said, very gently, "Silvia, I've been investigating this exact situation for a very long time, and I believe you, but we must talk. You're in terrible danger by knowing these things. It's much more complicated than you know. Please tell me where you are. I'll come and find you. We'll talk through everything. Where are you?" I closed my eyes. Hearing the General say he believed me felt like a huge weight off my shoulders. I was positive Omen wouldn't trust him to be involved and I didn't want to drag him into this either, but I could see the rebellion desperately needed him. If I started telling everyone the truth, people might think I'd just lost it, but when a man like the General spoke, everyone listened. He could change everything.

"I'm in a house on Bank Terrace—I'm with a group of walts who have broken-thru and survived. They're trying to stop what's happening, but we're being hunted."

"I understand," the General said. "Just stay put, and I'm coming to you. I'm with you, okay?"

"Sir, it's too dangerous," I told him. "I'll call you when I'm clear. I'll come to you instead. I'm scared for Dark … I don't know where he is."

"We'll find him," the General said. "But first I'm coming to get you."

"No—" I started to say again, but he hung up, leaving me twisted with anxiety that I may have just done exactly the wrong thing.

I lowered the phone and stared out the window into the garden gradually taking shape in the new daylight.

My phone buzzed with an incoming message and I tensed thinking again that it could be Dark, but the ID was Byter. The message said, *I'm sorry :(*

I wrote back quickly: *I'm the one who should be sorry. Things are happening I can't explain. Don't trust anyone.*

Then I sent another message that said, *Get armed and get as far away from Headquarters as you can.*

I sensed someone behind me and looked over my shoulder. Rocco stood beside the couch, silently watching.

"Hi," I murmured.

He walked around to sit down beside me, so close our arms were touching. He took my hand in his. He had a warm, strong grip.

"How's Marco?" I asked.

"Angry," Rocco said.

"Do you blame him? We left those people there," I said to him. "Those children …"

Rocco nodded. "We left them," he repeated. "We could have stayed and we would have been killed, then what about all the humans we're trying to save—thousands, millions of other people, including children?"

I rubbed my eyes and nodded. The theory sounded right, except this was actual life and not a hypothetical.

"It doesn't seem like it yet," Rocco said, "but we're already at war, and at war the decisions you make aren't right or wrong, just bad and worse ..." He paused. "If you'd known this was happening, would you have done something?"

I nodded. I would have. I knew that much. "Does that make any difference?" I said.

"It does," Rocco said. "I'll find a way to get them out. All of them."

"Why would the Horseman do that to his own kind?" I asked.

"I think he'd do anything to anyone to accomplish his mission."

"His mission—turning humans against each other? I don't understand. Why would he bother taking us out in such an insidious way when he could just attack directly? Humans don't have any weapons that could fight the Shaman."

"I don't know for sure," Rocco said. "But my instinct is that he doesn't want a Shaman versus human battle—he wants to sit back and watch humanity turn itself inside out on a mass scale."

"Why?" I asked.

Rocco looked at me, his eyes shimmering silver in the dim light. "Because his power has made him unbalanced. Because he's angry about how humanity chose to treat us when our mutation was revealed. Because it requires less effort than taking the world by force. All of the above and probably many more reasons we don't yet understand."

"And Omen?" I whispered.

Rocco paused. "He wants to stop the Horseman. Right now that's enough to keep him directed."

"Do we seriously have a chance?" I asked.

"There is always a chance," Rocco said.

His eyes lingered on mine. He was so close. Another time I would have been thinking about kissing him, but this wasn't another time. This was now—and as he'd said—we were at war.

Rocco jolted.

"Omen wants us," he said softly. "We have to go."

"Awesome," I murmured. "Can't wait."

I thought I saw a faint smile form on his lips.

I dragged myself up and shuffled after Rocco into the dining room. All the Shaman were gathered around the table where Omen was standing in front of his laptop. His expression was its usual mocking sneer, but with an added twist of bemusement. I didn't like it.

"Agent Silver," he said. "I'd like you to see something."

"Where's my partner?" I demanded. "I've done everything you've asked, now I want to know."

Omen completely ignored my question. Instead he turned his laptop toward me and gestured.

"Have a read," he said.

I approached the computer and saw a database file with lists of names—the White List. I glanced up at him and he gestured again. Reluctantly I started to read the names on the screen. At first I had no idea where he was going with it—it was just a bunch of names that meant nothing to me—and then I saw it, on the list of Shaman: my grandfather's name—my mother's name—my brother's name, my name—the due date of my brother's unborn baby and the scheduled date of its capping. The room spun around me and I had to hold the table to steady myself.

"Is this a joke?" I asked Omen. He narrowed his eyes, studying me closely.

"I didn't see it," he said. "Which means you're above me in the Order—and the fact you haven't broken-thru yet means you were capped by the Horseman himself."

I heard his words, but they didn't quite sink in. My thoughts were speeding through time, through my life, looking for signs that it could be true—that we were Shaman. Right then one thing stuck out in my thoughts—my grandfather—the lunatic. My mother said he'd once made their entire family home shake by summoning the devil. I'd always dismissed the notion of it. Mom had been very young at the time and I'd never believed in supernatural power like that, but with this information in front of me I saw it must have been his own unstable strengths bordering on a break-thru. I held my pounding head.

"Does it hurt?" Omen asked.

I raised my eyes to his, the pain obvious in my stare.

"It's your mind trying to wake up, but it can't. The Horseman has capped you. He's too powerful. You'll only wake if he lifts it," Omen told me. "How does it feel?" he asked. "Being one of us?"

His bemusement was gone, all the mocking gone—it was a straight question to which he wanted an answer. How does it feel?

All the lights in the house suddenly blinked out.

Omen's voice came out of the darkness. "They've found us."

33

All the windows in the house simultaneously imploded in a shrieking, shattering fall-out of glass. The whole place shook violently, bringing plates smashing off shelves and cabinets toppling.

"Scatter!" Omen yelled and there was a stampede of boots crunching on glass as everyone fled the quaking house through windows and doors. Rocco held my arm tightly and guided me through the chaos to the back. We pushed through with a group of others onto the porch. The Horseman's soldiers immediately attacked. Their forms, surrounding the house, were visible silhouettes in the gray light of dawn. As the rebels fought back, the sounds of war rose loud through the silence of the early morning—the sharp retort of gunfire, the smashing of projectiles, the ripping, rending, screaming, yelling. Ordinary suburbia had become a battlefield. If the neighbors weren't cowering under their beds, they were calling the police. And if they had any sense at all they were running away as fast as they could go.

"Stay low—get clear and run!" Rocco shouted and shoved me to the ground. He and Omen pushed to the front of the rebels to face the soldiers head on. I slithered on my stomach toward a nearby row of hedges. A boot came down on my arm, another kicked me in the face, but I managed to make it to the bushes. I pushed my way through to the fence and saw a similar anarchy at the front of the house—rebels battling soldiers, mind against mind, using every strength they had, but we were outnumbered at least four to one. As I watched, another huge military truck full of the Horseman's people rumbled up the street and stopped to let a mass of soldiers out, making it more like six to one.

A terrible dread seized my throat and squeezed. I leaped over the fence and ran for the cover of a tree trunk. I had to get the resistance some help, but from who? This was a war of supernatural powers: any human would be as good as dead. Even our deadliest weapons wouldn't stand against the Shaman. Then I saw headlights and glimpsed a familiar car driving up the road. My heart froze. It was the General's Cadillac, his personal vehicle. He was heading unknowingly right into the war zone, and it was my fault. As he neared, I took a chance and stepped out onto the street, waving him down frantically. I could see him squinting through the windscreen. He spotted me and shrieked the brakes to a stop. I darted to the driver's side window and crouched low.

"Sir, you have to get out of here!" I told him.

There was a massive booming explosion as someone threw a car into the rebels' house.

The General's face glowed with the reflected flames. He took out his gun and pushed open the door. I tried to shove it back closed and make him stay inside, but he was too strong.

"You don't understand," I tried to tell him. "You'll get killed."

He forced his way out and crouched down beside me, behind the idling car. Gas fumes filled the air. The General peered over the hood toward the house.

"They've all broken-thru," he said, watching the two Shaman groups fighting in the brightening light of the morning and the blaze of flames consuming the house.

"Did you know this was possible? Did you know what was happening—that there was someone controlling everything from inside the agency?" I asked him.

"Silvia, I've known for a very long time," he said. "The Chapter has been trying to dig the Horseman out for as long as I've been an agent."

"Do you know who he is?" I asked.

He gave a grave nod. "I know him well."

"Who is it?" I uttered. If he had been an agent at the same time the General had joined C11 then he had to be one of the senior bosses.

Another car came flying through the air, hurtling from the direction of the house, and crashed down onto the road, skidding toward us on its roof, stopping just before it hit the Cadillac.

"You need to get out of here," the General said to me. "Take my car. I'll stay and call in my team."

"I can't leave," I told him. "I need to help the rebels."

"You don't have to. They can't hurt you now. I know that Dark is clear—they're not watching him any more."

Relief surged through my body, but my mind went to Rocco. "Their boss, Omen—he's messed-up, but the others—they just want to save people. I believe in their cause. We have to stop the Horseman. We can't let him hurt anyone else."

The General looked down at me and I saw sadness in his eyes. He shook his head. "There's that heart again, Silvia," he said. "It's been your downfall since day one. You're a prisoner to your emotions."

"Sir, what do you mean?" I asked him.

"I've been waiting—waiting to see that change in you, that shift to indicate you were ready and I would have woken you up to join us. But it never came—the strength is there, it always has been, but your heart is weak."

"What are you talking about?" I demanded again. "What change? What shift?"

"You said their leader, Omen, is messed-up. He's not, he's evolving, coming into his true power, becoming enlightened, as I was—divorced from the emotions that keep humans crawling through the primordial sludge. With your strength, I thought you would evolve too—I was so sure." He shook his head. "But you kept hanging onto this?" He tapped his chest over his heart.

I stared at him, shocked, the words gradually sinking in.

"It's you!" I hissed and scuttled backward along the tarmac road. "You're the Blood Horseman."

The General's steady blue stare didn't falter for a second.

"You sent Annrais Pope to kill me," I said in disbelief.

"You weren't changing, but you were starting to question. You were linked to me and bringing attention to yourself," he said. "So I had to speed up my plan against the rebels. I did send Pope after you, but I didn't think she would succeed. I thought if you suddenly came under threat then Omen would step in."

"I can't believe this," I said and the General continued.

"After I dug him out of the agency, I found out he'd been watching you for quite some time. But after he ran, his cloaks were still so strong even I couldn't find him. And so I thought of you, and please don't be offended, as my Trojan horse. And here we are, through the gates, thanks indeed to you, my dear.'

I felt the betrayal sharp like a knife cutting inside me. I'd worshiped this man. His words were like gospel to me. He'd put everyone I loved in danger to use me for his purposes.

"I'll never join you—ever," I told him, my eyes locked with his.

"I believe you, Silvia," he said, and pointed his gun at my head. "And believe me when I say you're like a daughter to me. I love you like family, but I am a man of purpose and if my own hand got in the way of that purpose I would chop it off. You're too strong. I can't have you joining them." He cocked the trigger of his gun.

"First tell me why you're doing this?" I demanded, looking down the barrel and trying to stall him. "Why are you trying to kill humans?"

"Because," the General said, "this world is full of nothings, full of wastes of space and air and life—going to work, coming home, going back—doing nothing, going nowhere. I have a dream about a different world, a new kingdom, with all the dead branches cut away."

"With you as the king, right?" I said bitterly.

"I'm at the top of our Order. Who else could lead like I?" he said.

"What about your family? Your grandchildren?"

"Well they're precisely the reason for my actions—I'm preparing a world fit for them to live in."

"They're Shaman," I realized.

I stared at him, searching for the monster I now knew he was, but all I could see was him—the same unfashionable dresser, the same sharp but sparkling blue eyes, the same gentle question in his expression. There was no monster hiding behind the man—the man *was* the monster—with all its sides and shades, its abilities to love and show concern, then turn and stab you in the heart if you don't fit into its scheme—all the while saying he loves you. My head was pounding so badly my vision blurred out. I struggled to blink back to focus.

"You capped me," I said to him.

"Yes," he said. "I held you as a newborn baby, when you were only this big." He measured it with his hands, sounding so fond and grandfatherly. "And I thought, One day this girl will be a force to be reckoned with." He shook his head. "There's still time," he said. "You can still join me." His finger tensed on the trigger.

"You're the reason I am who I am," I said, my voice like ice.

"Well I did try to guide you—"

"No," I cut him off. "That's not what I meant. I meant that you are the monster I wanted to kill. You're the time I wanted to turn back. You're the wrong in everything and everyone that I swore I'd make right. You're telling me that I have too much heart but there's no such thing. A heart can love, but it can also hate and I hate you and everything you are!" By the end of my speech I was shouting, screaming, and as the echo of my voice faded to silence, the pain in my head peaked and then exploded into blinding white lights behind my eyes. The streetlights all around us blew out. I gasped, staggered and fell to my knees, alien sensations running through my body. The pain trickled away to nothing and I looked up at a changed world.

"Yes—well done!" the General said with genuine excitement. "You've woken yourself up. Outstanding! I think there's still hope for you, my girl, if you could break through a cap of my making. You're confused now, but I'll help you understand my vision, I promise. Come with me." He held out one hand while keeping the gun still trained on my head.

I stared toward him, but his image kept jumping from one side to the other, from far to very near. Time and space distorted around me. I couldn't see anything clearly: everything was rocking, colors running together like wet paint. My body felt completely disconnected, as if my head was floating in the sky and my legs and arms were somewhere far below. I couldn't control the feelings, but I did understand one thing. If I was going to strike, it had to be now. And I wanted to strike—more than anything I'd ever wanted.

I gathered my rage and lurched to my feet. I tried to rush the General, but I found I was stuck to the spot and everything around me was rushing toward him instead. The force hit him hard and knocked the gun from his hand. His expression registered some shock. He looked back at me and the sadness came back into his eyes.

"Shall I take that as a final no?" he asked.

I gave a very animal growl and sent my powers at him again, but this time he blocked it and threw it back at me. His movements were effortless, a minimal brush of his hand, but the force he sent was nuclear. My tiny attempt was like a butterfly's breath in the hurricane of his power. His psychokinetic force hit me and I flew—for yards—until I struck the fence of the besieged rebel house and crashed to the ground.

I managed to raise my head and saw the General moving toward me. His steps were unhurried as always, but purposeful. I struggled up, one arm holding my chest, and leaped back over the fence. I broke through the hedge into the backyard. Here, the fight was continuing. There was no sign of Rocco, but Omen still stood in the center of the grassy square laying waste to every soldier who came at him. I spotted Eric charging at him. With a flick of his hand, Omen snapped my former supervisor in half. Sensing the General closing in behind me, I stumbled out into the fight, running the gauntlet of flying objects and crashing powers toward the rebel leader. It felt like I was running on a lurching ship. I couldn't regulate my speed or even judge the distance. I ended up smashing hard into someone's back and the two of us rolled across the ground, lunging up at the same time face to face. I stared at Feng.

"Tell me you're not one of his?" I said.

"I told you I was seeing one of the big bosses," she said.

"Feng, no," I whispered. "What about Jovic?"

The hard stare of her eyes faltered and she said, "You should get out of here—you're going to get yourself killed."

She jumped up and tried to run past me but I grabbed onto her, hugging her against me. She tolerated it for a moment then pulled away.

"I was wrong," she said. "You can't learn how to care."

"But you do care," I told her. "Don't let the General convince you that you don't."

She looked into my eyes and said, "Goodbye, Silver."

Feng pushed past me. She ran across the yard and, using her Shaman skills, uprooted a tree and hurled it at a group of rebels.

Feeling an ache in my chest, I hauled myself up and ran to Omen, almost colliding with him as well. He spun around super-fast and grabbed me around the neck, then saw it was me and loosened his grip, fractionally.

"It's him. It's the Horseman," I managed to say. I pointed back toward the fence as the General appeared through the row of hedges.

Omen stared at him, confusion in his eyes. He knew the General the way I did. Then the lines of his face smoothed out and he breathed, "It's him."

A snarl set onto his face. All along his arms and up his body, tattoos appeared of roses thick with thorns. They grew thick around his neck and he gasped as though they were choking him.

He dropped me to the ground and I was rocked by a rush of air as he literally flew at his nemesis.

The two superpowers met with a collision that ripped through the yard, throwing everything and everyone in all directions. I landed back out on the sidewalk with a crash that knocked the air out of my lungs. Rebel corpses lay everywhere, there were a few still standing, fighting. I struggled up, searching the knots of people for Rocco or Marco or Willow, but I could barely see anything. My vision was blurring then focusing in on the minutest detail. My body was sending me a thousand conflicting messages—run, stop, attack, cry, lie down, jump up ...

Without warning something struck my shoulder with staggering force. I stumbled back and was hit again in the stomach. The impact knocked me onto my back. I grasped at the pain and my hand came back red and wet with blood. I'd been shot. I raised my eyes and saw Annrais Pope standing across the road, holding a rifle. This psycho just never gave up. She was like a freaking Terminator.

A smile crept across her lips and she came toward me. She seemed completely oblivious to the chaos around her—her tunnel vision was extraordinary. I tried to scramble back, but my coordination was worsening. I was just sliding around on the spot. She stepped onto the curb on my side of the road and closed in, wanting to be as close as possible for the death shot. I heard a car speeding up the street. Pope stood over me. She took aim at my head. Tires screeched so close. Pope lifted her head, distracted. I managed with supreme effort to land a savage kick to her leg. She stumbled backward. At the same time, a car mounted the curb with a massive crash, and slammed into her. I didn't see her flying, but I heard the dull thud a few seconds later.

The car door flew open and a figure jumped out. The person ran through the haze of smoke billowing from the car's hood. I stared up into sharp green eyes—Dark. I started crying, probably hysterically. I couldn't control anything. My partner, still battered and bruised, wearing casts and struggling to move fast, closed the distance between us. He fell down to his knees beside me and I hugged onto him so tightly. Scents of leather and peppermint chewing gum filled my senses. The familiarity helped me gain some focus. He was my anchor in the storm.

"How did you find me?" I whispered.

Dark lifted my arm—the tracer. He'd tracked me the same way I'd been searching for him.

"I thought the app was malfunctioning," I said.

"It was. Byter called me and gave me a location." He glanced around us. "I'm out of it for five seconds and the whole world goes to hell."

"Perfect reason never to leave again," I told him.

He smiled, but it faded immediately as he saw the blood pooling around us. He grabbed up my shirt. He gritted his teeth. There was a gaping bullet wound in my stomach. Dark ripped off his jacket to stem the blood flow, but before he could press it to the wound, the hole began to shrink, smaller, smaller until the bullet itself popped out and the wound sealed over. Dark's eyes widened. There was a *whoosh* of air and I dragged him down beside me as a massive tree trunk flew just over our heads.

"We have to get out of here!" I yelled to my partner.

He didn't question or argue. He just hauled me to my feet and helped me run to the car. We leaped in and he started it up. Through smears of Pope's blood on the windscreen, I finally spotted Rocco, Marco and Willow at the end of the cul-de-sac. They were surrounded on all sides by Shaman soldiers, and taking hit after hit. Rocco was trying to shield the other two. He was fighting their every move, but there were too many of them. I saw him stumble and fall. Fear choked me.

"See that guy there? We need to help him!" I said to Dark. "He saved me."

Dark nodded, grim resolve tightening his face. He grabbed something off the back seat and handed it to me. I held up the machine gun.

"Always come prepared," I said.

"Always," Dark said. He revved the engine and threw the car into gear. He skidded the tires across the grass and we flew off the curb toward the embattled group. I leaned out the window and opened fire upward. I didn't want to shoot Rocco and the others while aiming for the enemy. Taken by surprise, the Horseman's soldiers scattered and we screeched to a stop beside the trio. Willow and Marco dragged Rocco into the back seat and Dark hit reverse, speeding us backward. The smell of burning rubber thickened the air. I could hear a helicopter flying overhead. I turned to the others.

Marco was hugging onto his brother. Rocco held a hand over his neck, over a wound that was literally spurting blood. His eyes met mine and I understood the look. He was bleeding out. Modern medicine was not going to help. He couldn't regenerate himself fast enough and neither Willow nor Marco were strong enough healers. I looked around desperately for something to help him and grabbed up an oilcloth from near my feet.

"Bos, get us to a hospital!" I said, lunging back to press the rag against Rocco's wound.

As my fingers brushed his neck, his whole body convulsed off the seat. I gasped and pulled back, unsure of what I'd done to him, but when Rocco straightened up, not only had his neck healed: but all his minor scratches and all his old scars as well; even the tips of his fingers had grown back. The three Shaman stared at me in shock, and I stared back at them just as surprised. The General had said I was strong, but I hadn't had the time to really consider what that meant.

Dark looked back and saw Rocco was healed. "Where to now?" he asked, slowing the car.

"Back I think. The Horseman and Omen are fighting behind the house."

Willow's eyes welled up with tears.

"He needs us," Rocco said.

"Back, Bos!" I confirmed to my partner and he slammed the car into reverse and sped us back the way we'd come until I pointed to the rebels' house, on fire and half collapsed and said to my partner, "Can you ram the fence?"

"Not a problem," Dark said. He shifted the car out of reverse and into gear and sped toward the house. We crashed over the gutter, and tore through the fence and shrubs. The car stalled and we looked out on what had once been backyard. Now it was just dirt, with no one and nothing left standing except Omen and the General. The Horseman. They were throwing everything they had at each other, their powers so advanced that time itself seemed slowed around them. We witnessed each blow—the projection, the impact, both of them regenerating, transforming themselves so quickly they were just buzzes of light.

"Is that ...?" My partner hesitated, pointing to the General.

I just stared, still unable to really believe.

Omen got in a fast blow. He threw the General forward onto his hands and knees. I held my breath. The rebel leader moved in fast to strike again, but the General was faking. He shot up and grabbed Omen by the neck, lifting him into the air.

They were face to face—eye to eye—mind to mind, struggling—equally powerful, equally matched—then the General said something. We saw Omen falter. His control crumbled. He yelled out a word. Then he gave in. He lowered his head. The General squeezed his hand and Omen exploded into a million pieces of dust. And he was gone. Willow screamed. Marco turned away. Rocco watched, expressionless.

I was pretty sure what the General had said to Omen. I saw an image of a girl in red in my mind.

My ex-mentor started to turn toward us.

"Bos—go!" I shouted at my partner.

He snapped the engine on and hit reverse. We scraped back out through the fence and over the gutter to the road. He swung the car in a shrieking circle and took off. I turned to look through the back window. I saw the General stepping out of the yard, a gathering of soldiers around him. He walked with his usual casual gait to the helicopter, which had landed at the end of street. The General—the Blood Horseman—the Shaman—the man and the monster got in and it lifted up. It flew in the opposite direction from the way we were traveling, toward the rising sun. I looked at the others and saw it in their faces. The resistance had failed—the era of the Shaman had begun. I collapsed against the seat and closed my eyes.

*

Anger is a funny sort of thing—not ha-ha funny, as Dark would say—funny as in twisted and paradoxical. It drives us forward and it holds us back. It burns hot and it burns cold. It's our natural defense against pain, yet it hurts so much it can send us crazy... And I think I reached crazy several times in the first ten minutes of staring anger in the face. Then I felt regret—another awesome feeling that gnaws at the soul, like rats with razor teeth and a bad attitude. And betrayal. Another good one. And I wallowed in it deeply as Dark drove us down the highway with no particular direction, until somehow I drifted to sleep or it drifted over me. Either way I crashed out.

The dreams that came were vivid. Mom, Dad, Gemma and Benicio, their baby. It was a happy mind-film at first—a birthday party for their baby, for Lily Grace—somehow she was already a year old. Dad was bringing the loud and inappropriate jokes, trying to start up a round of "happy birthday to you" before the candles were even lit, and Mom was shooting him looks. Gemma had Lily on her lap, Benny stood behind them with his hand on Gemma's shoulder. I kept to the back of the gathering, looking through the gaps in the crowd to the end of the table where my family was. I felt a sense of something good as I watched my brother, who'd had times in his life where he'd struggled so badly, when he'd been overtaken by fears and obsessions that had haunted him, hunted him to the edge and back. I felt a sense of pride in him—he'd made it—he'd fought his way back and here he was. He was a good husband and a great father. Lily Grace looked in my direction and as she did, a camera flash lit up her face—and then all the camera lights started blazing at once and I heard Dark talking behind me, saying, "It's time to go." And Rocco's voice as well—"It's time to go."

But all the lights were scaring the baby and my brother's forehead had furrows in it—the crowd was pressing too close. I started fighting my way forward through the people, trying to reach my family, but someone was holding me back. I spun around to face them—then I wasn't at the party anymore. I was in the warehouse, in the middle of all the trapped Shaman, the imprisoned, the tortured and tormented—and my family was there. All of them. The baby too. I put my hands to my head and screamed. I woke up screaming with Dark shaking me and shouting, "Open your eyes!"

When I did, I was lying by the side of the road and the car was just ahead of us. It had crashed into a guardrail, and smoke was coming from its smashed up hood. Rocco was right beside me—his eyes like the dead of night, and as I stared into them I thought it was true what Mom had told me once, that silence is the loudest scream of all. Willow and Marco stood further back. Willow was sobbing, Marco had his hands on top of his head and was staring in shock.

"What happened?" I asked, and the words burned my throat.

"You flipped right the fuck out is what happened!" Dark said. Panic stared from behind his dark green eyes.

"I'm okay." I sat up and winced. My chest hurt, my lungs hurt, my stomach muscles felt knotted.

"You've been screaming without taking a breath for an hour," Dark said. "Literally without taking a breath." I could see all the little veins in his forehead standing out in a way that was never good, but then I noticed something else, all his injuries had healed. He looked perfect. Sweaty, shaken and pale, but perfect. He saw me staring at him.

"You ..." He couldn't finish the sentence and just stood up, running his hand down his face and holding it over his mouth for a few moments before letting it drop to his side with a thud. When he looked at me again I remembered my dream.

"They're out there," I said and Dark knew immediately who I meant. In his heart, they were his family too. "I sent them away and they're out there alone." I started to feel myself losing it and tried to stand up, trying to escape breaking down in front of Dark and the others, trying to escape myself, impossible as it was. I slipped on the sidewalk, the rain drizzling from a dark gray sky above. I couldn't tell what time it was. Rocco grabbed my arm to steady me. Dark saw and took hold of my other side, trying to drag me away from him, but I kept a grip on Rocco. Dark looked from my hand to me and back to Rocco. Dark didn't let go either, saying, "You did what you had to do. What else could you do?"

"I don't know," I said, the words sounding hollow. "I don't know."

I looked around us, down the empty highway and up at the distant black shapes of birds flying through the storm far above. A feeling came over me, a feeling like a shout pushing upward through my throat, but I shoved it back down, terrified of what it meant. I needed to call my family. I had to find them. I had to get to them before *he* did. The General wanted me dead and he'd follow assassin protocol—just like Pope had. I felt over my jacket searching for my phones, but my pockets were empty. I looked to Dark and saw him exchanging a glance with Rocco over the top of my head. It made my heart sink.

He saw I'd caught them and explained, "We've already tried to contact them. We couldn't reach the ship, and Gemma's mother said they'd gone to the family cabin. It doesn't have a phone."

It was typical of my brother and Gemma to be difficult to contact. They were both suspicious of cell phones and social media and hardly ever checked their emails. So short of sending a note via snail mail or carrier pigeon, it was next to impossible to get a message through.

"They had to have taken some form of communication," I said. "With the pregnancy and everything."

"The mother told me they had a phone with them, something they brought over there—but she didn't have the number," Dark said.

"How could she not have the number?"

He shrugged. "It's for them to call out not for anyone to call in—you know what they're like."

I nodded. I knew. "But why couldn't you reach the ship?" I asked, feeling sick.

"Maybe they're going through rough weather," Rocco spoke up beside me, "and it's disturbing the satellite signal."

"Rough weather or something else?"

Rocco didn't respond, but I caught a flicker of something in his eyes.

"He'll go after them," I said. "The General."

"We don't know that," Dark said, then repeated. "We don't know that."

"I need to go. I need to get to them."

Rocco and Dark looked at each other again and I felt a surge of anger. It made me tremble and then the ground started rocking, my vision blurred, and my head felt too heavy to hold up. I crouched down and sensed Dark kneeling beside me.

"Please don't start screaming again."

"I will if you don't tell me what's happening."

I raised my eyes to him. He noted my expression, then looked behind him to Marco. The younger brother came forward clutching his laptop. I noticed for the first time that it had stickers on it—the World Wildlife Fund Panda Bear, a rabbit sticker with *free* beneath it and other animal ones too.

"You okay?" he whispered, sitting down beside me.

I nodded. "You?"

"Still here ... If that counts for anything."

"It does," I reassured him.

He opened up the computer, moving it toward me. The screen was split into many small boxes and I recognized each one—the criminal hit-list of the city, state, country and world. We were on the most wanted list of every law-enforcement agency in the entire universe. Terrorists. The General's work, no doubt. Anything we said would now be discredited, and getting out of the country would be next to impossible.

"Bastard," I murmured, rubbing my eyes. "What are we going to do?"

Rocco crossed his arms. "We don't have the numbers for anything except retreat."

"Retreat how?" Dark demanded.

"I have a boat," he said. "Big enough for us. We can get away—re-group—try to wake some others to join us. That was Omen's plan."

Willow sobbed. She went over to the car and leaned against the back of it crying. Then I saw a flash of something beside her—it was Omen standing there. He looked up at me and smiled—that deadly smile—and vanished.

"I'm getting some kind of Star Wars visions happening here," I said to Rocco.

"What are you seeing?" he asked, concern in his voice.

"Him. Omen," I said and Willow looked up at me sharply.

"He was here?" she asked, her voice choked.

"Right beside you," I said. "What does it mean?"

Rocco shook his head, but the heavy grief lines on Willow's face seemed to ease a little. As I watched her, more of the dream came back to me—the warehouse, the imprisoned Shaman, the children ...

"We have to go back for the trapped Shaman," I said and Marco's eyes darted to mine.

Rocco shook his head. "We can't. We don't have the numbers."

I'd spent a great deal of my life second guessing myself, down-playing myself, disliking and distrusting the face staring back at me in the mirror, but I felt something now—a certainty. I stood up.

"We are going back for them," I said to Rocco. "Except you. You're going to the docks. I have a plan."

*

I'd tried to prepare my mind before reaching the warehouse. I thought it would be somehow less horrifying the second time around, but it wasn't. It was even worse because I had more time to look at the General's victims—his experiments, treated no more than pieces of inanimate flesh and left to rot. I didn't know where to run first, who to try to help and how. They were all so hurt and weak. From a distance, I heard the thuds of Dark's boots as he ran and his voice calling my name and when I looked up he was right in front of me.

"They're here," he said, breathless, showing me his cell phone, which was streaming CCTV footage from the front of the Dunbar Road facility. I watched the screen as a line of cars and trucks pulled up at the gate of the compound and the General's soldiers started to pile out. I spotted Feng, but then I saw Jovic as well, and other C11 agents who weren't Shaman—I could sense it. And then I realized the General had sent in human agents so that we would hesitate to attack, to fight back. He was using them like shields for his people. It was his usual cunning.

"He knew we were coming," Dark said.

I watched the soldiers trying to open the gates but it wasn't working for them. Marco had hacked the system and locked everything down from the compound's central control room. Some of the soldiers began climbing over the fence and running toward the front of the facility, but they didn't get far. Strange figures started appearing from the fog and dark of night—unnatural others, brought into sight by Willow, who was standing hidden in the shadows near the gates. The soldiers baulked, raising their weapons at the apparitions. Fear held them back—but it would only be temporary.

I stared around us, then checked my watch. Six minutes left to get all the prisoners out to the back of the warehouse to wait for Rocco. Impossible. Most of them wouldn't even be able to walk. My breathing sped up. My chest crushed in, throat tightening. Tremors wracked my body. And that feeling started pushing up again—the shout. Omen had asked what it felt like to be a Shaman, and I hadn't been able to give an answer at the time. I felt like shit—run over several times or more.

Dark stood watching me and I looked into his eyes, expecting to see suspicion or even dislike. I had become what we had spent years together hunting, after all. But instead he just looked worried.

"It's okay," he said. "It's all right."

"Everything's changing." I gasped.

He nodded. "Except one thing." He held his hand out to me. "I told you I wasn't going anywhere."

I put my hand in his and felt his strength radiating through me.

"Now do whatever you have to do to get these people moving," he said. "We can't leave them here like this."

I nodded but I didn't want to use my Shaman skill. The thought of it was terrifying. I checked my watch—four minutes. Marco and Willow would be heading to the meeting point. I looked around. I wouldn't even be able to run the length of the warehouse in four minutes. Or maybe I could. Was I faster than I used to be? Was that one of my enhanced abilities?

"There's only one way to find out," I whispered. I tried to calm myself, find that feeling I'd been trying to shut down. I felt it rising up within me and didn't fight it this time. I just took off running—my hand sweeping over the beds and bars and gurneys as I went. *Fast* as a descriptive really didn't cut it—I was supersonic and my touch sent healing power into the prisoners. Tubes started popping out, chains started breaking—they were sitting up, standing, older children helping the younger ones. Some looked more confused and lost than others. Some just looked angry. It was so surreal it felt like I was still dreaming.

"Come on!" I heard Dark shout. "Follow me out!"

I ran up and down both sides of the warehouse, then tried to stop but failed—skidding and smashing into the wall. Dark dragged me up.

"I'm fine," I said.

"Two minutes," he told me.

"So let's go!" I said, then shouted out to the prisoners who had started to huddle behind us. "We're breaking you free. Keep up!"

We headed, in a stampeding mass, toward the back of the compound. I started thinking we were going to make it. They weren't going to catch us. But then a locked gate rose up before us, blocking off the exit. I slammed into the steel and was immediately shunted back by a volt of electricity.

I scrambled up to my feet and blocked Dark from getting any closer. "It's electrified."

"Can you shut it down?"

A sudden faintness swept over me and I half collapsed, smashing my knee on the concrete. I closed my eyes, trying to fight the way everything was rocking and shaking. I could hear the people around me breathing heavy, starting to panic, and I could hear the footsteps of the soldiers closing in behind us.

"Marco!" Dark shouted into his phone. "You need to shut down this gate!"

Marco's muffled reply came through. "I'm trying!"

"Try harder!" Dark demanded, just as we heard yelling behind us.

"Freeze! Get down on the ground!"

"I can't do it!" Marco yelled through the phone. "Something's crashing my computer!"

The gate suddenly sparked up with a loud drone that zapped into silence. I couldn't hear the electricity humming anymore.

"It's down!" I said to Dark and he ran forward and kicked the gate, smashing it open. The prisoners crashed through as shots rang out behind us. Screams rose from the crowd and I ducked low, drawing my TRANQ gun. I aimed toward the oncoming soldiers and started firing, dropping one after the other. I saw Jovic and Feng diving behind a row of desks and felt a momentary flash of pain for Jovic. He didn't know.

"Sil! Come on!" Dark shouted behind me. We ran through the gate and out of the warehouse, down the stairs to where the prisoners had gathered. Willow and Marco shoved through the crowd toward us.

"You did it," I panted to Marco.

"No—someone else hacked in. You know a Byter?"

Dark and I exchanged a quick look and I nodded.

"Where's Rocco?" Willow asked, her voice rushed and shaking. The rain began to pelt down heavier, as the shouts from inside the warehouse started closing in.

Beyond the compound fence I spotted something moving—growing larger and darker by the second. Shock and amazement blazed through me.

"He's here," I murmured.

The ship was gliding forward, just hovering above the road, with Rocco standing at the front. It wasn't a six person deal either—it was huge. Dark cursed beside me just before it struck the fence, ripping it down and flattening it. The ground trembled as Rocco extended a ramp from the deck high above. We heard him shout—

"Move!"

No one needed more motivation than the gunshots behind us. Dark and I stayed at the back of the pack—shoving people up ahead of us, shouting for them to move faster. The General's soldiers and the C11 agents burst out the back of the facility, opening fire. It was company policy—shoot first, ask later. Dark started returning fire, live rounds that made the soldiers lunge for cover. It gave us a chance to run up the ramp with Willow and Marco, the last ones aboard.

"Hang on to something," Rocco shouted as he used his skills to send the ship speeding backward. I stumbled and fell onto my hands and knees and saw several others do the same. Some were clinging on to ropes and planks and objects, their faces pale and eyes wide with fear.

The ship was really gliding now—moving down the streets, past cars and apartment buildings. I caught blurry glimpses of shocked faces staring at us from windows and it made me smile. Let C11 try to cover this up—let the General try to explain a ship cruising down Main Street. Dark looked over at me, his hair blown back by the wind, and I could tell he was thinking the same thing.

"You okay?" he asked.

"Define okay," I replied.

He snorted. Some of the freed Shaman had started to ask questions, calling out for us to answer them.

"You rest. I'll talk to them," he said and I shook my head. Dark comforting the distressed and confused usually involved a combination of buck up, shut up, stop crying for nothing, get over it and move on. And none of these people needed that kind of motivational speech right now.

Another wave of disorientation struck me and I squeezed my eyes shut. When I opened them again I spotted Dark at the back of the ship awkwardly patting a sobbing man on the shoulder. Marco and Willow were among the freed as well. Willow was sitting cross-legged with a bunch of kids and Marco was showing them something on his laptop. It sounded like a children's program. It made me think of the dream and my brother's baby... Had I seen the future? And then Omen appeared behind Willow, just standing there with his hands in the pockets, present for a few moments before vanishing. We all suddenly jolted as the boat reached the shore, crashing into the water. We'd finally made it to the docks. Rocco didn't slow it there—he just kept sailing us through the water. I managed to scramble to my feet and went over to where he stood. His eyes were closed and he was concentrating deeply. I touched his arm and he raised his head, turning to me.

"Are they following us?"

"They're trying, but we're faster," he said. His eyes moved over my face. "I'll head for the cruise ship, but we have to expect it will be a trap."

I nodded and looked back to the young Shamans, the ones who had been imprisoned. "Are they awake?"

He glanced over his shoulder, "Some are, some aren't. We'll need everybody up to speed by the time we reach the ship."

"I don't want to be the one to wake them. I don't want to use these abilities." I held my hands out in front of me. "I'm going to end up losing it like Omen did."

Rocco shook his head. "That's no certainty of that. We're all different."

"But if I do?"

He stared across the dark waters and said quietly, "We'll deal with that if we come to it."

The dizziness threatened to drop me again and I stumbled against Rocco. "Sorry," I murmured, shaking my head, trying to get clear.

"Don't be," he replied, sounding closer than before.

I looked up just as he kissed me, warm lips pressing against mine. For a moment I was confused, the thought running through my mind that he didn't need to act as though we were together anymore, but when he pulled back I saw the look in his eyes. He wasn't acting. I was sure I was about to say something insightful, maybe even witty, but then a violent surge of disorientation collapsed my legs from beneath me and I ended up dropping to my knees in front of him and somehow accidently ripping down his pants in the falling process. It really wasn't the subtle segue into romance I'd been imagining, but I was too sick to register embarrassment. I collapsed down on one side with an inelegant grunt.

Rocco knelt beside me and said, "It'll get easier. Just breathe. Try to relax."

I closed my eyes and took in deep breaths of the salty sea air, my mind full of thoughts of my family. Were they safe? Were any of us safe? What was the General planning? One thing was for certain—whether the rest of the world knew it or not—we were now at war.

Acknowledgments

This book would never have seen the light of day if it wasn't for my incredible agent, Sophie Hamley—my deep gratitude again and always.

All my love to my family—my husband, George and my sons, Josef and Daniel, and to Mum, Dad, Berto, Emma and Charlotte.

My heartfelt thanks to everyone at Momentum, most especially Joel Naoum and Mark Harding for their ongoing support and creative brilliance, as well as the wonderful editors Tara Goedjen and Kate O'Donnell.

Much love to my friends and family for their encouragement and support, with an especially huge thanks to Barbara Pitt and Karla Johnston, the best friends a person could hope for.